OUR LOVE IS
The Realest
2

A NOVEL BY

SHVONNE LATRICE

CHAPTER ONE

Jonaya Goode

"I sucked his dick and that's it," Leighton replied, making me choke on my drink.

"How the hell did that happen? I wish I would suck a nigga up and he send me home." Wednesday sucked her teeth. I nodded in agreement. Leighton's ass was dumb.

"I was over his house, and we were watching a movie in the dark. So he was just like 'show me something' out of the blue, and was taking it out. I didn't know what to do, so I just started sucking it," Leighton explained as she rolled one up.

Wednesday and I doubled over in laughter at this bitch. I didn't like hearing about Nusef and other girls at the moment, but that shit was funny.

"Wow, he got yo' ass, and easily, too." I shook my head.

The three of us continued drinking, and then smoked as well. An hour and a half later, we were drunk, high, and running in and out of my stepfather's bar bathroom to pee.

"What's the worst thing you've ever done?" Leighton slurred.

"Who?" I inquired.

"Both of you. But since you asked, you go first."

"Worst as in like sex, orrrr?" I furrowed my brows. I was too twisted for this.

"Okay, I will go first so y'all can get an idea." Leighton sat up, eyes low as hell from the weed and drink. "I fucked my sister's boyfriend after I convinced him that she'd cheated on him."

"Leighton!" Wednesday screeched.

"Damn, bitch, you're a fucking hoe," I laughed.

"Just a little," Leighton chuckled. "Okay, Jonaya."

"Shit, umm... I was talking to this guy once, and when I went to his house, I saw his brother looked better, so when he fell asleep, I fucked his brother."

"What the fuccckkkk!" they both shouted in unison, making me laugh way too hard because I was under the influence.

"I think yours is the worst, Jo," Leighton said.

"I've never done anything shady like that." Wednesday shrugged. Her eyes were damn near closed because she was gone.

"It doesn't have to be sexual," Leighton exhaled.

"Okay, okay," Wednesday slurred and smiled. "You guys can't say shit though."

"Bitch, go! As fucked up as Jonaya's and mine were, we will not tell your little secret," Leighton assured her, and I nodded to agree.

"Okay." She sighed. "I lied to Waayil about Uncle Harry."

There was complete silence amongst me and Leighton as Wednesday chuckled with her eyes closed, head resting against the back of the couch. Leighton and I made eye contact, before turning our attention back to Wednesday who clearly... hopefully... didn't realize what the hell she'd just said.

"She's joking." Leighton chuckled, briefly glancing my way. "You're joking, right, Wednesday?"

Shaking her head 'no,' Wednesday finally picked her head up and opened her eyes. When she saw that Leighton and I weren't smiling or giggling like her, her laughter ceased. For a moment, it was like she'd sobered up, as she straightened her body and scooted to the edge of the couch.

"Fuck," she whispered, running her hands through her hair.

I hadn't said a word yet, but I didn't know what I *should* say. I was secretly waiting for her to admit that she was fucking with us, because if not, this was about to cause a whirlwind of trouble. What she'd done effected too many people, not to mention, it ended with someone getting murdered. I just refused to believe Wednesday would do something like this. Her explanation *had* to be plausible.

"Wednesday, seriously, you didn't do that." I got up and went to sit next to her. I rubbed her back gently as she kept her face planted in her hands. "Wednesday."

I glanced over at Leighton who was still stunned, staring at Wednesday.

Wednesday picked her face up, and when I saw the abundance of tears cascading down her face, I knew that what she'd confessed was in fact true. There was a large lump in my throat that was hard as hell to swallow as I stared at her, mouth ajar.

"Wednesday, why?" Leighton quizzed with a confused frown, before coming to sit on the other side of her.

Shaking her head as tears continued to drench her face, Wednesday replied, "I was stupid and I was young." She sniffled, wiping her nose. "You have to promise me you won't say anything to anyone." She looked to me specifically.

"Wednesday—"

"Promise me, Jonaya. Waayil is *not* your best friend, I am."

"But Yikayla is my sister, and—"

"So what! This has nothing to do with Kay! Waayil is out of jail and his life is getting back on track! What's the point of telling him this and making me lose my brother? He would hate me forever!"

I gazed into her glossy eyes as she explained her reasoning for wanting me to keep this a secret. I wanted to *not* understand where she was coming from, but unfortunately, I did. Waayil was doing fine now, and the only thing this secret getting out would do, would ruin his relationship with Wednesday. It's not like he could get the years back that he'd spent in jail, so honestly, what good would telling do? However, keeping something like this a secret felt like the worst thing in the world. I was stuck and I didn't want to be. I didn't even want to know this shit. Whose idea was it to play this damn game again?

"Jonaya," Wednesday interrupted my thoughts.

"I… I won't tell, I promise."

"Leighton." Wednesday turned to her right and stared Leighton in the eyes. "Don't tell Nusef during any pillow talk or anything."

"Girl, please, I won't." Leighton smacked her lips before giving a half smile. When Wednesday turned away from her though, she gave me a look that showed she was still shocked. I was the glue that held Leighton and Wednesday together, since I introduced them to one another. By saying that, Leighton's loyalty to Wednesday wasn't as stable as mine.

The night was pretty much over after that, so I helped Leighton and Wednesday to the guest room in my house where they were gonna sleep, and then I went to my bedroom.

While sitting on the edge of my bed, feeling paralyzed, I heard Rori's TV, so I climbed out of my bed and stumbled across the hallway to her room.

When I opened her door, she looked to me and then grinned before pausing whatever she was watching.

"Who did you fuck?" She laughed as I came and sat at the foot of her bed.

"Nobody. We were just downstairs in the bar." I smiled awkwardly. I had drunk and smoked a lot, but my high seemed to dissipate at the sound of Wednesday's admission. "I just want to ask you something."

"Okay." Rori sat back against her headboard and folded her arms. I noticed she had some hickeys on her neck and collarbone, but I would get to that later.

"What's the worst thing I could do to make you never talk to me again?"

"What?" She chuckled with her brows furrowed.

"What's the worst thing I could do to where you would wash your hands of me? Something that would make you never speak to me again."

"Jonaya, why—"

"Answer the question, please."

She looked off like she was thinking and said, "Kill my child or something, I guess." She nodded then added, "Yeah, that would make me hate anybody, even my little sister."

I contemplated telling Rori, but I couldn't. I knew she could keep a secret, but this wasn't something I was sure she would keep. Rori was always about doing the right thing, so it was a good chance that if I told her this, she'd go and tell Waayil like… tonight. As badly as I wanted to get this out of my system, I couldn't do that to Wednesday.

"Oh, okay, thank you." I got up.

"Why?"

"It's for a… school psychology project. I've been forgetting to ask, and right now I remembered so I thought I'd get it out the way before I forgot."

Rori nodded, even though her face said she thought what I'd said was odd.

I went back to my bedroom and lied down in my bed. As I stared up at the ceiling, I wondered how much longer I could go on keeping this to myself, all the while still in slight disbelief. If I could go back to an hour before I found this out, I would pay any price to do so.

CHAPTER ONE

Yikayla "Kay" Goode

A couple days later...

I woke up to the sound of my baby's laughter and squeals, and as soon as I sat up, I felt a throbbing pain between my legs. Waayil had done a number on me last night, and I wasn't even sure if I could walk right now.

I smiled upon hearing Waayil talking to Lonan, and Lonan responding in baby talk. I'd never woken up to anything nearly as adorable as that with Roscoe. He and Lonan just didn't hang together like that. Literally, the only time they did spend together was when we were a trio. The closest they got to being alone was probably when I got in the shower and had to leave them. Not to mention, Roscoe usually slept until about 2 p.m.

I climbed out of Waayil's bed and went right to the bathroom to pee, then brush, floss, and rinse my mouth with Listerine. He was still waiting for his rental home to go through, so for right now, he was staying at his parents' home. His parole officer made it clear that he wouldn't give him any more passes if he found out he was staying in hotels, with me, or with Nusef again.

"Could you two be any louder?" I walked across the hall to the bedroom that used to belong to Nusef.

Waayil was on the floor helping Lonan play with some little tricycle he'd gotten him. It was originally white, but Waayil had painted it black and put all these flames and shit on it like my baby was gonna be a part of a motorcycle club. He even painted his name on it, graffiti style. It was the cutest thing, watching Waayil be so focused when he was designing the tricycle.

"I hope you didn't inherit the hater gene from ya mama, Lonan." Waayil kissed my son's cheek and placed him on the bike.

Lonan looked so adorable, with his curly hair sticking out of the baby helmet. He had on a onesie, sweats, and his new Nike Huaraches Waayil got for him. They were so cute and small. I didn't even know they made them.

"Shut up," I finally replied, smiling at Waayil trying to get Lonan to put his little feet on the pedals. "I'm gonna take a shower, so when I get out, Lonan and I have to go to the store."

"Nah, leave him here."

"Waayil, I can't."

"Why?"

Waayil was seated on the floor, with his hands still on Lonan's bike. His honey colored eyes shot through me as he waited for my answer with a subtle frown. He was shirtless, wearing only gray sweatpants and socks. And even though he was seated, his tattoo-adorned chest was still looking as chiseled as ever.

"I don't know. You shouldn't have to watch him while I—"

"Yikayla, stop. If you and I," he pointed from himself to me, "are gon' be anything, then I'm gonna have to watch him sometimes. I need to bond with him and we're gon' be a family, right?"

Even though there was a bit of hostility in his tone, his words warmed my heart. I didn't think I could love Waayil any more than I already did, but every day that went by, I proved myself wrong.

"I know, I just don't want to force you."

"Nobody can force me to do a damn thing, Kay, and you should know that shit, ma. Not even you, and you got something I love."

I was blushing until I saw him nibbling on his lip with his eyes fixated on what was between my legs.

"Really, Waayil?" I chuckled and turned my back to him.

"I like that shit too."

We both laughed in unison as I left the room.

I gathered everything I needed from my duffle bag, then went to Waayil's bathroom for a shower. Once out, I quickly spread lotion all over my body, then put on a tube dress. It was still pretty hot outside, so pants or long sleeves were not an option.

Walking out of the bedroom, I peeked into Nusef's old room, expecting to see Waayil and Lonan, but they were nowhere to be found. Just when I was about to continue to look in other rooms, I heard them downstairs. Rushing down, I followed their voices, which led me to the kitchen, and I saw Waayil and Lonan eating, with Wednesday sitting at the table across from them.

"Morning, Wednesday," I smiled and she gave one back.

"Good morning, Kay. You look pretty. Where are you going?" She cocked her head.

"I look pretty?" I chuckled. "Thanks, I guess. And I'm just going to the store to get a few things. Your brother is in the mood for pork chops tonight."

"Oh." Wednesday nodded slowly. She looked like she wanted to say something else, but Lonan's loud voice yanked her attention away from me.

"Well, I'm gonna go. You sure you don't want me to take Lonan, Waayil?"

Typical Waayil ignored me, only making conversation with Lonan as he fed him as Wednesday watched. Smiling at the sight before me, I left out and headed to the store.

It was a weekend and mid-day, since I for some reason slept late, so the grocery store was a bit more crowded than I liked. I missed being able to shop on the weekdays, but with my new job holding me hostage during the week, I was way too tired to do anything else afterwards. Steaming dresses didn't sound like much, but when there are sixty of them, and then in combination with occasional deliveries, you do get quite tired.

When I got to the meat section, I slowly pushed my cart down as I browsed to see what I wanted.

DINK!

"I'm so sorry, sweetie, are you okay?" I frowned, filled with concern as the cutest little boy rubbed his arm. He'd run into my cart, hitting it hard, so I'm sure he was slightly hurt.

Nodding his head, he continued to caress his arm, so I came around to the end of my basket and squatted down to inspect him.

"Where is your mommy?" I questioned him. He looked slightly familiar for some reason and I didn't know why.

"At home," he pouted adorably, making me chuckle.

"At home? Well then who are you here with? I know you didn't drive all the way to the store by yourself, did you?" I grinned and he gave me one back before shaking his head 'yes.'

"I drive all the time," he smirked. I recognized that smirk.

"Aren't you too young to drive?" I asked, discreetly scanning the perimeter to see if I could spot a parent, an aunt, cousin, shit, anyone who he belonged to.

"No, I'm four. I'm a big boy now!" he shouted.

I looked to the floor and saw a package of Nestle cookies that he'd dropped, so I picked them up and handed them to him.

"Wow, four years old? I guess you *can* drive." I rose to my feet and towered over him. "No one came with you? Are you sure?"

He shook his head 'no' with a smile.

"RJ!" I heard someone yell, and when I looked to see who it was, my heart sank just a tiny bit.

"Daddy!" the little boy rushed to Roscoe and hugged his leg.

11

Roscoe picked him up, and RJ began whispering in his father's ear. I wasn't sure if Roscoe was listening though, because he was just as stunned and paralyzed as I was as we stared one another down.

Finally, he said, "Yikayla, I—"

"You what?" I shrugged, feeling hot and like I was about to cry. I shouldn't have even cared, but I did and a lot. "This is your baby?"

"Yes, but—"

"He's four years old, Roscoe!" I barked, making a few people look my way. Roscoe moved in closer to me and I stepped back. "He is four years old," I repeated, feeling the two lone tears travel down each side of my face.

"Yikayla, let me explain to you but another time," he spoke lowly as RJ stared down at me.

RJ... I'm sure it was a nickname for Roscoe, Jr. No wonder he went so hard about not naming Lonan that. He claimed his name was ugly and sounded like a cartoon character. Shit, I hated the name too, but I wanted my son to carry his father's name because I loved him.

Staring at RJ, I couldn't help but to produce more tears.

"Don't fucking touch me!" I hollered again, when Roscoe's stupid ass attempted to thumb my tears away.

RJ stared at me with bucked eyes. He had no idea why I was crying and yelling at his father. *His* father. The thought alone gave me a nasty feeling in the pit of my stomach like I was going to throw up.

"Yikayla, we can talk toni—"

I snatched my purse from the basket and rushed off before Roscoe could finish his sentence. I quickly made it to my car, cranked up, and sped out of the parking lot so I could get back to Waayil's parents' home. I wanted to get my baby. For some reason, I just wanted to hold him really badly.

Instead of pulling into Waayil's parents' driveway, I parked my car at my house and just went back across the street and down two houses to knock on the door.

"Damn that was quick," Waayil answered, grinning and holding Lonan on his side.

"Yeah, umm… I—come to Mama, Lonan." I forced a smile, trying to keep my voice from shaking.

"You aight?" Waayil frowned. When he tucked his lips in, his dimples appeared, making him look so damn adorable and sexy.

"Yeah, I'm fine. Can you just let him go?" I had my hand on Lonan's small wrist, but Waayil's grip on his body was firm.

"Fuck is wrong with you, Kay? Come inside."

"I don't want to come inside! I want you to give me my fucking baby like I asked you to!"

Waayil calmly turned his attention to Lonan, placed a kiss on his plump cheek, and then handed him out to me. The look he gave me as I adjusted Lonan on my hip gave me an eerie feeling. I'd never been afraid of Waayil per se, but right now, I was a little scared. However, what had just transpired back at the store had taken precedence over my fear of him at the moment.

I quickly turned on my heels and started off towards my house.

When I looked over my shoulder, Waayil was still in the doorway, watching me like a hawk. As afraid as I was of what he would do or say to me later, I just needed some time alone.

CHAPTER ONE

Waayil Christian

A couple hours later...

I'd finally calmed down enough after Yikayla came over here acting stupid and shit. I just sat there, smoking and playing the game to keep my mind off the shit. I wasn't a violent muthafucka, maybe only sometimes, but I didn't want to be that way with my girl. So it was best that I let myself cool off before going to say anything to her ass, because I just might... I just might have said some shit that I'd regret.

I ashed the junt I was smoking on and cut the game off so I could go brush, floss, and rinse with Listerine. Once I handled that, I went to put on my Gamma 11s since I was already dressed, and then grabbed my keys off my old dresser.

Being in my parents' house wasn't pleasant at all, and it had nothing to do with my family being here. I felt like a fucking failure being up under my parents' roof at my age, and needed to have my own shit before I went crazy in this bitch. I'd found a spot, and the old bitch claimed she was gonna give me a call but never did. I knew exactly why, but I wanted that place badly and I needed to make that shit clear to her ass.

I arrived at the real estate building the lady worked out of, and parked in the lot. The place I wanted was a single-family home for rent on McLean, here in Midtown near my parents. I had to get letters of recommendation from a few people, including my weak ass parole officer to even get considered for this shit, so I really wasn't about to lose it. The life of an ex-con was not the business.

After pocketing my phone and keys, I got out of the car and went straight for the rental office. I had a mind to bring my Glock, but then I had to remind myself that, that muthafucka was the reason I hadn't gotten a call back in the first place.

When I got to the floor of the rental office that old hag worked on, the door to her office was wide open, so I peeked in to see some younger woman sitting behind the desk. That shit caught me off guard because the bitch I spoke to was old, dried up, and clearly a muthafuckin' hater.

"Excuse me, can I get a word with you?" I stepped in, crossing my arms over my chest and turning my hat to the back so I could see better.

She raised her head up and when she took me in, the attitude on her face quickly disappeared. She set down the pen she was writing with, and then rose to her feet. She was pretty skinny, tall too, and had on a suit, but the kind that was a skirt and not pants.

"Hi, have we met before?" She spoke softly, tousling her long brown hair.

"Nah, we haven't. My name is Waayil Christian. I met with somebody else about one of the vacancies on McLean, and she ain't hit me back like she'd promised."

"Someone else? Oh, my grandmother, Barbara." She giggled and then sat on the edge of her desk. "My name is Eden. I'm actually the one who oversees that property, but my grandmother was just helping me out. She does that sometimes when I get busy."

"That's perfect, but I wanna see about getting that spot, ma."

I didn't give a fuck about her schedule, job title, or family history. All I wanted was to see about moving into that crib and not a damn thing else.

"Right." She hopped off the edge of her desk. "Let me just look up your file. You said your last name was Christian, right? Is it spelled weirdly in any way?"

"Nope."

She looked through this accordion folder, and after a minute, she finally pulled out some papers. I surveyed the office as she read over them, until finally I heard her voice.

"Okay," she sighed. "Yeah, you have pretty great credit, just not a lot of history. We have to—"

"Look, I know why ya grandma didn't call me back, and I get it. You don't want some criminal ass nigga in ya spot, selling coke out in the front yard and threatening the neighbors with a gun and shit. But I promise you it won't be any of that. I'm a regular dude, working at a tattoo shop, and I'm just trying to get my life back together."

She stared up at me, hand still holding one of the papers, before she placed it back down and sat back.

"And you have a steady income from tattooing, right? You wouldn't be late on the rent or anything due to not having any clients?"

"I co-own the shop, so even if I don't have any clients, which will never happen, my employees will."

Nodding with a smile, she got back up from her chair and said, "Okay. I will go ahead and give you a chance. But you have to do something for me first."

Frowning, I asked, "Like what?"

"Have a drink or something with me." Her grin was so wide that I already felt bad for the way I was gon' have to shut her ass down.

"Oh nah, I can't do that. I got a girlfriend."

"Girlfriend," she repeated and nodded. "Sorry. I'm just a tad bit embarrassed," she chuckled.

"It's aight. So what do I need to do now?"

"Do you have time to go over and look at the place again while I explain some things to you and have you fill out some more documents?" she asked as she gathered some paperwork and keys.

"Yeah, of course."

"Great. Follow me." She rubbed her hand down my bicep and gave me a half smile.

In my own car, I trailed her to the spot I wanted, and after getting there, she let me inside so I could take a look around again. She talked the whole time as I looked, explaining and showing me the same shit her grandma had already shown.

"Yeah, I remember everything. She told me $995 a month, is that still the same too?" I leaned up against the wall.

"Yes, it is, but I can give you a discount—"

"I don't need that, but thank you. So, $1,990 upfront; I can give you that this evening in a money order."

"Okay, sure. Then I can have you fill out some forms and get you your keys since we've already ran a credit check." She walked to the door and placed her hand on the knob. Before turning it, she asked, "Is your girlfriend something serious or is it something new?"

"Eden, the only thing I want from you, ma, is this house, aight?"

She turned to leave, but I stopped her and stared down into her eyes with a serious ass expression. I needed her to not only hear what I'd said, but comprehend that shit too. I had enough muthafuckin' women problems and didn't need this bitch trying to add herself to the list. In a minute, I was just gon' exterminate every bitch that wasn't Yikayla.

"Yes, okay. I understand," she finally responded and nodded.

I saw a slight smirk lingering somewhere in her face, but I was gon' let that shit slide because I needed this spot. However, if she tried anything else, I was definitely gon' have to hurt her tall ass feelings.

***

Later that night…

I pulled up in front of Yikayla's parents' crib, and as soon as I shut my car off, I saw Dree coming out dressed like she was about to walk a damn runway or some shit. I didn't even notice the clean ass black truck, until some cornball ass nigga jumped out and opened the back door for her. I could have sworn she was back fucking with Canyon, but shit, that was none of my damn business.

I made my way up the driveway as the car left out, windows tinted dark as fuck, so I couldn't see whom Dree's companion was up close. Before I could even knock on the front door, Jonaya opened it and stepped back to let me in.

"What's good?" I smiled and reached for a hug as I made my way inside. I noticed she wouldn't look at me and her hug was light as hell. "You aight? That bitch nigga do something to you?" I asked her.

"What? Who? Marquise?"

"Who else? Only other nigga really checking for you that I know of is my brother."

"Oh well, no, Marquise is just fine."

"Just checking. If not, don't hesitate to let me know," I smirked, slipping my hands into my jean pockets.

"Waayil, you shouldn't go around always trying to save people," she scoffed and walked off towards the den.

I couldn't even respond because I didn't know where that shit came from. Shrugging that shit off because I didn't care enough to keep pondering, I made my way to Yikayla's bedroom and slipped in. It was dark, but she had a candle lit, as she lied on her stomach in her bed.

When she noticed me, she pressed her chin into her forearms to prop her head up.

"I've been texting and calling you all day," she whispered, as I moved towards the bed after taking my shoes off.

"I didn't answer because I needed time to cool down, Kay." I sat on her bed.

"I upset you that much?"

"Yeah, ma, you did. Had I answered your texts and shit, I might have said something I could never take back."

I lied on my back and turned my head to the left so I could see her face.

"I'm sorry, Waayil."

"Tell me what was wrong with you."

"Waayil, it's noth—"

"Tell me, Yikayla, or I can't do this shit with you. You not gon' be pulling up on me acting stupidly as fuck, and then expect me to just let the shit go because your pretty ass apologizes. Tell me what the fuck had you tight, or I'm leaving," I stated sternly.

Exhaling heavily, she replied, "I met Roscoe's four-year-old son today."

"What?" my brows dipped.

Nodding, she said, "Yeah. It's funny because he ran into my basket, and I started talking to him. Then lo and behold, here comes Roscoe calling his name, and the boy ran to him saying 'daddy.'"

Turning onto my side, I ran my hand down her smooth back and kissed her cheek.

"Damn," was all I could think to say at the moment. "You never suspected anything, ma? I mean, there had to have been some type of clue that he had some other shit going on outside of what y'all had. Niggas ain't that smart."

"No… I mean, I don't know. We spent almost every day together. The only time we were apart was when he was… doing his music out of town." She whispered the last part slowly as if she was coming to some sort of realization.

I chuckled at the mention of that nigga being a rapper. Shit made me wonder about Yikayla sometimes. I wasn't sure how a muthafucka like Roscoe had even gotten her out of her panties. Shit was baffling as fuck to say the least.

"I'm sorry that happened to you."

"No you're not, Waayil. You want me to hate Roscoe."

"Shorty, I admit I don't fuck with his ass and never will, but I don't ever want something happening to you that would break yo' heart, and that's on God. My job is to protect your heart, so why would I want anything to happen to it? Yeah, I wish I could just walk up on his bitch ass and smoke him, but that doesn't mean I want you seeing shit like what you saw today, just so you can dislike him. Long as I got yo' heart and I'm the only nigga you spreading ya legs for, then I'm good."

"Of course. I'm not angry because I love him or anything, I'm just… I don't know. I just don't feel good about it."

"You can be sad, baby. Don't hide how you feel because of me. You been with that nigga for longer than that child has been here, so I expect you to feel down."

Smiling as she scooted her body closer to mine, she said, "Your job is to protect my heart, huh? I like that."

"Yep. You gave it to me, so I'm gonna do that. I expect the same from you. My shit is more fragile though, because I'm a nigga with an ego," I smirked, making her flash her beautiful smile as she laughed.

I didn't know if Roscoe was retarded or what, but many niggas, including myself, would kill to have a family with Yikayla and Lonan. Niggas really didn't recognize the shit they had until it was too late. I was never like that. Never would I jeopardize a relationship with a good woman to fuck another bitch. Yeah, I loved pussy, but some shit just wasn't worth it. Niggas would sabotage their whole shit just to bust; not Waayil.

As Yikayla and I started to kiss, Lonan woke up and started to whine a little bit. Yikayla was about to get out of the bed, but I stopped her and went to pick homie up out of his crib. When I did, he slowed down his attempted cry as he played with my facial hair, but then when that got boring I guess, he started crying again.

"He just needs warm apple juice with cinnamon. I will go get it." Yikayla sat up.

"No, I got it."

"Waayil, don't make it too hot."

"I got it. Damn."

I took Lonan with me to put some warm apple juice in his sippy cup that I'd seen him drinking out of before, and then I added some cinnamon. I tested the shit on my wrist like them hoes do in the movies, and when I saw it wasn't too hot, I put it in his small hands and then grabbed him up from his highchair. He immediately started drinking it like a muthafucka who had been stuck in the desert and had finally gotten their hands on a water bottle, which made me laugh as we entered Yikayla's room.

"Does he like to be sung to?" I asked Yikayla once Lonan finished.

"Uh, I don't know. I haven't tried."

"Hopefully you didn't, ma."

"Fuck you," she chuckled.

I sat on her bed with my back against the headboard, with Lonan chilling in my lap. He was much calmer, but still talking a little bit as he stared at Yikayla.

When I started to sing "Ain't No Sunshine" by Bill Withers to him, he tilted his small head back to stare up at me with his mouth open. I gave him a half smile before continuing, and he watched me the whole time until he started to doze off. When he finally passed out, I kept singing just in case, as I carefully got off the bed and placed him in his crib.

Yikayla grinned widely as I sang the rest of the song to her, while I removed my shirt and jeans before getting into the bed.

I finally stopped to kiss her lips, as I got between her legs and said, "That song reminded me of you when I was in jail. Especially that first year."

"Really, babe?" Yikayla's eyes widened a little as she caressed the side of my face.

I nodded and started to kiss her collarbone, just as the door flew open, catching us both off guard.

"Boy, why did you stop? I was jamming!" Yikayla's mom squealed as Buddy hugged her from behind.

"Ma, get out," Yikayla said as the four of us laughed in unison.

CHAPTER ONE

Nusef Christian

It'd been a couple damn weeks since I'd ate Jonaya's pussy and had her squirming and shit. A nigga was feeling some type of way because I honestly thought she would have come around by fucking now. I was starting to see that me ambushing her wasn't fucking working, but it was hard as hell for me to sit back and leave it be. Some days I hated her ignorant ass for trying to pretend like she didn't feel the same, and others, I remembered how much I loved her, and the thought alone would have me smiling like a hoe ass nigga.

Something inside of me wouldn't let me give up on Jonaya Goode, and I hated that shit. I never in life chased a woman, because not only was that not my style, but I never had to. Ever since I started getting hard from the sight of a woman, which was around eight years old, I never had to beg or chase a bitch to do what the fuck I wanted her to do. By saying that, Jonaya was turning my ass crazy. I felt like a real-life stalker 'round this bitch, and sometimes wondered if maybe her ass just honestly didn't reciprocate my damn feelings.

Rori told me Jonaya was in the backyard swimming, even though it was 7 p.m. at night, so I headed back there so I could talk to her ass. I was tired as hell of the bullshit and was about to make her woman the fuck up tonight.

When she came up from under the water, she ran her hand down her face but stopped at her mouth when she saw me standing over the pool.

"Sef, what the fuck?" she hissed.

"Get out so I can talk to you, Jo."

"I just got in, Nusef. What did you need?"

"Get out the damn pool before I come in there and pull you the fuck out, Jonaya. I'm dead serious, ma."

She stared up at me as if she was trying to figure out just how serious I was, and then she swam to the steps that led into the pool. I couldn't help but to lust over her sexy ass frame as she sauntered up the steps in that skimpy ass bathing suit. When I finally got to fuck Jonaya, I had a feeling I would nut as soon as I got in. There was so much sexual tension that it was fucking ridiculous.

After throwing her towel around her shoulders, she followed me to the outside table, and we both sat down. She looked beautiful as fuck with her hair sticking to her face and shit.

"Jonaya, you know how I feel about you, ma." That was all I could say at the moment. I was frustrated with her stupid ass.

"What do you want me to say, Nusef? I mean, we've been friends for years and I have a boyfriend. You expect me to dump him and then start dating you after seeing you as just a best friend for this long?"

Squinting my eyes, I asked, "So you don't feel the same is what you're telling me right now?"

"I have a boyfriend. Marquise, remember him?"

"I don't give a fuck about that nigga! He's the least of my damn worries when it comes to you. I proved that shit the day I had his ass on the ground outside of Monarch."

"Nusef, why do you have to do this!" she yelled, suddenly throwing away her calm demeanor she had just possessed. "We were fine as best friends and now you fucked it up with all of this!"

"I fucked it up? How the hell did I fuck it up? I was honest with yo' ass about my feelings, and now I don' fucked everything up? Okay." I nodded. I had to tell myself to stay calm.

"Yes, because now we barely hang out or talk because you don't want anything to do with me unless I do what you want or say what you want to hear."

"I want you to be honest, Jonaya. I love you and I wanna be with you, ma. Do you feel the same or nah? Tell me, and let me know so I can proceed correctly."

I was done with this shit.

"I would rather we stay friends. I want to be with Marquise—

Nusef!" she called my name when I abruptly got up from the table. "See! Now what? We're not gonna be friends anymore?" She got up from her seat as well.

Chuckling, I replied, "Nah, you right, ma. We can still be friends. My bad for even bringing this shit up. You stick with Marquise, and I'll do me."

"But we're still best friends, right?" she half smiled, looking up at me.

I couldn't help myself, so I moved in a little closer and pecked her lips. Them shits were like pillows right now. She froze up as I continued to kiss her gently, before starting to suck her lips. Not but seconds later, our tongues were tangled and a few moans slipped out here and there. Like the last time though, she pulled away suddenly.

"Sef, please," she begged.

Without another word, I turned on my heels and left her crib. I was finished with my Jonaya mission once and for all. I loved her, but I wasn't the type of nigga to be made a fool of. If she didn't want it, then I'd just have to accept that and keep it pushing. There were plenty of bitches around this muthafucka that were ready and willing, so there was no need for me to be up Jonaya's ass when she didn't even want me to be.

As soon as I hooked my phone up to the car charger, it beeped and I saw Leighton had texted me.

Leighton: My parents left town today, wanna come over and chill? My dad has a cabinet full of wine and cognacs.

With my phone in hand, I looked out my passenger window at Jonaya's parents' home and contemplated. Yeah, I let Leighton suck me off, but that was just because I was thinking with the wrong head at the time, and she kept licking her full ass lips. I ain't wanna really fuck with her because I wanted Jonaya, but now I was starting to see that Jonaya and I weren't gon' happen, so fuck the la la.

Me: Yeah, I'm on my way.

Leighton: *Yes! Okay.*

I shook my head at her response and then texted her for her address. I'd been over there before but I didn't remember where the fuck her ass lived.

Leighton's people stayed in Cooper-Young, which was pretty much Midtown where Jonaya and her family resided; also, where I used to live when I stayed with my parents. So it didn't take me long at all to get there. When I did, I took a moment before telling Leighton I had arrived because I wasn't sure if I wanted to smash her tonight, or try to slide up in Rebecca. I decided to go ahead and stick with Leighton, because Rebecca had feelings for me, and me getting some pussy from her would make her think I'd changed my mind about us.

"I almost thought you weren't coming." Leighton answered the door wearing what looked like a bikini top and a tight ass skirt that looked like t-shirt material.

"Nah, I wouldn't lie to you." I stepped in, scoping the scene, as she closed and locked the door behind me.

The living room was dark, with the TV flickering to light up the room. I saw she had a bottle of champagne, one of wine, and two types of cognac; Hennessy and Remy. Also on the table was a bowl of popcorn, a bowl of tortilla chips, and what looked like a plate of mozzarella sticks from afar.

"Have a seat." She reached her hand out to the leather couch.

It smelled like roses or some type of garden shit in here. It was a real-life family home, and the shit made me think about how my life would be with Jonaya. I couldn't stand her right now because she had me feeling like a weak ass bitch.

"Did you for real make some damn mozzarella sticks?" I chuckled, kind of liking how her ass went all out. Shit reminded me of Rebecca a little bit.

"Yeah, but they're just the freezer kind, so relax. Not like I made them from scratch or anything."

I shoved a tortilla chip into my mouth as she talked and sat next to me.

Everything she'd said went in one ear and out the other when I got a better view of how her hips looked in that too tight skirt. Then the way she was sitting gave me a glimpse of her pussy, covered in some thin ass panties. Just that quickly, my dick was hard as fuck and I didn't want to chill, talk, or eat; I wanted to fuck.

"So where—"

I cut her sentence off when I yanked her closer to me and started kissing on her neck, while my hands quickly and easily untied her bathing suit top. As soon as that shit fell, my mouth gravitated towards her nipples, and I began to suck the shit out of them muthafuckas hungrily. I groped them as she moaned and caressed the back of my head, before I let one of my hands travel down and between her legs. It was like a furnace in that shit, and I could feel her wetness seeping out onto the seat of her panties. Fuck.

In one motion, I laid her on her back, and rose to my feet to unbuckle my jeans and release myself through my boxer's slit. I got back onto the couch as Leighton stayed on her back staring up at me, titties out and looking edible as fuck. Pressing her thighs into her stomach, I slowly moved her panties to the side to get a view. Licking my lips, I smirked at how pretty that shit was. No way was I gon' eat her pussy, but it was tempting for sure.

"You're so sexy, Sef," she whispered as I opened and slid a condom down my shaft.

I tugged her panties down her legs, then roughly pressed her thighs back into her stomach. Looking down between her legs, I watched myself as I entered her slowly. I knew as soon as I got in that shit that I was gon' be hitting this for a minute and a couple more times.

"Mmm," she whined as I moved in and out while holding her legs down against her body.

Pussy was nice and tight, and not to mention, spilling with her nectar damn near. Once she started to open up some, I began pounding her hard as fuck. She came only a few seconds in, but I just kept going, beating her pussy out the frame as she whimpered and moaned.

"Damn," I mumbled to myself, watching my dick penetrate her forcefully.

Faster, harder, deeper, described my strokes, and soon enough, I was filling the condom up. She'd cum about three times, and every time it made it harder to hold my nut back.

I slowly pulled out of her, and then stood up off the couch to remove the condom. I glanced her way once I got it off, and the look on her face as she breathed heavily told me I had fucked up. If I thought she was on me before, shit was about to get worse. Her eyes told me so.

CHAPTER TWO

Yikayla

I was at work but I could barely concentrate because Roscoe and his baby were still on my mind. He, of course, had been texting and calling me so much that I had to turn my phone off when I was with Waayil. If Waayil knew how much that nigga hit me up, he would for sure whoop his ass, and as much as I despised Roscoe right now, I didn't want that.

Waayil was crazy before he went to jail, but after going, he seemed to be a bit more unhinged. Unfortunately, it turned me on though, and it felt good to be with a real man for once. Being with Roscoe was like dating a little boy, or having two sons instead of one. Waayil was nothing like that, and I felt safe with him. Not to mention, I was deeply in love with him, even after all of these years of not seeing or hearing from him.

I saw myself in the small mirror nearby, and realized I was smiling at the thought of him. I didn't know if it was healthy to love someone as much as I loved Waayil, but I didn't care right now. And at least the feelings were mutual.

KNOCK! KNOCK!

"Come in!" I yelled, hearing someone knock on my door. I prayed to God that it wasn't Jerica's assistant coming in with another rack.

I was suspicious about why she had so many dresses needing to be steamed if they were all handcrafted and one of a kind. I didn't know anyone who could sew a damn dress that quickly, and I was sure I'd seen the same dress twice. That wasn't any of my business though. I was just here to steam.

"Hey, are you busy?"

I turned around at the sound of Brynn's voice, and turned the steamer off before setting it down. She and I hadn't said two mumbling words to one another since our little spat that one day, so I didn't know why the hell she was creeping back in here.

"Yes, I'm busy, Brynn. We're at work, so you should be busy too."

"Yikayla, I'm sorry for what I said that day. I was just dealing with some things at home and I brought it to work."

"It's fine."

I was being short with her because I honestly didn't care too much about our little altercation. On the flip side, I was a bit interested to know why she was in my work room looking like her damn dog had died.

"I just…" She took a seat and I rolled my eyes when she wasn't looking. "My child's father is stressing me out and I don't know what to do."

"Well, baby daddies are only really good for one thing: sex and headaches."

"You have a kid?" She smiled and wiped the lone tears traveling down her face as I sat across from her.

"Yes, a little boy named Lonan. He's one."

"Wow, I would have never guessed. You look so young and your body doesn't look like a bag of oatmeal." She chuckled, making me do the same.

"Neither does yours, Brynn."

"Not according to my baby daddy," she sighed. As much as I tried to keep my disdain for her alive and thriving, I was starting to feel bad for her. "He bought me a gym membership the other day."

Brynn was definitely plus size, and she dressed really well from her head to her toes, so I was surprised by her self-esteem issues. But I guess if a man I loved told me I wasn't attractive or fat, it would hurt my feelings too. I couldn't imagine Waayil treating me that way. That was what I loved about him; however, I knew that if I did change physically, he would still feel the same about me. Our connection ran very deeply.

"Girl, you need to let him go. I know plenty of men who would be interested in you, just the way you are."

"No you don't." She smiled brightly, making her caramel complexion glow a little. It was no longer flushed, and I was proud to be the reason for that.

"Yeah, I do. Why don't we go somewhere one of these weekends?"

"Like to a club? I don't really do clubs."

"I think it will be fun, Brynn. And how else will you see all the niggas that I'm sure will be drooling over you?"

"I'm sure my sister can babysit, so I guess I can go."

"So it's settled then," I smirked. "I will let you know when."

She nodded with a smile in response, and we continued talking for a little bit as I got back to work. Brynn was actually really cool, and it felt good to have somewhat of a friend outside of my sisters.

It wasn't long before Jerica made Brynn get back to work, because the phone had been ringing off the hook.

By the time the clock hit 5:30 p.m., I was finished with all the racks, which was record time compared to my usual. I couldn't wait to get home to my baby, and then eventually, my man.

Waayil had gotten the house, but he was still getting it furnished, so at the moment, our living arrangements hadn't changed.

As I walked to my car, my phone started ringing and I looked down to see it was Roscoe's ass, yet again. I was so tired of this nigga, but I knew a conversation needed to be had. Regardless of what he'd done to me, he was still Lonan's father, and if I wanted them to have some kind of a relationship, Roscoe and I needed to be able to talk to one another.

"Hello?" I answered as soon as I got into the driver's seat of my car.

"Hey, baby—"

"Roscoe, keep the terms of endearment, please. What do you want?"

"I wanna talk to you, but in person, Kay. Can you just meet me somewhere so that we can do that? I'm at home."

"Which home? The one with your mother or the house you have

with *Shamaria*?"

"My same crib that you've been to a million times. My *only* crib, Yikayla."

"I will be there in a little bit. I'm leaving work right now and it's not too far from there, okay?"

"Perfect. See you later, bab—Kay."

I hung up the phone and just stared straight ahead for a couple moments. I was hoping I could face him without taking off on his ass.

After calling my mother to see how Lonan was doing, I headed towards Roscoe's mother's house. Speaking of his mother, I wondered if she knew about his pre-school aged son that he'd had. I'd been with him for five damn years, and his son was younger than our relationship. Every time I thought about that, it infuriated and disgusted me.

And this Shamaria character still stuck with me. I didn't believe that she was related to him on his father's side. Roscoe barely mentioned his father to the point where I'd even forgotten he had one. Yet, now all of a sudden, he's close enough to people on his paternal side of the family to have a key to their home?

And Lopez? That wasn't even Roscoe or his father's last name. But then again, I felt like I didn't even know the nigga anymore. I just… I didn't know what to think. It was too much.

HONK!

Some car behind me honked loudly and sped around me like a maniac. I looked to my left to see a bitch with braids and a stank face, so I flipped her ass off.

Finally, I'd made it to Roscoe's, so I parked, said a prayer to God to keep me calm, and then got out of the car. I knocked on the door, and when his mother answered with a smile, it took actual muscle work for me to deliver one back to her.

"Yikayla, baby, I haven't seen you over here in a while. I almost thought Roscoe had lost you," she added as I walked in and hugged her lightly. "And where is my grandbaby? I haven't seen him either."

"He's with my mother since I had to work, Miss Laughton."

"Oh, well, why don't you let me watch him some days, sweetie? I'm his grandmother too; plus, I'm sure that mother of yours values her free time."

I was gonna let that one slide. She always made snide remarks about my mother, and I think it was because she was jealous. Miss Laughton wasn't ugly by any means, but she was alone and slightly older, with a grown ass baby man for a son. My mother was beautiful, only in her forties, had a rich handsome husband, pretty well to do daughters, and she owned a poppin' ass waffle house.

"Ma, leave Mrs. Vaughn alone." Roscoe came from the back looking nicer than I wanted him to. His caramel complexion looked vibrant, just like his soft curly hair. He smelled really good, and it permeated the air as soon as he entered the living room. Lonan looked just like him. "Come back here, Kay."

"I don't think that's appropriate, Roscoe."

"Oh, honey, don't mind me. I know you guys do y'all thang. Lonan is proof of that, Yikayla." Miss Laughton chuckled.

"No, I have a new boyfriend, Miss Laughton, and I don't think he'd want me alone in a bedroom with my ex-boyfriend. Waayil Christian, do you remember him?" I smiled at her, enjoying the shock in her expression.

"The young man who murdered his foster mother's brother?" She frowned in disgust as her eyes searched my face. "And you're okay with a man like that being around your son, honey?" She turned her attention to Roscoe.

"Nah, actually, I'm not—"

"Well, he doesn't have a choice. Waayil is my man and he and Lonan have a very strong bond."

"Ma, give us some privacy, please." Roscoe stared hard at me like he wanted to fight. I didn't care though. I was angry about his other son.

"Alright." Miss Laughton threw her hands up in mock surrender, and got up from the couch to leave. She was shaking her head as she went to the back, and I just wanted to punch the back of it.

"Talk, Roscoe. I'm actually interested to hear what explanation you have for your situation. By the way, how is RJ?"

"Look, we had just gotten together—"

"A year is just getting together?"

"It wasn't a year yet, Yikayla. He's four years old, so you and I had only been together for a couple months when I got his mother pregnant."

"Who is his mother?"

Sighing, he said, "That's not the point, Kay, damn! You need—"

"Who is she!" I barked.

"I'm not telling you who his mama is, mane. Not right now." I scoffed and shook my head as he exhaled heavily. "But look, I met her and I was fucking around with her for a minute, then she got pregnant. By that time, I realized I wanted you and only you, but I couldn't ditch her, obviously."

"Roscoe, just stop. I really don't wanna hear anymore." I felt a tear drop from my eye, but not because I was sad, it was because I was furious with him. This whole time he had this whole other family.

"But, Yikayla, I love you, not her. I know what you got going with Waayil is a part of some obsession you've had with him since when you were younger. I'm willing to give you time—"

"What?" my brows dipped. "I love Waayil! I have loved him since I was sixteen years old! Every day that I spent with you, I wished I'd spent it with him! You were nothing but something to pass time! The only good thing I got from you was my baby, and even though I love him, I wish Waayil was his father!"

We both stared at one another in silence. I couldn't believe that I'd said what I'd said, so I was just as surprised as Roscoe was right now. I hated to tell him that I wished Waayil was Lonan's daddy, but it was true. Roscoe didn't care for my baby the way Waayil did. I'd never seen Lonan laugh and smile so much with someone that wasn't my sisters, his grandmothers, or me. I hated to say it, but Roscoe didn't love Lonan; he tolerated him because he happened.

"Yikayla, you're just mad right now." He tried to touch my hand but I snatched away.

"Look, Lonan is your baby so I won't keep him from you, but I am with Waayil and I will be forever, Roscoe. We can set up a schedule for you to see your son and spend time with him." I got up from the couch.

"Aye, come here!" He shot up from the couch and roughly pinned me against the wall. With his teeth clenched, he said, "You gon' always be mine. Now like I said, I'll give yo' little ass some time, but when I'm ready for you, you best be ready too, Yikayla Goode."

"Get off me!" I screamed, trying to release my wrists from his hold.

"Roscoe Jermaine Cousins!" His mother shouted his name as she marched to the living room.

He quickly let me go and I rushed my ass out of there. I'd never seen Roscoe like that, and I hoped this behavior soon passed because not only would he not see my son, but if Waayil got a whiff of that shit, it would be another murder on his hands.

CHAPTER TWO

Dree Goode

That weekend...

Sean and I were at his house studying, since I'd gotten a B- on the last test and he'd gotten an A. I didn't know how that was possible since we studied together all the damn time, but it happened.

I'd been spending a lot of time with Sean and I must say, I enjoyed the high life. Granted, my stepfather gave my sisters and me a great life growing up and even now, but with Sean, things were different.

My stepdad only provided the things I needed, whereas with Sean, it was more of the shit I wanted. He bought me things, took me to nice places to eat, and we even planned to travel to France next summer. I'd only been out of the country once, and that was when my stepdad took the whole family to Turkey for Christmas when I was around eleven years old.

"I think I've had enough for the night." I closed my book and sighed. It was now 9 p.m. at night, and my head was hurting from trying to remember all the laws, how and when they should be applied, and when they didn't apply. It was just too damn much right now.

"You're sure? You were pretty upset about that B-." Sean smiled and pulled me closer to him.

We were in the big ass den of his parents' home with the fireplace on, as we sat on the big plush white rug. His housekeeper had made us snacks all day, and then we'd had dinner just a couple hours ago. I think I was getting used to the way Sean lived.

"Yes, I'm sure. My brain feels like it's turning to mush right now. I'm barely caught up, and on Monday, we're gonna be learning even more. I think maybe I need a tutor."

"No, I'm your tutor." Sean hugged me tighter from behind as I stared at the burning flames.

"No you're not. Plus, you distract me."

"Excuse me, Miss Goode, I have some of those puff pastries you love. Would you like me to wrap some up for you?" Sean's housekeeper entered the den, smiling.

"Yes—"

"No. They're a little fattening. She's had enough for today," Sean cut me off. The housekeeper nodded as I stared back at him like he was crazy.

"Sean, seriously?"

"What? I'm trying to keep you from becoming overweight and failing out of law school at the same time." As rude as the former part of his sentence was, the latter took over my brain. I could not flunk out.

It wasn't an option. "I have to ask you something, Dree."

"Go ahead," I spoke lowly, mind going crazy. All my life I'd dreamed of becoming a lawyer, and for the second time in my life, the first being, when I didn't get into Harvard Law, I wasn't sure if I could do it.

"Are we like together or what?" Sean's soft yet masculine voice broke me from my thoughts.

Moving from his embrace and turning to face him, I said, "I don't know. Do you want to be? I mean, we just met so I don't want to rush it."

"Yeah, I wanna be. You think I do all this for women I'm not interested in?" He showed his sexy smile.

"No, I know you're interested, I just don't want us to rush into anything like I said. But I like you, so yeah… I guess we are together."

"Good."

He took my hand and pulled me back closer to him, before pressing his lips against mine. Our pecks turned into full on French kissing, and before I knew it, he was on top of me and in between my legs, tugging on my tights.

"Wait, Sean." I pulled away.

I liked Sean a lot, but I couldn't get to the sex part with him yet. I didn't know why, but for some reason, after Canyon, I didn't want to be touched. Canyon still crossed my mind every now and again, and it was almost like, if I let someone else go there with me, it would erase the nights I'd spent with him. I didn't want to be with Canyon because Sean was a better deal, but I just couldn't help but to hold back. I needed to be sure that I wouldn't regret anything.

"Are you alright, Dree? I mean, I assumed you tensed up whenever we got this close because I wasn't your boyfriend, but now I'm confused."

"I'm just not ready, Sean. I will be soon, I promise, but just not tonight. I have a lot on my mind with school and everything."

"And I can help you with that." He tried to kiss me but I turned away, so he rolled off of me and sighed dejectedly. "Dree, I'm starting to think this is all because of your situation you mentioned."

"What?" I sat up. "No it's not. Why can't I just not be ready?"

"Because it's not like you're a virgin, Dree! And I'm sure you slept with that *situation,* so what am I doing wrong? Do you not like me?" Sean hissed.

"So just because I'm no virgin means I have to sleep with every man who shows interest in me? You know what, I'm leaving."

"Dree—"

"No, it's fine." I stood up and began messily shoving my shit into my Louis Vuitton messenger bag that my mother gifted me with this year.

"Baby, I'm sorry." Sean grabbed my arm gently. "I'm just a little bit jealous of this guy you used to mess with, and knowing he had you in a way that I never have, irks me a little bit."

"Well you need to grow up, Sean. And I never said I slept with him."

"Did you?"

"Yes, but I've known him for a long time. He and I used to be good friends since I was like fourteen years old. So when we reconnected, it just felt right."

"So things don't feel right with me?" Sean palmed his chest, making me groan in frustration because I didn't know how to explain this.

"No, what I mean is I need more time. And you pressuring me and questioning my motives is not helping you in any way."

"I'm sorry—"

"See you Monday." I quickly slipped my feet into my Nike slides and darted from the den, through the foyer, and out to my car.

That nigga had me hot with his comments, and for the first time, I was furious with him. How dare he insinuate, that just because I'm not a virgin, I should be spreading my legs for any man that I date. I shook my head and scoffed as I hightailed it out of his long ass driveway and down his street.

There was a little bit of traffic since a lot of people were running the streets tonight, so it took me almost fifteen minutes to get home from Sean's house in Belle Meade.

When I pulled up, I saw Canyon's car outside out my house, along with Nusef's, Waayil's, and some others I didn't recognize parked along the street.

When I entered the house, I heard music, conversation, and laughter coming from the back, so I went right towards it. Peering through the sliding doors, I saw Canyon, Waayil, Nusef, my mom's boo, Buddy, and Eko playing cards or Dominoes at this table, and then Rori, Jonaya, Yikayla, Leighton, Wednesday, plus this girl named Jodi that worked at my mom's waffle house. My mother was even out there, dancing with Yikayla and Lonan. I felt some type of way about everybody out here having fun and not even sending a memo to me about it.

Stepping out back, the smell of food hit my face just as I spotted the grill. Buddy hopped up and went to tend to it, as I walked slowly towards where everyone pretty much was.

"What's going on out here?" I approached the guys first, standing by Canyon.

"Nothing. Shit just turned into a little something," Nusef replied to me. I looked to Canyon who acted like I wasn't even standing there as he shuffled with his cards.

"I see." I nodded. "What are you guys playing?"

"Blackjack," Waayil replied. I realized Canyon wasn't gonna answer any of my general questions.

"How is work, Canyon?" I moved back from him some so that I could see his face. He looked so good dressed down in a wife beater, basketball shorts, socks, and slides. His strong caramel arms, which were covered in tattoos, were on full display.

"It's good, Dree," he responded dryly as fuck.

I felt stupid standing there because the nigga wouldn't even look at me, so I walked away to see what Rori, Jonaya, Leighton, and Jodi were doing. As I walked to them, Jodi got up and went towards the table where the guys were. My eyes followed her for a moment, and my stomach dropped when she stood behind Canyon and placed her hands on his shoulders.

"What, are they dating now?" I quizzed my sisters and Leighton, as I sat down on one of the lawn chairs.

"Probably." Rori shrugged, texting on her phone.

"No, they just met tonight. I introduced Jodi to everybody, and he was the only one she didn't know. They did converse for a little bit, so I think she likes him," Jonaya answered.

I raised my brow as I watched them closely. She was joking and laughing with the guys, and every time she made a comment, Canyon laughed sexily and looked up at her. Finally, she pulled a chair up to sit next to him, and brushed her hand down his freshly cut fade which had my skin boiling.

"Is this bitch serious?" I frowned deeply, lip turned up so high it was damn near touching the tip of my nose.

"Dree, you stopped talking to him for your nerd nigga," Jonaya said, making Rori and Leighton laugh.

"So that gives this hoe the right to push up on him? We're friends!"

"Friends?" Rori laughed. "Dree, you barely even acknowledge Jodi when you come eat at the waffle house. I'm surprised you even know her damn name."

Rori was right. I didn't give a fuck about a damn Jodi until now. Shoot, I surprised myself when I remembered her name.

I tried to stay calm and ignore the interaction, even when it was obvious they were exchanging numbers. She stuck by him for the longest as he played cards with the boys. Finally, he got up to go to the bathroom so I got up too.

"Dree," Rori called my name to stop me, but I ignored her.

I followed Canyon into the house, and waited outside of the bathroom. Hearing his pee hit the toilet water made me roll my eyes for some reason. I hated him right now and everything he did, including peeing. When I heard him washing his hands, I straightened up a little.

"Ooh shit." Canyon jumped a little after coming out of the bathroom. "Fuck you standing out here like a parole officer for?" he hissed, face looking like he was disgusted by the sight of me.

"So Jodi is your new thing?" I folded my arms. He stopped in his tracks and turned to face me. The hallway of the downstairs bathroom was pretty narrow, so he was on one side and I on the other, but we were still pretty close.

"Excuse me, but why the fuck would that shit matter to you, ma?"

"It doesn't. I'm just wondering." I shrugged, trying to play it cool.

"So you followed me to the bathroom and waited outside just to ask me about Jodi, but you're just wondering? Wonder about that bitch ass nigga that got muthafuckas driving you around Memphis and shit."

"Canyon, don't be like that."

"Dree, what I said on the porch that day, I meant that shit, ma. I don't fuck with you. So the next time you feel the urge to wonder about me, don't."

He quickly walked off, slapping me in the face with his cologne.

I stood there for longer than I wanted to, baffled and feeling some type of way for sure. I didn't want to care because I had who I wanted, but Canyon's words made my stomach ache and my heart beat rapidly.

Feeling too mentally and physically sick to return to the backyard get together, I retired upstairs to my room for a hot shower. I tried to go to sleep after, but instead, I stayed up for hours, in the dark, replaying what Canyon had said to me.

CHAPTER TWO

Jonaya

I walked out of my chemistry class, smiling down at the A I'd gotten on my test. Because I didn't broadcast it like Dree, people thought I was just some wild child with no plans for the future. That couldn't be further from the truth; I just liked to leave school at school, and keep my party life where it was. Plus, I liked surprising people by telling them I had a 3.8 GPA and was majoring in Chemistry with a focus on healthcare.

"I was looking for you!" Leighton shouted, walking up to me. She was glowing and smiling hard as hell.

"I told you we'd meet at Subway." I snapped a picture of my test and then sent it to my step dad. I was just gonna wait for his congratulatory comments, and then for the money he was gonna put into my checking. I loved chemistry and healthcare science, but getting money for good grades was definitely motivation to stay on it. I just couldn't wait to graduate so I could get a car.

Leighton and I went to Subway, got our sandwiches, and then found somewhere to sit. We didn't have the same classes, but as fate would have it, we had the same length of a break between classes.

"So I've been keeping a secret." Leighton smiled as she unwrapped her sandwich.

"A secret? How dare you keep a secret from me?" I playfully rolled my eyes before we both laughed.

"Remember how I told you that Nusef and I were talking again, and how I stupidly sucked his dick and got nothing back?"

"Yes, I remember."

My heart started to thump rapidly as I waited for her to continue. I had no idea what she was about to say, but seeing how brightly she smiled let me know that it was a positive thing in her eyes. The last time I talked to Nusef, outside of the little barbecue we had this past weekend, he appeared to be done with chasing me. By saying that, there was no telling what he'd gone and done with or said to Leighton.

"Well, he came over the night my parents went to Ohio, and we had sex. Girl, your best friend has some good ass dick." She sucked her teeth and shook her head like she was in church receiving the Holy Ghost. "I have never came multiple times, but I did that night."

Hearing about Nusef fucking her angered me, but then it brought back memories of him eating my pussy, which made my clit throb. I bit down on my lip, unintentionally, as I reminisced about the way he ate my pussy with so much passion and a little aggression.

"Are you listening, Jo?" Leighton ended my trip down memory lane.

"Yeah I am. So damn, what now?"

"I don't know. We still text a little bit, and we even fucked again but I don't know. I kind of feel like that's all it is."

As bad as it sounded, that made me smile knowing Nusef wasn't taking her seriously. I knew I shouldn't have cared since I was pushing him away, but I couldn't help how I felt. And he had me a little crazy from the head he gave me. I'd never experienced head so good in my life, and I'd gotten it plenty of times.

"Well, maybe you should just move on from that dream. You want a relationship and Nusef doesn't—"

"Oh shit, this is him. He just texted me."

"For another booty call?" I rolled my eyes.

"No, he asked me to the movies and to get something to eat," she beamed, staring down at her phone with her mouth ajar.

"You're lying!"

"Nope!" She turned her iPhone to me so that I could see, and sure enough, he'd asked her out.

"Well, looks like you're gonna get what you want." I fake smiled as she giggled.

***

Later that night…

There was a house party tonight, and I planned to skip it since I had to study for an exam that I had in two days. However, I was sure Nusef was going because I saw him talking about it on Snapchat.

I wanted to talk to him about dating Leighton because I didn't appreciate him stringing my friend along. I loved her and she deserved

55

better than what he was trying to do. That's what I told myself, and even thought it was partially true, I was angry with him for moving on I guess.

"Cute jacket, where are you going?" my mother asked as she sat at the table with Dree, Yikayla, and Lonan.

"Thank you. And just stepping out for a moment."

"I thought you had an exam to study for, Jonaya?"

"Study and Jonaya should never be in the same sentence," Dree scoffed and shoved some mashed potatoes into her mouth.

"Fuck you, Dree. And I do, Mama. I will study when I get back. I shouldn't be gone long."

My mother nodded as I grabbed her car keys off the key rack. Rushing outside, I hopped into my mom's Mercedes and peeled off. The party started two hours ago, and I was sure Nusef's ass was just arriving. When I made it to the Southside, I smiled upon seeing him and Sax walking up the sidewalk to the house. I knew his stupid ass so well it was scary.

I parked in someone's driveway since I wasn't gonna be long, and then got out to jog across the street. I got right in the yard of the home, and yelled over the loud music to get Nusef's attention. He and Sax both turned to look at me, before Sax continued into the house party and Nusef came back down the porch steps begrudgingly. I hated that he acted like he hated me now.

"Hey, I just wanted to talk to you." I smiled when he got close enough to hear me without me having to yell.

"Talk, Jo."

"Sef, I thought we could still be friends." I exhaled. "Just because we're not gonna be together, we have to throw away almost a decade of friendship?"

"Yeah, uh, I thought about that shit and I can't be ya friend right now, Jonaya. I gotta let this shit pass and then see what's up. But what you call me over here for?"

He was so nonchalant and I didn't like it. Not to mention, I didn't like hearing that he didn't want to be friends anymore. The thought of him dating Leighton, while not talking to me, made my head hurt.

"What are you doing with Leighton?"

"Oh my gosh." He chuckled, flashing his perfect smile and making his hazel eyes light up. "Jonaya, don't come at me with this bullshit. You don't tell me who the fuck I can talk to, ma."

"You don't even like her! You're just using her and then you're gonna hurt her feelings in the end! I cannot let you do that!" I shouted.

"No, see, the problem is that you're jealous." He grinned cockily with his fine ass. "But look, ma, I'm gon' fuck and date whomever the fuck I want to and you ain't gon' say shit about it. I told you I loved you and since you don't want that," he shrugged, "I'm moving on."

The way he was smiling and shit, I knew he could tell that what he was saying bothered me.

"With Leighton? You're moving on with Leighton?"

"Yep." He put an emphasis on the P. "You look tense, like you need your pussy ate again." He licked his lips slowly, sending chills down my back. "Aye, we done? I came out to turn up, not to be out here talking to yo' confused ass."

"Nusef, leave Leighton alone."

"Pussy too good," was all he said before he made an about face and started back up into the house.

I stood there for a little bit, admiring the smooth way that he walked, and how beautiful his smile was when he turned to the side to greet some hoe. I loved him, but being with him would be too much for me. I didn't think I was mature enough, but that didn't mean I wanted to sit by and watch him fuck my best friend. And what if they fell in love? I wouldn't know what to do. There was no telling how much longer Nusef would love me.

I finally got back into my mom's car, and planned to sit there for a little bit until the person whose driveway I was in, flicked on their living room light and peeked through the blinds at me. Letting out a frustrated sigh, I reversed and started back towards my home.

On the way there, I decided to stop for a Starbucks drink since I rarely ever went there and was in the mood for it. As I got my drink from the window, my phone started to ring. I almost burned myself with this chai tea trying to hurry and answer, thinking it was Nusef.

When I saw it was Marquise, I rolled my eyes but answered anyway.

"Come over," he said before I could even greet him.

"Umm, I have to study. I can come tomorrow, babe."

"Just for a little bit. I haven't seen or talked to you all damn day because you've been busy."

I pulled out onto highway 70 and said, "Fine, I will be there in a little bit."

Marquise lived near where the party was, so I had to go back that way. I parked outside of his spot, and then got out with my drink in hand. I texted him as I walked to his door, and by the time I got to it, he was opening it for me, wearing a sexy smile. We kissed, and then he led me to his bedroom, which was really dark, except for the time on his cable box.

"Where you coming from?"

"Home. Just stopped at Starbucks on the way," I lied, sitting in the chair across from the bed where he'd sat. The setting was eerie, and he was acting kind of weird.

"How you get here so fast then?"

"I drove fast, Marquise."

Laughing, he said, "Oh, 'cause the homie said he saw you outside that house party on Dison Avenue."

"No—"

"Said you were all up in that nigga Nusef's face."

Marquise's voice was calm, but sitting here in the dark and with the way he was looking at me, had me scared as hell.

"Well, I stopped by the party and I ran into him, so we chatted for a little bit. It was nothing major, Marquise. Your friends need lives of their own."

Again, he chuckled.

"You my girl, right, Jonaya?"

"Of course."

"Good," he smiled. "Come over here."

Hesitantly, I rose to my feet and placed my drink on his nightstand near the bed. I sat down slowly, and Marquise helped me out of my jacket before tossing it across the room. He started to kiss on my neck as he laid me back, and then he climbed on top of me.

He stopped kissing and groping me to say, "I don't know if I told you this, Jo, but I love you. And when I love something, I'm very serious about it." He looked deeply into my eyes, and all I could do was nod.

I didn't know if he was being romantic or threatening me.

CHAPTER TWO

Waayil

The next morning…

I pulled up into the parking lot of Monarch Tattoo at around 10 a.m. I had a gang of fucking clients today, and I wanted to start early. Most of them wanted small shit done, but a few wanted shit that would take me a minute.

As soon as I threw my car into park and reached for my water, my phone rang. I already knew who it was, so I reached to hit ignore but saw it was my parole officer instead. I let out a sigh of relief, happy as a muthafucka that I didn't ignore that uppity ass nigga. Swear he had a stick up his ass and was always throwing warnings out like a nigga didn't understand how the game went.

"Hello," I answered.

"Good morning, Christian." He called me by my last name like some kind of a sports coach or some shit. "I know you said you found a home, but I do have to come out and take a look at it."

"Yeah, I know that." I was hoping that because he'd given me a recommendation letter that he'd pass on inspecting, but I guess I was wrong.

"I can't get out there to do it until next Friday."

"Wait, what? I don't have that much fucking time, Bradley. Come on, mane," I grunted but tried to keep my cool because this nigga stayed ready to add days to my probation. Calming down, I said, "Bradley, is there any way you can come out earlier?"

"Unfortunately, no. I even moved things around to get you the date you *do* have. You need to understand that you work on my time and not the other way around, Christian."

On God, it was taking everything in me not to drive over to that nigga's location and snatch his skinny bitch ass from his cubicle. And what made shit worse was that he knew I could only say and do so much, so he took me there. I wasn't sure how much longer I could go on being told what to do by this Napoleon Dynamite ass nigga.

"Aight, I gotta get to work, Bradley."

"Of course. Have a good day and remember, do not sleep at that house. You should be living with your mother and father until I give you the okay."

"Yep." I quickly hung up, fearing that some shit would uncontrollably slip from my mouth.

I sat there, just taking a moment to myself, so I could get back in a positive mood as I watched Rebecca come and open the shop. She was totally different now that she and my brother weren't together. She barely talked, and she dressed like she was preparing to be shipped off to a nunnery somewhere. I didn't give a fuck though. Long as she brought that sad ass to work and on time, she could dress and act however the fuck she wanted to.

My phone rang in my hand again, and when I looked down thinking it was Bradley's ass, I saw it was that nigga Neo... again.

Neo was locked up in prison with me, and he had a lot of connections. Nigga had been in and out of jail starting from his late thirties, but was in his fifties when I got in. To make a long story short, he watched how I moved through the jail, keeping to myself and checking niggas when they got out of hand from trying to show out on the calm, quiet nigga. At the same time I earned everyone else's respect, I earned Neo's, which was a big deal around the prison.

Every nigga locked up wanted to be liked or respected by that nigga as if he were the King of England or some shit. I never cared, but I got the shit anyway. He came to me, telling me how he respected me, and how I was the perfect nigga for his daughter. How a nigga locked up in prison for life was perfect for his daughter? I didn't know, but I was miserable and felt like my life was over, so him offering to get her to come through and fuck with me sounded like the move at the time. I couldn't fuck Alba because they wouldn't allow it, and Neo only agreed to help me if it involved his daughter, Zia.

So after greasing a few palms and shit, Zia and I became pretty close, if you know what I mean, and I was smashing a few times a week, which was unheard of for a nigga in prison; especially the one I was locked up in. I would treat her like my bitch because shit, why not? I wasn't going anywhere and I couldn't have the woman I wanted anyway. Shit was cool, but then I got that new lawyer, and as you know, I was released. Neo had gotten out about ten months before me, and I was holding up our deal to be with his daughter during that time. But now that I was out, shit had changed lanes of course, and that nigga was still expecting me to be with Zia, and I'm sure so was she.

"What, bruh? I'm busy," I spat into the phone.

"We need to meet up," Neo replied.

I honestly didn't know shit about Neo or Zia like that. Like I said, my life was over and I was just doing whatever to get by. By saying that, I wasn't quite sure how Neo got his money or what he did exactly to be so powerful. And I knew he wasn't bluffing because he got me the ability to smash Zia for one, and then he got my number when I got out, which was baffling as a muthafucka. Either way, the nigga didn't scare me and he wasn't about to bully a nigga into being with his daughter.

"Nah, I got a lot of shit going on, and making time for you ain't at the top of my priority list. But I work at Monarch Tattoo. Google that shit and drop by."

"Waayil, do you think this is a game? We had a damn deal, and—"

"Ain't no damn deal no more, my nigga! Realize, I agreed to that shit because I thought there was nothing else out there for me! I'm done talking about the shit! If you gon' move something then move it, my nigga! You should know better than anybody that threatening me ain't gon' get you shit but a well whooped ass, bruh!" I roared into the phone, ready to jump through this bitch and fuck his ass up.

"What kind of a man—"

"Make a move." I cut off his hollering with a calm tone before hanging up the phone and getting out of the car.

Just as I locked my whip and started towards the door, Chiara walked up in one of her tight ass dresses. She looked good, better than usual, and I didn't know what it was. I inspected her as I held the door open for her, while she looked up at me smiling and shit.

"You look different," I said as we walked towards the back.

"You don't know what it is?"

"Nah, I don't."

She sucked her teeth as she shoved her stuff into her designated locker and said, "I dyed my hair golden blond, Waayil."

"Oh shit, you did." I chuckled subtly at myself as I leaned against the wall. "Why are you frowning?"

"Because it shows that you don't pay any attention to me! My hair was red and now it's blond, Waayil, and you couldn't even tell?" she pouted and whined.

"I'm sorry," I laughed because she was for real upset. "Why you care if I pay attention to you or not?"

"You know why, asshole." She moved closer to me, and I stood firm with my hands planted deeply in my jean pockets. "You still have a girlfriend?"

"I'm pretty sure I'm gon' be with her forever."

"She's crazy." She chuckled, still standing close as hell to me with her hand lightly touching my abs through my shirt.

"Yeah, but I like it. You better get that hand off me though, before she breaks that shit." I lifted her palm from my midsection.

"Whatever. You just remember what I told you. If that goes sour, I will be here waiting for you."

I didn't say anything as I went back to my room because… uh… never would I make her my girl. I stopped to get a look over my shoulder to watch her ass as she went back to the front. I had a mind to tell her ass not to dress like that, but a lot of times she got male clients for our artists that weren't as established as Nusef, Sax, and I, so I let it go.

By the time I finished getting my room ready, my first client had arrived. After that, it was almost like back to back, especially because I added a couple of the homies from way back in between my breaks.

I was so hard at work that I'd forgotten to get food. However, Chiara's thirsty ass went and got me something from Krystal burgers, which I appreciated very much, but still wasn't gon' fuck with her.

I was done with my last person around 8:30 p.m., and when I checked my phone on my way out, I saw Alba had texted me. I wanted to forget about her stupid ass sometimes, but I knew I couldn't. Some days I hated the evil thoughts I had about her, simply because she *could* be carrying my kid. My mama told me to refrain from saying certain things, because if that baby was mine, I didn't want him or her thinking I hated them at one point. That was very true.

Instead of texting Alba back, I decided to just call her because my hands were a bit full.

"What's good?" I said, walking through the lobby. Rebecca gave me a nod that she would lock up, and Chiara rushed to walk out with me so I shook my head in irritation.

"Hey, I'm sorry to bother you, but can you stop at the liquor store and get me some Ginger Ale and crackers."

"Fuck wrong with yo' car? I ain't yo' muthafuckin' errand boy 'round these parts. You better—" I frowned and then remembered my mother's words so I relaxed. With my eyes closed, I let out a breath and said, "Yeah... give me like fifteen minutes, ma."

"Okay, thank you."

"Bye." Chiara touched my arm on the way to her car.

"Bye," I responded dryly, replying to the plethora of texts I had, starting with Yikayla first. I heard Chiara smack her teeth at my dryness, but I really didn't care. Her thirstiness was so fucking unbelievably unattractive, and I wish she could see that.

I stopped by the store to get the shit Alba needed, then raced over there. I just wanted to get home to my girl, and maybe play with little man if he was still awake. I smiled thinking about Lonan. He was cute as hell, and smart too. Niggas like Roscoe didn't understand how lucky he was to have that boy as his kid.

"Thank you," Alba whispered lowly as she answered her door to let me in. She was hunched over, wrapped in a blanket and looked like shit.

"Here. You need anything else? I'm about to bounce."

"No, just this. I've been throwing up all day. Your baby is killing me."

I declined to respond to that bullshit because I just had a feeling that, that wasn't my kid. But what if it was? I would feel like shit for all my thoughts.

"Did you wanna touch my stomach?" she offered with a weak smile.

"For what, Alba? I'm sure ain't shit poppin' off in there yet. Stop trying to get me to feel on yo' stupid ass."

"You are such an ass!" she shouted.

"And you a stupid ass. Trying to get me to feel on yo' stomach when you ain't got shit going on. I know that baby ain't got no damn legs yet, so what the fuck would I be feeling for, huh? What you had for lunch? Shit, in that case, come feel my shit."

She stared up at me for a minute and then burst into tears. Not in the mood for any of this bullshit, I left her ass just like that and went home. Ignorant ass bitch.

CHAPTER THREE

Rori Goode

"Just one more." Eko bit his lip as he looked me in the eyes.

I playfully rolled mine before laying another kiss on his lips. He was so damn fine, and it seemed like every time I saw him, he somehow got even finer.

We'd been spending a lot of time together ever since he'd saved me from Gavin's wrath, and sadly, I hadn't been this happy in a long time. I didn't notice how much I was settling until I started hanging with Eko tough. Of course, Gavin called me and texted me 24/7 damn near, but I just blocked his number a couple days ago, so that shit stopped.

"Okay, I have to go or I'm gonna be late for class." I smiled, one leg hanging out of Eko's car.

"What time should I be back to get you?"

"Eko, you don't have to pick me up. Jonaya and I get out of class at the same time, and my mother let her use the car this morning so she's gonna drive me home."

"I don't mind picking my girl up."

Him calling me his girl made me pause for a moment. He noticed, and a smirk spread across his face.

"Eko, let's just relax for a moment. I don't wanna hop from one relationship to the next so quickly."

"Okay."

"Are you mad now?"

"Nah, I'm not mad, ma." He kissed me again, making goosebumps rise on my forearms, and then I got out of his car.

As he sped through the parking lot blasting his music, I stood there watching him. I wanted that man badly, but I had a feeling he would hurt me. Gavin had done enough damage to me, and I wasn't sure if I was ready for round two just yet.

Plus, Eko was *that* nigga, and I didn't know if I could live up to being his girl. The way he tossed poor Jenni to the side like that was scary to say the least. I didn't know what I would do if he got tired of me. Then, not only would I be known as the hoe who left her boyfriend for his best friend, but I would be heartbroken yet again. So no, no fucking way was I getting into a relationship just yet. I needed a small break.

I only had one class today, Math, which was why I agreed to spend the night with Eko last night. I knew he would keep me up, but it didn't matter since this class was so late in the afternoon.

"Hey, Rori!" this girl from my class named… I guess I forgot, was waving me down.

"Hey," I smiled, slowing down so that she could catch up.

"Girl, who was that? He was cute as hell!"

Carissa, that was her damn name. I only remembered because she had it written all over her book cover.

"He's just a friend. How did you even see him? His windows are tinted."

"Oh, I saw him when he dropped you off last time, two days ago. He opened your door and walked you to class."

Damn, stalker much?

"Right. Well yeah, he's just a friend."

We entered the class, and since the teacher was conversing with another staff member, the students were just having conversation amongst themselves until he was done. Carissa and I sat down, and of course she wanted to continue talking about Eko.

"Does he have any friends or anything? I'm so tired of these square ass college niggas, girl."

"I will ask him."

"Good, thank you. You have my number, right? Text me what he says."

"Actually, no, I don't have it." Before I even got my sentence out, she had snatched my iPhone up, waving it for me to unlock it and store her digits.

Thankfully, as soon as I had it stored and texted her, the professor was ready to start class, which meant we had to be silent.

Class seemed to take forever to end, but when it did, I hightailed it out that bitch. I met Jonaya in the parking lot, who was flirting with some guy like she didn't have enough nigga problems.

"Excuse me." I slipped between her and the dude she was smiling up at. "I wanna drive. I can drop you at home."

"Oooh, where are you going?" she grinned.

"None of your business, bitch."

"To see Ekoooo." She dragged it out, and the simple sound of his name had me smiling hard as hell. "Ahhh! See! See!"

"Aye, ma, can I get your number or nah?" the boy finally spoke up.

"Maybe, if I see you again." Jonaya winked and rounded the back of the car to get to the passenger side.

"Then what about you?" He ran his tongue across the golds on his top row of teeth, as he looked me up and down lustfully.

"Nigga, if you don't scram." I sucked my teeth as Jonaya laughed.

My sister and I got in the car, and I quickly sped home because I *did* want to see Eko. He told me he only had a few heads to cut, and then he had some business to handle, but that by the time I got out of class and to him, he'd be there or on his way.

As I pulled into the driveway and waited for Jonaya to get out, I noticed a familiar car parked across the street. As I stared hard in my rearview mirror, a loud knock on the window made me damn near jump out of my skin.

"Gavin, what the fuck!" I shouted.

He smiled widely, and then pointed to the door so that I could open it. I hit unlock, and as he slid into the passenger seat, I stared off, arms folded.

"You smell good," he spoke softly as if that was supposed to make me forgive him for threatening my life and cheating on me.

"Thanks. What do you want? I have somewhere to be."

"Rori…" He took my hand into his. "Look, I know me pulling a gun on you was a bit much, and I apologize for that shit. It's just that I love you so damn much, and the thought of you leaving me drove me crazy, ma."

"It can't drive you that crazy, nigga, because you cheated on me with some hoe that wears cheap ass beauty supply hoops!"

"I told you, the homie and his girl came over to use the bedroom and she must have left them."

I threw my head back laughing at this man right here. He clearly thought I was a damn fool to believe some shit like that.

"So you let your friends fuck in your bed?"

"Yeah, sometimes, but I always change the sheets and shit. This has never happened; one of their bitches leaving shit behind."

"Gavin, I don't believe you and even if I did, I don't want to be with you anymore. You pulled a gun on me, and you don't treat me like I want to be treated. You act as if I'm your business partner and not your girl."

"I know. I know that, Rori, and all that shit is gon' change, ma. I promise."

"No."

"Is this because of Eko? You fucking him?"

"No, I'm not fucking him! What do you take me for?"

"Someone told me y'all have been rocking a little bit. Couple people seen y'all out at places, so I had to ask."

"Yeah, because we're friends. I go out with my friends."

"You know he wants you though, right? You need to be careful." I didn't respond to him, so he exhaled as he looked out the window, then turned his attention back to me. "Rori, I swear to you that I'm gon' do better, baby. I love you, and these days without you have really fucked with me. I'll give you some time to think about it, aight?"

"Yes, Gavin. Just get out of the car."

I felt him staring at the side of my face, before he let my hand go and got out like I'd asked him to. I waited until he got back in his car and drove off, before I cranked back up and started towards Eko's place.

I got us some food from expensive ass Chick-fil-A because I knew he loved their chicken sandwiches, and I wanted to surprise him.

I parked my mom's car across the street from his house, gathered the food, and then went towards his spot.

As I started up the steps to knock, I heard loud female moans coming from the side of his house where his bedroom was. My breathing became shallow as my suddenly sweaty hands gripped the food I'd bought. I rounded the corner of the house, and walked down the side through the backyard gate. The moans were louder, and whoever it was, was getting fucked the shit out of. I finally made it to the window the sounds were coming from, and when I looked through the swinging blinds, I could see Eko giving Jenni the business doggy-style.

The food slipped from my hands, which went right to banging on the window. I watched Eko stop, pull out his thankfully condom covered dick, and slightly fix himself as he made his way to the window. I continuously banged on the glass, hoping the shit would eventually shatter.

"Baby, what is it?" Jenni panted, looking like she was about to pass out from that good dick I knew Eko had.

"Rori, baby, I'm about to come around—"

"No, fuck you! Don't you ever hit me up or talk to me again you whack, lying ass nigga!"

I ran basically because I wanted to leave before he got out the house. Unfortunately, he'd moved too fast, and by the time I got into his driveway, he was there too, snatching me up.

"Rori, you said we wasn't together, ma! What the fuck! You wanna be with me then say that shit!"

"I don't, and let me go!" I yanked my arm from him. He was strong though so I had to yank extra hard, which sent me on my ass in his lawn.

"Eko!" Jenni came rushing to his doorway.

He paid her no mind as he squatted down to look me in the eyes.

"Rori, say the word and it's me and you."

"Only words I have are fuck you, bitch ass nigga."

I hopped up, dusted my jeans off, and walked my ass back to the car. As I put my seatbelt on, I saw Eko still in his yard, pants unbuckled so you could see his boxers, wearing a deep sexy frown while Jenni continuously called his name like an annoying alarm. I was done with Eko. He was just the type of nigga I knew he was.

CHAPTER THREE

Canyon Dennis

I'd just gotten out of the shower and finished brushing, flossing, and rinsing my mouth, when I heard some stupid muthafucka banging on my damn door like they'd lost their mind. I tightened my towel around my waist, and walked through my living room to look through the peephole. I was surprised as hell to see Dree's fine ass standing there with a plate covered in foil.

As mad as I was at her, seeing her had my dick rising like them damn zombies in *Thriller*. She knew what the fuck she was doing coming over here in them little ass jean shorts and a top that barely covered anything. Licking my lips at her dark cognac skin, I yanked the door open, praying that my mans down below didn't greet her before I did.

"What?" I hissed.

"I was making breakfast for my family this morning, and I made way too much," she smiled. Her hair was pulled back into a ponytail, and I loved that shit. Her hair being out of her face showed just how beautiful her bougie ass was.

"Fuck that got to do with me?"

"I brought some over here for you. I know you love my waffles and scrambles, so I have some here. Can I come in? If it's too cool, I can warm it up for you."

"Why you didn't take that extra food to your nigga?" I smirked, knowing she wouldn't take kindly to what I'd said.

"Because this isn't his favorite, it's yours."

"Well maybe you should start making what that nigga likes instead of what I like, so you won't have to make pointless ass trips to my crib, ma."

"Canyon, can I please just come in and warm this up for you?"

Thinking with the wrong head, I stepped back and let her in. I wasn't gon' let her ass stay long because I had some shit to deal with regarding my baby mama. I wouldn't dare mention that shit though, because I didn't want Dree thinking her ass was right about me.

My baby mama, Luna, and I didn't have much drama really; she would just have her moments where she gave me a hard time, and then she'd fall back. Right now was one of her, give-my-baby-daddy-a-hard-time moments, and I just had to wait it out. I was going to try to wait it out at least. Because I was extremely fucking close to reverting to the old Canyon and bodying her ass then tossing her limbs into the Mississippi River. You know how much easier life would be?

I watched Dree as she walked in, taking my food to the kitchen. She had on some high ass heels that had her ass sitting upright in them tiny ass shorts.

Adjusting my dick, I went to my bedroom to slip on some clothes and by the time I was finished, the smell of the food had filled the air from her warming it up. Returning to the kitchen, I saw Dree had set my plate down, accompanied by a glass of juice. She was smiling widely as hell, as if I'd forgiven her and all was well. Not returning the gesture, I sat down at the table, said a prayer, and dug in.

"Oh, you can bounce if you want to. I'll drop this plate off at ya crib to ya mama or one of your sisters," I said as soon as her sexy ass sat down. The look on her face was jokes, but I played it cool.

"Dang, I can't sit here with you for a moment?"

"For what? I told you I don't fuck with you no more. You think 'cause you lied yo' way into my crib with some food, shit has changed, shorty?" I frowned. Her mouth opened and closed, but no words came out. "Well it hasn't. I'm off you, and for good."

"So you deal with Jodi now?"

Laughing on the inside, I decided to fuck with her.

"Don't worry about who I'm fucking."

Granted, I did smash Jodi but only because I was drunk. The shit happened in the back seat of my truck, and I swear to God it wasn't planned. Bitch was fine as fuck and on me tough at the right time, so I busted her down. But it was definitely a one-night stand type of deal.

In response, Dree just sat back pouting, while folding her arms. I polished that good ass food off, and she sat there the whole time, watching me like a dummy.

"You're leaving?" She stood up right along with me, eyes full of hope as if we'd been conversing this whole time.

"Yeah, I got shit to do."

"Can I come? I'm free today." She followed me out of the kitchen, and I stopped in my tracks once my mind processed her question.

Turning to face her annoying ass, I said, "What don't you get about me not fucking with you, ma? We can't be friends, and we can't be anything else. I don't wanna see you. If you spot me at the university, act like you don't fucking know me, period. I appreciate the food, but don't pop yo' ass up over here no more on that bullshit." Looking over her head to see the plate she brought sitting on the table, I added, "Matter fact, get that damn plate so I don't have to drop it off and see you."

I low-key felt bad seeing her eyes become glossy at my words, but that was only because my stupid ass still had feelings for her shady ass. But fuck that. She wasn't the type of bitch I wanted to build a life with. Dree was that muthafucka that would leave you when you were down and out, and that was the last thing I wanted. I don't know what the hell I was thinking trying to be with her honestly. She was better off with whatever rich nigga she'd bounced on me for.

"Canyon—"

"Get ya plate and go, Dree."

She turned around to slowly pick the plate up off the table, and then somberly grabbed her purse before slipping past me. Once outside, we both went to our cars, and I sped off, not even staying to make sure she left. I cursed her ass on the way to my baby mama Luna's house. I had two bitches I didn't fuck with in my life at this point.

Luna's stupid ass was supposed to drop my son off to me yesterday evening, but she didn't. She wasn't answering her phone, and I guess she'd told her sister, Rain, not to answer hers either, because she, too, didn't pick up when I called. I didn't go hard on this bitch yesterday because my son needed to spend more time with his mama.

See, every time I got him, something would always come up on Luna's end, leaving me to have my son to myself for weeks at a time. Trust me, I didn't mind, and would much rather have Luna disappear into thin air, but it wasn't about what I wanted, it was about what Cade wanted and needed.

I hit ignore on a phone call from Jodi as I pulled into Luna's driveway. I grabbed my hat from the seat and pulled it down before exiting the car and trucking it up to her door. Her fucking doorbell had been broken for years, so I beat on her screen like I was about to break that shit down. Shit, I was about to break that shit down.

I heard low talking and the sound of rustling, which made me raise an eyebrow. Just as I was about to say something, I heard Luna unlocking the door. She answered, dressed up in some cheap ass Instagram boutique lingerie, smiling all hard and wide and shit.

"Move the fuck out my way. Where is my son?" I snarled, barging in and almost knocking her delusional ass over. "You had me waiting outside so you could put some damn lingerie on? Fuck is wrong with you, Luna?"

She always did shit like this when she thought I was moving on with a new bitch. Ever since she saw a woman in my whip, she'd been on her "seduce my baby daddy" tip. But when she thought I was single and only focusing on Cade and my job, she didn't give two fucks about sleeping with me. I honestly didn't know what the hell was wrong with her ass. Luna was a special kind of person, and not the good kind.

"You don't like it?" She spun around, dropping the robe.

The lingerie was cheap as fuck, but the way them lace shorts cupped her plump ass was nothing to shake a stick at. Luna would always be fine as hell with her light bright ass. She'd had her share of bad weaves on occasions, but everything else was always on point.

Realizing I was actually admiring the sight before me, I quickly came to my senses and turned my lip up in disgust. It was too late though, because Luna was already wearing that lustful smirk on her face.

"Cade!" I called my son's name.

"Shhh, shhh, Canyon! He's napping. He should be up in like ten minutes. He fell asleep about an hour and a half ago."

I glared at Luna as she tousled her hair, before I sat down on the couch and hit ignore on Jodi's fifth call of the day. I hadn't said two words to her ass since I fucked, and now she had me worried that she was on some fatal attraction shit.

"You got some water?" I quizzed, tossing my head back. This house was always so damn hot.

"Of course."

Luna pranced off, letting her ass jiggle wildly as she walked to the kitchen. Her crib was small as hell, with an open floor plan up front so you could see into the kitchen from the living room. She brought me the water bottle, and then sat next to me, allowing me to take in that loud ass perfume.

"How was your day?" She rubbed her hand up and down my leg.

"Why you ain't drop my son off yesterday like you were supposed to?" I gave her the side eye as I downed that good ass water.

"Because he and I were having so much fun yesterday."

"Nah, you just like getting me over here to act a fool on yo' stupid ass." I shook my head. "You like when I talk roughly to you."

"No I don't!" she grinned, obviously lying.

"Yeah, the fuck you do, ma. But look, one of these days I'm gon' choke the shit out of you."

"No you wouldn't. You love me too much."

Snickering to myself, I said, "Sure."

"You do. That's why you asked me to have your baby, and then I did," she replied proudly. Just like a hoodrat.

"No, I said that shit because ya pussy was good, I was in the moment, and I was drunk and high as hell."

Her jaw dropped which prompted me to laugh. Shit was funny but it was true too. I wanted Dree back then, but Luna had some good ass shit between her legs that kept my mind off Dree for a minute.

"Canyon, why do you always—"

"Daddy!" Cade cut his mama off, running up to me while rubbing his eye.

I scooped him up, and started right towards the door, happy as hell he'd saved me from his crybaby ass mama. As she tried to finish her sentence, I left out. I never took shit of Cade's from her crib because he had plenty at mine.

"I hate you, Canyon!" Luna yelled from the doorway.

"Why does Mommy always say that?" Cade quizzed as I buckled him in the back seat.

"Because yo' mama is a hater," I answered once I was in the driver's seat.

"A hater?" he repeated, face frowned in confusion.

"Yep. Next time yo' mama is telling one of her bunion footed friends about me, tell her she's a hater so she'll stop aight?" I looked in the rearview mirror at him.

"Okay," he nodded seriously.

I chuckled subtly to myself because that would be the one phone call from Luna that I would be looking forward to.

CHAPTER THREE

Nusef

*T*onight the homie, Sax, was having a birthday party, which meant every muthafucka from all over Memphis would be in the building. He'd rented out this big ass space downtown, and had caterers and everything. Nigga was smart about it by charging people to get in too. Shit was legit, so he didn't have to worry too much about making people pay to get in.

Currently "Fight Night" by Migos was playing over the whole place, and a bunch of nasty bitches were dancing hard in their skimpy ass outfits. I hated hoes, but my dick loved them a lot. Sax's ass was in the midst of it all, getting freaked by a couple of bitches that I knew wanted to get in his mediocre pockets.

"Now why the fuck she here?" Waayil quizzed as he sat next to me, Canyon, and Eko in the sectioned off area. Sax knew better than to try to make us chill with the regular folk. I wasn't having that shit, especially because my brother and I put in on his liquor so that he'd have top shelf shit.

"You know anywhere she hear you gon' be, her ass is gon' be there too," Eko replied, as I nodded in agreement.

Alba never missed an opportunity to kick it or be around Waayil. I think it was more of an obsession than love.

I don't know what it was about my brother, but ever since he'd started dating, women always became obsessed with his ass. Even Chiara back at the tattoo shop was showing signs of being obsessed with him. It never failed. That was probably why he didn't wanna fuck a lot of bitches growing up like me and the homies did, because every time, that hoe would turn crazy.

I didn't know what this nigga did to these bitches. I think it was because Waayil wasn't the thirsty type, so you'd never catch him obsessing over a woman... ever; except Yikayla. Even at the strip club, while all of us were hooting and hollering, throwing dollars, Waayil would be chilling, drinking, and watching. What made shit funnier was that the nigga barely talked, but still got bitches that he barely even wanted. I chuckled at my thoughts.

Waayil was always focused on his goals and shit, and I think women gravitated towards him because of that. Whatever it was, I was just happy as hell I didn't get that damn gene; too damn stressful for me. Maybe it was them damn dimples.

"Well, I'm tired of that shit. I hate that we both know everybody. I should have fucked with an unknown ass bitch so she could be somewhere across town with her own muthafuckin' friends," Waayil spat as he refilled his glass using the bottle of Hennessy we had sitting on the table in front of us. "If Yikayla and I split, which won't happen, my next girl is gon' be the type of bitch that has no profile picture on social media. The type that just like shit and don't post."

Canyon, Eko, and I doubled over in laughter and shook our heads at Waayil's crazy ass. My brother was a crazy one with his usually mute ass. But put him around Yikayla Goode and he was like a damn kitten or some shit. It was literally like magic on God.

I adjusted my sparkling watch after refilling my own glass, taking in the dark scenery that was lit up by glow sticks. Shit was high key gay as fuck, but that was Sax for you.

"Them shoes is dope." Canyon nodded down to my Gold Nike Air Max 97's and I nodded to him with a smirk.

"Had to use Waayil's shoe plug for these," I responded.

I was fresh as hell tonight, and scoping the scene of bitches to see what I wanted. A lot of them were looking to get chose, which made me a picky ass nigga. I had fucked with some of the baddest hoes, so there was no room for me to bed the butterface ass bitches; that was some high school shit, when I was just looking to bust a nut on anything.

"How the fuck you still got a plug and you've been locked up for six years, mane?" Eko frowned as he rolled up. We all burst into laughter because that shit was true. Nigga still had connects fresh out the pen.

Waayil just shrugged with a grin, taking down his drink.

As I scanned the room, I saw some dude in Rebecca's face that she clearly didn't want there. She'd been acting like she was gon' kill her fucking self these past few weeks, so I was surprised she'd even come out.

"Be right back," I said, rising to my feet and making my way across the room to the bar where she and that thirsty ass nigga were. "Aye, she's good, bruh." I approached them, staring down at him because the nigga was on the shorter side, looking like a light-skinned Boosie; golds and all. Jeans were so damn baggy that it made no sense.

"Who the fuck are you?" he hissed, spit flying every damn where.

"Nigga, back yo' ass up and get that damn saliva in control. You spit on my clothes again and I'm gon' rock yo' shit, bruh," I gritted, moving his way a little bit more.

"Mane, fuck outta here." He waved me off but walked his whack ass away, looking both ways for a new bitch to bother.

"Thank you." Rebecca smiled when I turned to look down at her. She looked good tonight.

"I see you're not sick anymore," I smirked.

"Sick? I was never sick." She frowned and then her face softened. "I just wasn't wearing makeup, asshole!" She struck me and I moved some.

"I know. I'm fucking with you. But I'm glad you came out tonight. We got plenty of shit at the table over there if you wanna drink in peace." I nodded towards where Waayil, Canyon, and Eko were.

"Okay, thanks."

I led her to where we were, and she took a seat in between me and Canyon. She made herself a drink and moved her body a little bit to the music. It felt good to see her happy for once, especially because I was the reason for her acting so glum and shit.

"Taste this concoction I made." She smiled and placed her cup to my lips. I took a sip and turned my lip up at how weak it was.

"Shit is like water."

"No it's not, nigga," she giggled. "Not everybody drinks lighter fluid like you, okay, Nusef?"

I laughed at her and she pressed her lips against my cheek. She did it again, and then gently turned my face towards hers to peck me. I'd kind of missed them soft muthafuckas of hers. Before I knew it, she was straddling my lap and we were tonguing it up like crazy. The feeling of her plump ass in my hands had my dick hard as a brick.

"Let's go to the car," I whispered as I sucked on her neck, which smelled like some cotton candy.

She nodded and then got off my lap, so I took her hand in mine and led her to the car. Once in the back seat of my whip, we got right back to kissing and I was damn near trying to tear that dress off of her. As I laid her on her back and started to pull down her panties, she unbuttoned the top of my shirt.

"Baby, I'm so happy you changed your mind."

"Wait, what?" I pulled away, leaving her panties at her knees.

"About us. You said you couldn't do it but—"

"And I can't, Rebecca." I felt my face twist up. "Fuck!" I plopped back down into the seat as she pulled her underwear back up.

"So you thought we were just gonna fuck tonight and that was gonna be it?"

"Uh, yeah, pretty much. I don't know how you thought me

fucking you right now meant that we were gon' be together. I told you I couldn't do it."

"Why, Nusef! You obviously have feelings for me so I don't get it! This is so fucking stupid! I'm tired of you little ass boys out here!" she fussed as she fixed her dress. "I just don't get why you can't be a man about yours and try to make what we have work! It's almost like—"

"Because I love somebody else, Rebecca." I turned to face her, and her mouth was ajar. "Is that what you wanted to hear?"

I tried to let her ass off easy by making her think I just couldn't be with her nagging ass because I was a player, but she had yanked the truth out of me.

"Who?" her voice trembled. When I didn't reply right away, she yelled, "Who is it, Nusef!"

"Calm yo' ass down, aight?" I spat before turning my attention back straight ahead. "It's Jonaya."

Laughing loudly, she said, "I knew it! Oh my gosh, how could I be so stupid. I knew you were fucking her hoe ass the whole time."

"Aight, first off, don't call her a hoe. Secondly, I have never fucked Jonaya, even to this day."

"Wow, you're defending her now?"

"Hell yeah! Didn't I just tell yo' ass I loved her? Fuck I look like, letting you talk shit about the bitch I'm in love with?"

"Whatever, Nusef." She shook her head like she always did before she was about to cry.

"Rebecca, get out the car."

She shook her head at me with tears pooled in her eyes, before shoving my back-door open and getting out. I did the same and hit my alarm to lock my shit, before buttoning my shirt back up. Instead of going back to the party, Rebecca went to her car to leave. Just as I was walking back up, I spotted Jonaya, Leighton, and my little sister, Wednesday.

"Sup." I greeted Jonaya with a head nod before hugging and kissing the top of Wednesday's head.

When I turned my attention towards Leighton, we both smiled widely before I pulled her in for a hug. She was looking better every time I saw her ass, and now that I knew how good that pussy was, she was almost a straight up and down ten. Get her some ass shots and she'd be wifey material.

"You look good as fuck, ma." I bit my lip, eyeing Leighton.

"Thank you, and so do you," she blushed. I'd definitely be in them guts tonight.

I felt Jonaya's eyes on me as I draped my arm around Leighton and walked back into the venue. When I got to the section I was sitting in, Yikayla was straddling Waayil, and them niggas were kissing so hard I couldn't tell where her face began and his ended. I accidentally checked out her little plump ass because of how roughly he was squeezing on that shit.

When I sat down, I pulled Leighton into my lap, with my eyes hard on Jonaya. She was hot as fuck, I could tell, and that shit was making my night so much damn better. Just as I started feeling good about fucking with Jonaya's head, Marquise called her name and she rushed from our section to kiss and greet him. She glanced over her shoulder at me as he attacked her neck, and I just scoffed lowly.

"I'll be right back," I told Leighton, moving her out of my lap and to the side.

"What happened?" she questioned, but I just kept it pushing towards Marquise and Jonaya.

Jonaya's eyes were wide as hell as I got closer, because I guess she thought I was about to fuck Marquise's ass up again. Shit, if he said or did something I didn't like in this moment, it was bound to fucking happen.

"Jonaya, let me talk to you for a second," I stated once I made it to them.

"Nah, nigga, what the fuck you think this is?" Marquise barked, grabbing Jonaya's arm. His actions pissed me off more so than his slick ass words.

"Get yo' damn hands off her, my nigga," I spoke calmly as I pried his fingers from her body. As I started off with her, I realized he was following, so I turned around, getting in his face, and spat, "Bruh, you wanna go at it again in front of all these muthafuckas?"

"Baby, it'll be just a second," Jonaya told him.

He stared down at her and then nodded as if she was really the one to change his mind. What changed his mind was when I reminded him of how he got that ass whooped in front of all them damn people outside of Monarch.

"Stop all that shit you're doing in my face," I hissed to Jonaya once I got her in the abandoned hallway of the venue.

"Doing what? You were the one pulling Leighton into your lap!"

"So! You don't wanna be with me so why the fuck does it matter when I pull a bitch into my lap, ma?"

"Why does it matter when I let a nigga kiss on me?" The way she rolled her neck made me want to snatch her smart ass up.

"Because I love you. I explained that shit to you forwards and backwards, so stop with the extras."

"Fine. Sorry. But as far as Leighton, you need to… Nusef! Nusef!"

I didn't even stay to listen; I just walked off. I'd said what I'd needed to say, and if she wanted to play with Marquise's life tonight, then that was up to her.

When I came back to sit down next to Waayil, who still had Yikayla in his lap only she was talking to someone else, he gave me a look.

"What?" I frowned.

"You need to boss up on Jo's ass."

"I can't make her be my girl!" I hissed lowly since Leighton was on the other side of me dancing and conversing with Wednesday.

"Shiiiit. Why you can't? She would have been having my baby by now fuckin' around with a nigga like me. Find ya balls muthafucka, or are you walking 'round here with a pussy between ya legs?"

"Fuck you." I shook my head, taking in his words.

I didn't know what the fuck to do. All I knew was if we kept up with the bullshit, we were gon' drive each other crazy.

CHAPTER THREE

Yikayla

Lonan cried hard as hell every time his daddy tried to take him, so I had to get him to sleep before Roscoe could slip out with him. I just couldn't bear seeing my baby cry so hard while calling my name, so I made Roscoe wait until I'd gotten him together. It was crazy how Roscoe couldn't even hold him, yet, Waayil could. As much as I loved that Lonan was becoming close with Waayil, I wanted him to like his daddy too.

"We shouldn't have to do this shit, Kay." Roscoe sighed once I had Lonan buckled into his car seat inside of Roscoe's car.

"Roscoe, please don't start." I looked down the street at Waayil's parents' home, making sure Waayil wasn't home yet. As many times as I'd told Waayil he needed to behave in the presence of Roscoe, I knew my words went in one ear and out of the other.

"I'm just saying, we're torturing him by pushing him back and forth when we need to be raising him together."

"He was crying because he doesn't want you to touch him, Roscoe.

95

He's afraid of you. And raise him together? What's the last thing you did for him? Keep in mind that the car seat he's buckled into right now is the one from my car. You still haven't gotten one for him. Your mother even has one for him in her car, yet, you don't. Plus, how would Shamaria and RJ feel about us raising Lonan together?"

"That was the old me, and I don' told you Shamaria is not my son's mother."

I burst into laughter and shook my head at him.

"Boy, go home."

"Aye, wait." He grabbed my hand but I snatched it from him. Moving in closer to me, he stared down into my eyes and said, "We love each other and we need to do this together. Don't break our family up just yet over small shit."

"Small shit? I hope you're referring to your four-year-old son's height and not the fact that he actually exists, because there isn't anything small about that. Have my baby back in two days and FaceTime me when I request it. Goodnight."

I knew Roscoe was still watching me as I went into the house, but I didn't turn around. Once inside, I looked out of the window and watched until he'd gotten into his car and drove off. I could bet my whole weeks' worth of pay that he was going straight to his mama's house to get her to help with Lonan. Although I appreciated Miss Laughton's hating ass, I wanted Roscoe to build a bond with our baby on his own so he wouldn't have to wait until he was asleep to take him.

I went upstairs to get into the shower because tonight Brynn, Rori, and I were going out. I tried to get Dree to come, but she said she had too much studying to do, and Jonaya really hadn't been in the partying mood lately. I didn't know what her deal was because it seemed like every time I wanted her to come out with me, or go anywhere, she couldn't go. It was almost like she was avoiding me, but I knew that couldn't have been the case… right?

"Are you wearing a dress?" Rori yelled through my door as I tightened my towel around my body.

"Yes, I am."

"K! Oh, and Waayil is here."

Her question reminded me to text Brynn what the attire was, because I didn't want her rolling up in pants or something more laid back when Rori and I were gonna be dressed up.

After sending the message to Brynn, I slipped on my burgundy colored thong since it matched the dress I was wearing tonight. The dress was really tight, short, and had no straps. I was hoping Waayil didn't get done working until I was already gone, but that wasn't the case. This dress would not get his approval, but I was wearing it!

Speaking of the devil, I heard him knock on my bedroom door and then slip in. When I looked over my shoulder at him, a sexy smile covered his handsome face as he leaned up against my door. His deep dimples were so adorable, standing out amongst his facial hair. And I loved the way his tattoos looked on his deep cocoa skin. He was wearing a wife beater, gray sweats that showed a nice healthy bulge, socks, and some black Huaraches. The wife beater clung to his six-pack, making me nibble on my lip at the sight. He was so tall and built that it was ridiculous. His scent traveled from where he was, and danced up my nose, giving me chills.

"Don't put that dress on yet," he said, moving closer towards me.

I was in front of my mirror, wearing only a thong with my hair tied up. As soon as he made it to me, his big hands traveled down the front of my body as he pressed his hard dick against my ass. His dick was so hard that I was surprised it hadn't ripped through his boxers and bottoms.

"Waayil, Brynn is gonna be here soon."

Ignoring me, he groped my breasts and kissed on my shoulder sensually. As badly as I wanted to stop him, he had me feeling so good already. Dropping his hands to my waist, he craned his neck around to kiss me gently, and I could taste the candy he must have eaten before coming here. Waayil could make me cum from the way he kissed me; slowly yet hungrily was his motto. His soft, thick lips traveled down my neck until he vacuumed my nipple into his mouth, sucking passionately.

"Mmm," I moaned, lips tucked in and eyes closed, as he attacked my nipples while still gripping my waist.

He turned me to face him, and then pushed me down onto my tall king-sized bed. Grasping the waistband of my panties, he tugged them down past my thighs and placed them on the bed. Yanking me to the edge, he pressed his mouth against my lower lips and began to French kiss my pussy softly, which sent chills down my spine.

"Waayil," I whimpered when he slowly began to suck on my clit. Waayil could eat pussy like no other. He knew when to be gentle with it, and when to aggressively eat.

Closing my eyes, I caressed the back of his head as he buried his face further, making my legs spread wider. He was flicking, sucking, groaning, and slurping hard as he passionately ate my pussy. I loved when he moaned while eating me out like he was just that hungry for it.

I looked down at him, loving the way his hands moved up and down my thighs, roughly grabbing at them every now and again.

"I'm gonna cum, mmm." My voice trembled as Waayil went hard in the paint. I began to wind my hips a little against his mouth, feeling like my eyes were gonna roll into the back of my head.

Next thing I knew, I was exploding hard. Waayil attacked me into another orgasm that had me damn near biting a hole in my lip. He then cleaned me with his tongue, leaving kisses here and there as he lapped up my juices.

"You taste so fucking good, ma," he growled in between soft sensual pecks to my pussy. My body was still trembling a little from the two orgasms he'd brought me to.

Finally, he pulled away and stood up with a smile. Seeing his facial hair glistening was so sexy to me.

I grinned back and then went to clean between my legs, while he brushed his teeth in my bathroom. We spent so much time together that he left little toiletries like that here just in case.

"You're lucky I have another pair of maroon colored thongs for my dress, Waayil," I hissed, as I came out of the bathroom, seeing him seated on my bed. "Waayil!" I shrieked when he pulled me towards him by my waist, and then groped my ass roughly. He laid his head on my ass with his freaky ass. "Waayil, if you don't leave, I'm never gonna be ready," I whined.

"I could go to sleep just like this." He squeezed it before laying his head back on it. Every time I felt his strong hands grope my ass, I got hornier.

Laughing, I replied, "Waayil, goodbye."

"Aight." He stood up, towering over me like a skyscraper.

He gave me a kiss that was getting me hot again, so I pulled away and then turned him around. I tried pushing his big ass towards the door, but I wasn't strong enough, which he found funny. He got to my door and went out, before peeking his head back in.

"I love you, Yikayla." He cheesed, letting his dimples take center stage, as his hazel eyes brightened.

"I love you too, baby," I blushed. Embarrassed, I covered my face, which made him laugh a little in his sexy deep voice.

He came back into the room to give me one more kiss before leaving my bedroom and eventually the house. I walked to the window to look down, and like always, he was smiling up at me with his perfect grill, before walking down the porch steps. I felt so stupid and ridiculous from smiling as hard as I was. He literally didn't have to say anything to make me weak, which is why I guess he never said much.

I spotted Brynn's car pulling up as Waayil jogged his sexy bowlegged ass across the street, so I rushed to put my dress and jewelry on. My clit was still throbbing from that head, and now I was horny as hell.

I usually didn't care about my hair, but it was in need of a wash, so

I just put it up into a slick bun on top of my head. I then put on maroon lipstick to match everything else, and by the time I was fastening my shoes, I heard Brynn downstairs talking to my mother.

"Nasty ass," Rori commented to me as we both walked out of our bedrooms at the same time. She was wearing a white skirt, with a matching white top and white heels. Her dark curly hair hung freely, and had a sheen to it.

"You could hear?" I chuckled.

"Umm, yeah, bitch. I thought you were crying until I got closer to the door and realized what your ass was doing," Rori grinned.

"Hey, Brynn," I greeted her when I got downstairs. "I see you've met my mother. This is my little sister, Rori."

"Nice to meet you," Rori smiled.

"Wow, you guys look just alike." Brynn chuckled, looking at all three of us.

Brynn was wearing a black halter dress that showed every part of her curvy frame. She paired it with matching black stilettos. Her brown curly hair was sweeping her shoulders, right along with her big ass gold hoops.

"Say 'thank you,' ladies. You should be happy to look like me," my mom jokingly replied, making us chuckle.

"Well, let's go, y'all. I was able to get a table tonight."

"Okay. Nice meeting you, Mrs. Vaughn." Brynn waved to my mother as we left out of the house.

"Who was that guy leaving your house just a minute ago?" Brynn asked once Rori and I were in her car.

"Oh, my boyfriend Waayil that I told you about." I couldn't help but to beam at the thought of him.

"Ohh wow. Yeah, he was very sexy from what I could see." She said it lowly like she was thinking to herself.

I nodded as she started towards our destination.

It was Friday, which meant Privé was having its very popular Toxic Fridays tonight. I hadn't been in a long time, and honestly, I was excited. Brynn wasn't the only one who needed to get out tonight.

When we arrived at the club, it was packed as hell. I was surprised that we were even able to find a park. After letting them know I had a booth, we were escorted to our section and given bottle service. My mom had made a nice dinner, so I was prepared to drink as much as I wanted to.

"Yikayla, girl, you were so right! I needed this!" Brynn laughed as she danced to "Everyday We Lit" by YFN Lucci.

I smiled back and began to move a little as well, with my drink in hand. I couldn't help but to look at this girl from a little ways away, who was watching me closely. I figured maybe she was a lesbian.

I noticed Rori was babysitting her drink, and checking her phone every ten seconds it seemed.

"Waiting for Gavin to call?" I raised a brow.

"Ugh, no. I couldn't get him to *stop* calling, so I blocked him. And I'm not waiting for anyone to call me. I'm done with guys until I graduate college."

"So, what's going on with you and Eko? I've never seen y'all two hang out this much."

She sighed as she stared out at the people dancing and singing along to the music, before she finally turned to look at me.

"I had sex with him. But no, it's not like what you think, Kay!" she shouted when she saw my jaw drop.

"You fucked Gavin's right hand? Rori, what the hell?" I frowned because I didn't know who this Rori was. This wasn't like her at all.

"Hey! I'll be right back!" Brynn cut into our conversation as some dude led her out of our section for a dance. I simply nodded and turned my attention back to Rori.

"I didn't expect it to happen. Gavin doesn't pay me any mind, and Eko does, so it just happened." She shrugged. "But I like him now and I don't want to."

"I mean, Eko is a sweet guy, but I thought you loved Gavin."

"I thought I did too, but Eko is just…" She cheesed and sighed. "I mean, he was what I wanted until I caught him fucking his ex earlier this week."

"Maybe you just like him because he was there when Gavin wasn't."

"No, I don't know. Maybe. Anyway, I just want to have a good time so…" She stood up and began to dance and sing along to the current song, so I joined her.

Brynn eventually came back, and I let the two of them get drunk as we all had a good time. It was a bunch of fine niggas that I had to turn down, but it was okay. I thought about dancing with some, but Waayil was pretty well connected in Memphis and it was nothing for one of these hating ass bitches to snap a photo and get it to him. Waayil was too crazy for all that. I highly doubt any of these niggas were willing to get fucked up or killed over a dance.

"Going to the bathroom. You two stay here!" I told Brynn and Rori as I headed to the restroom. I'd only had one drink, but it'd run through me quickly.

I peed then washed my hands, and as I was coming out, that same girl who was staring got my attention.

"You know Roscoe?" she asked, but the look on her face told me she already knew the answer.

"Girl, get out of my face," I frowned and started off, but this dummy grabbed my arm. "Don't touch me!" I shoved the shit out of her and she hit the wall.

"Bitch!" she shouted back and pushed me too.

WHAM!

I socked her ass in the head and she fell into a group of guys who then got in between us to prevent things from going further.

"Stupid hoe," I said, straightening my dress and starting off.

"Damn, shawty. Let me get yo' number since I broke that shit up for you." One of the dudes smiled in my face, grill shining brightly.

"I didn't want you to break it up." I tried to walk off but he gripped my arm tightly.

"I didn't say I was done."

"Well I'm done, nigga. Let me go!"

"Fine." He thrust me back some like a little bitch. What nigga shoves a woman? I can't even right now.

I grabbed the drink his friend was holding and tossed it into his face. He was about to try and hit me, but his friends stopped him and got in his face as I switched off.

This was some kind of fucking night. It seemed like I would never be free from Roscoe and his bullshit.

CHAPTER FOUR

Eko Bennet

Rori hadn't answered any of my damn texts or calls since she pulled up on me while I was smashing Jenni. I wished I could take that shit back, but shit she'd just told me she didn't wanna be with me like that. How the fuck was I supposed to know that she didn't really mean it? Females killed me with that reverse psychology shit. I had enough bullshit on my mind and didn't have time to be deciphering codes and shit. If Rori wanted this dick, she needed to act like it.

"Fuck," I grunted, slamming my iPhone onto my desk in the back, irritated that Rori really wasn't answering any of my communication attempts at all.

I was at Coney Barbershop, which was the barbershop I managed and would hopefully own. I'd been stacking and saving for years now, and after a few more runs in this here drug game, I'd be good to go.

I wasn't like Gavin, in the sense that I didn't want to do this shit forever. I wanted to make an honest living and not have to look over my shoulder every damn day. It wasn't even just about me though because best believe no nigga pumped fear in my muthafuckin' heart. But if I had a wife or some shorties, I couldn't imagine being worried about them all damn day due to my line of work. And if they were to get hit because of me, I'd never forgive myself.

"Aye, Luke is here, Eko," one of the other barbers named Chris let me know.

"Aight, bet." I nodded to him before sending Rori a text.

Me: Let me talk to you ma.

I stared down at my phone for a little bit even though I knew her ass wasn't gon' reply. A couple minutes passed with no response, so I pocketed my phone and went out front to cut the homie's hair.

As soon as Luke sat his ass in my chair, he asked, "What's good with that thick white junt you was smashing?"

Of course, these nosey muthafuckas in the shop roared with laughter as they listened in. I could never understand how a grown ass man would wanna gossip. I never gave a fuck about what the next muthafucka was doing unless it affected my cash flow. Other than that, the shit was none of my business.

"Jenni. Damn, man, she's fine as fuck. Bitch must have been raised by a black family," Chris commented as he cut some nigga's hair.

"Hell yeah, nigga. Bitch is corn-fed like a muthafucka," Robert added as he swept the floors.

"Aye, nigga, I don't pay you to run yo' muthafuckin' mouth. I better be able to eat off these damn floors by later tonight, or I'm knocking yo' ass out," I hissed at Robert. Nigga was nineteen years old, in and out of jail, and always crying about getting work to feed his baby and girlfriend. He had no room to be chilling and shooting the shit.

Robert got right back to sweeping, while bobbing his head to the Young Jeezy song that was playing.

"Ayyyyee!!!" a bunch of niggas in the shop hollered as some pretty thick bitches walked by the shop. That was why I hated leaving the door open some days, because these muthafuckas acted like they ain't ever had pussy in their lives.

"Them niggas is crazy." Chris chuckled and shook his head as two of the niggas waiting, rushed out to catch up with them bougie hoes.

"So answer me, nigga? You still smashing that?" Luke inquired as I started to work on his head.

"Yeah, sometimes, nigga. Fuck you all in my business for?"

"I ain't never smashed a white bitch before. Their pussy better or worse?" Luke quizzed, and even though I didn't want to, I joined the fellas in laughter at his ignorant ass.

"Pussy is pussy, my nigga," Chris replied.

"Nahhh," a couple of us said in unison.

"I mean, I feel like black girls get wetter, so the pussy feels better. The head is better from white hoes though because they don't give a fuck," I added, and a few of them nodded and commented in agreement.

Suddenly, I thought about Rori and how good her pussy felt. Shit stayed wet and was super fucking tight. I didn't know what Gavin was doing, but maybe that nigga had been sliding up in her belly button because the pussy felt untouched.

Damn, and them faces she makes when I'm deep inside, pounding her shit like it's no tomorrow. Fuck. Her little ass needed to answer my call because fucking these thots wasn't enough for me no more.

"Damn, I need to find me a white girl," Luke sighed.

"Shit, take Jenni," I half joked.

"Nigga, you'd be hot as fuck if I fucked her," Luke replied. His tone made it obvious that he was checking to see if I was serious or not.

"Nah, I really wouldn't. If you're trying to fuck with that, I can let her know for you or hook you up." I chuckled to myself because I knew Jenni wouldn't be down if I approached her about it. But if Luke hit her up on the low, ain't no telling with her track record.

"All jokes aside, you would do that shit for a nigga?"

"This muthafucka is excited as hell." Chris and his client laughed.

"Yeah, I got you, Luke."

Just as the conversation switched, I saw somebody come into the shop out the corner of my eye. When I looked, I spotted Gavin, mean mugging like he wanted the fade. A couple people spoke to him as he made his way further into the shop, and he replied with his eyes on me.

"Let me talk to you, Eko," he finally said once he got by my station.

"I need to finish this cut then I'll holla at you."

He stared at me as I continued lining Luke up, but then he turned around and went to sit at one of the abandoned stations towards the back by my office. I finished with Luke, and then once he paid, I pointed to my office to let Gavin know he could go in.

As soon as I closed the door behind myself, I asked, "What you need?"

I was on the defensive a little because I didn't know where we stood. We hadn't talked for a week after I picked Rori up from his spot, and he caught on to my feelings for her. After that, we met up to do business, but we grazed over the situation and never talked about it. But right now, in front me, he was looking like he had an issue.

"Did you say something to Rori?"

"About what?" I furrowed my brows. Even though, technically Rori was his, I didn't like him speaking on her, especially not while she was ignoring a nigga.

"Did you say anything to convince her not to get back with me! I've been—"

"Whoa, hold the fuck up, bruh. Don't come in my shit yelling at me! I didn't have to say shit to Rori! You ran her off on yo' own by treating her like garbage, and then pulling a gun out on her when she found another bitch's shit in yo' crib!"

His demeanor changed once I'd said my piece, because I guess he realized he'd done enough to Rori for her to never want his ass again. There was nothing I could have said to add to that, because the damage he'd done was insurmountable.

"I know." He plopped down in the old chair. "Fuck, I know." He dropped his head into his hands and then picked it up. "You really got feelings for my girl?"

"Gavin, I got work to do. I'm losing money sitting back here with you, talking about some bitch shit."

"I love her, man, and I can barely handle my business because I'm always thinking about her. I caught up with her the other day and

111

spilled everything, but she basically spit on me."

"Nigga, what happened to that side bitch you were feeling so tough?" I frowned.

Before all this shit went down, Gavin was fucking with some bitch that he claimed he was starting to love. Was talking about how he didn't know if he was gon' stick with Rori or leave her. Shit had me hot when I was listening because Rori was better than that shit. She was the type of bitch niggas prayed to have, and this muthafucka was acting like she was just an option.

"I don't know about her."

"She dropped you too?" I chuckled, irritated by this nigga.

"Nah, she just be acting funny as fuck. But even if she wasn't, I know I want Rori. What you think I should do?"

"Gavin, get up outta here and handle the traps like you're supposed to be doing, nigga. This is my legit work day, and I can't let you fuck shit up for our other business over a female."

Nodding, he replied, "You right. Yeah. Aight. Well, thanks for taking the time anyway, my nigga. And thank you for not pursuing whatever feelings you have for her."

I opened the door, gesturing for him to leave, and he walked out briskly. For a minute, I watched him, wondering if I should just come clean now and whoop his ass. However, I needed him on my side until I dealt with some underground shit. Not to mention, I hadn't discussed shit with Rori. If she would answer her fucking phone, there wouldn't be so much damn confusion.

Shaking my head, I went back on the floor and called my next head to cut. About three and a half hours later, I was done with all my clients and closing down the shop. Robert had come through with the sweeping and all the other shit he was supposed to clean, so once I paid him, I locked up and left.

I drove straight to Rori's spot, and as if God was on my side, I saw her sitting on the porch with her older sister, Dree. They were drinking what looked like iced tea, and talking about some shit. Getting out of my car, I hit the alarm and walked up the driveway, then up the porch steps.

"Eko, what are you doing here? Serving the people your street drugs?" Dree fake smiled. I fake laughed and sneered, which caused her to chortle loudly. She loved fucking with people, with her bougie ass.

"Rori, can I talk to you for a minute, ma?" I slipped my hands into my jean pockets.

Rori stared up at me, and then gave her sister a look.

"Okay, I guess I will go inside." Dree got up with her glass in hand. "Yell 'help' if you need me, Rori."

"Fuck you," I hissed to Dree, taking her seat as she chuckled while going into the house. "I miss you." I pulled Rori's chair closer to mine so that the arms of our chairs were touching.

"Oh yeah?" she looked away.

"Yeah." I kissed her neck gently, and saw a small smirk appear on her beautiful ass face. "Why are you so damn pretty, Rori?" I looked her up and down in them jeans and that top. It was simple, but I swear

113

someone pulled her sexy mocha ass from a magazine. And she smelled like sugar and coconuts too.

"Where is Jenni?"

"Fuck do I know?"

"You should since that's your little girlfriend!"

"That's not my girl. I was horny and needed to bust one right quick before I ran the streets, so I hit her up."

"Why you didn't hit me up?" She finally looked my way, pushing her brown curly hair from one side to the other.

"Because that's not the type of woman you are."

"Please, Eko. That's just an excuse for you to have sex with another girl. And one who is supposedly your girlfriend."

"I'm dead serious about you not being that type of girl. I would never hit you up just to bust one and send you on yo' way. When I fuck you, I wanna take my time with that shit. Bask in that pussy."

Laughing, she said, "Eko, shut the fuck up."

"So what's up?"

"I just need to be alone for a little bit to make sure I'm thinking clearly. We started messing around while I was still with Gavin. I need to be sure that I'm not just using you to get over him."

Shit low-key hit me in the chest like a bullet.

"Wow."

"Not like that, Eko. I like you, I do. But I don't want to rush into something without knowing if I want it for sure or not."

"So what, like a week?"

"Maybe, I don't know. And that situation with Jenni just... it messed things up." She fidgeted.

"She don't even mean shit to me, Rori. I can drop her at any time. Shit, I've dropped her ass already."

"And I don't want to be with a nigga who would drop his girlfriend for someone else so easily. Who's to say you won't leave me when another bitch comes along? And how do you know you're not just interested in me just because I needed saving?"

"Rori."

I exhaled and then rose to my feet, looking down at her.

"Just a little space, please."

As badly as I didn't want to grant her request, I nodded. I leaned down to kiss her lips and then snaked my arms around her body. She hugged my neck, caressing my fade a little, and then we let go.

"If I find out you're fucking another nigga, Rori, I'm killing him."

"Oh my gosh, and you're serious!" She threw her hands out.

"I am." And with that, I left her crib.

Shit, let me even *think* she's letting another muthafucka smash. That nigga is gon' be dead so quickly, niggas are gon' wonder if he was ever alive.

CHAPTER FOUR

Dree

Two nights later…

Sean and I had just come from having a nice dinner out, and for the first time in days, Canyon wasn't on my mind. I actually was able to laugh and enjoy myself with Sean, without Canyon lingering in the back of my head.

I wanted things with Sean and I to work because I was hooked on this fantasy of a life that he and I could build together. I wanted to be like his parents, rich and in love, living in a beautiful home in Belle Meade, with maids and servants tending to my every need. It may have been shallow, but I liked nice things, and the life Sean and I could build together was the life I was supposed to have.

Sean did have his drawbacks though, like his constant monitoring of what I ate, or how I talked or reacted to things. He was a bit too controlling for my liking, but I was hoping I could change that in him. Canyon could be dominant too, but it was sexy, and he didn't try to control things like what I ate or how I said something. Not to mention, I was pretty close to perfect, and Sean made me feel like I had a lot of flaws sometimes.

"I have some champagne in the den that we can open," Sean offered as we walked through the foyer.

"I saw your parents' cars outside. Can we open the champagne?" I whispered to Sean as he took my hand into his.

"Yeah, it's fine. I'm grown, Dree. I can do as I please."

I followed him to the den area, and then took a seat on the buttery leather couch that reminded me of the one in my stepfather's office. As he made the drinks, I smiled, loving how handsome and clean he looked.

"I have to pee really badly. Can I use the bathroom right out here?" I quizzed, standing up and fixing my dress.

"Yeah, go ahead."

I got up and left the den, making my way down the long hallway where the study and his parents' offices were. When I got ready to go into the bathroom, I heard loud voices, which stopped me in my tracks. Checking over my shoulder to make sure no one was close by, I followed the voices, which brought me to Sean's father's office door. Placing my ear to it, I could hear Sean's parents arguing. The door was thick as hell though, so they sounded like they were under water.

"Fuck," I mumbled, mad that my nosey ass couldn't make out what they were saying.

I went to use the bathroom then returned to the den where Sean was. He had the fireplace going, so it was nice and toasty. I sat down next to him on the couch, and picked up my flute with the strawberry on the rim.

"Are you feeling better about school?" Sean inquired.

"Yeah, I am, finally. My brain is actually starting to retain the information so much better." I set my flute down. "You know a couple of the people in class are having a study group and I think I'm gonna join."

Frowning in confusion, he inquired, "Who told you about it? Tyson?"

"Yeah, how did you know?"

"Because I see him always looking at you in class. I've been meaning to talk to him about that. And I don't think the study group is a good idea." Sean downed what was in his glass and added some more.

"Why not?"

"Because we've been studying together and you've already improved, so there isn't a need for you to do it with Tyson."

Chuckling, I said, "Do you really feel that you're helping me, or do you just not want me to study with Tyson?"

"Both."

"Sean, if I want to join the study group I will. You can't just make decisions for me like that."

See what I meant? I had a father in Jasper and didn't need another one.

"You're right. I'm sorry." He leaned over to kiss my lips before sliding his tongue into my mouth. Our kiss became hungrier, and his hand started up my dress so I stopped it. "Dree."

"I'm not really in the mood, Sean." I pulled my dress back down. "But I will be soon, okay?" I cupped his chin when he groaned.

He reached for the bottle of champagne and said, "More?"

"Yeah. I have to pee again though. Hopefully your parents aren't arguing again." I got up.

"Oh, they always do that. My mother complains that they don't spend enough time together, but then she gets over it."

"I see."

I left out to the bathroom with Sean's words on my mind. Hearing his mom and dad argue gave me a bad feeling in the pit of my stomach. I'd been looking up to them this whole time, but I was realizing I didn't know anything about them outside of their occupations. I wanted to be a power couple, but I wanted to be a happy one. I guess with all that they had, I assumed there was no way they could be miserable. I was somewhat wrong though.

I came back from the bathroom after relieving myself, and when I got into the den, Sean was typing on his phone. I sat next to him and downed the flute of champagne with a lot on my mind.

Tonight was making me feel like I'd chosen the wrong guy. For the past few weeks, I'd already been feeling that way, especially when I saw Canyon, but right now it was the strongest it'd ever been. The simple thought that I'd possibly lost Canyon for the second and probably last time, made me sick. I was even starting to get light headed as I polished off the flute.

"You okay?" Sean inquired.

"Perfect." Setting the empty glass down, I added, "I think I'm gonna go home now."

"No, baby, stay for a bit more."

Looking at his adorable baby face, I responded, "Okay, just for a little bit. But no more champagne."

***

Around 3 a.m. in the morning...

I woke up in a dark bedroom that I didn't recognize, and my head was pounding hard. I scanned the room, trying to get my mind together so I could remember it. I knew it wasn't mine because it was much larger, even though mine was pretty big too.

Looking down on the carpet, I saw my dress, underwear, and shoes scattered, which made me look under the covers to see that I was ass naked. Looking over my shoulder, I saw Sean passed out next to me, mouth all open.

"What the fuck," I mumbled, head feeling like someone had hit me with a hammer.

I could barely see, but thanks to the moonlight shining through his window, I could still navigate around the room. I slowly crept out of the bed and slipped my panties on, along with my dress. Putting on my shoes as I sat on the carpet, I tried to remember what happened last night. All I recalled was dinner, Sean's parents bickering, and then drinking two measly glasses of champagne.

I rose to my feet and turned around to look at Sean, who was still knocked out. I had no recollection of ever coming up to his bedroom, or even worse, sleeping with him. I felt weird, and I really wanted to go home, so I rushed out of his bedroom and down the stairs in search of my purse. The home was dark, and very quiet, which was scary right now because I was somewhat half asleep. Not to mention, I felt like I was high or something; just very discombobulated.

"What the fuck? What the fuck?" I kept repeating, trying to remember where the den was without crying. I was panicking right now.

My breathing pace picked up as I darted towards the den, and then grabbed my purse. I frantically searched it for my car keys and phone, as if I were worried they wouldn't be in there. Once I had them both in hand, I quickly ran towards the front door, feeling like someone would stop me and try to keep me here.

Something like this had never happened before because I was very responsible when it came to drinking. I knew my limits and once I started feeling warm, that was my signal to stop. I don't ever remember getting that warm feeling, but somehow, I'd drank enough to sleep with Sean? I was losing my damn mind right now. I wasn't ready to be with him like that. He'd erased the nights I'd spent with Canyon and I wasn't ready to let that go yet.

"I'm never drinking again," I sniffled, fumbling in attempt to put my keys in the ignition.

I cranked my car and barely got the gear into reverse before I was peeling out of that long ass driveway. I floored it all the way back to my home in Midtown, and had never been so happy to see my house. I parked, hopped out, and rushed inside, but was caught off guard at the sound of loud voices coming in from the backyard. Of all nights, why did they decide to have a party? And why did it last so late?

I booked it in order to get away before anyone coming inside saw me. Unfortunately for me, I ran dead smack into what felt like a damn elevator door. It was like a steel plate that sent me to the laminate floor on my ass.

"Damn, Dree. Somebody chasing you, ma?" Canyon quizzed.

"No, no, move," I sniffled, rising to my feet and trying to move past him. I could tell by the look in his eyes that he wasn't gonna let me pass.

He took my hands into his and lifted them to show me that I was shaking badly. He'd put his be-mean-to-Dree campaign on hold as he pulled me into his chest for a hug. At the scent of his cologne, I burst into tears. He held me tighter, strong ass arms feeling like a safe barrier that wouldn't let anything happen to me.

"Baby, it's okay," he spoke lowly, voice still deep and commanding.

Scooping me up, he carried me upstairs as the loud voices from the backyard got louder since everyone was walking through the house to leave.

Canyon took me to my bedroom, and closed the door by kicking it. He laid me down on the bed, and removed my shoes as I continued to sob. I was so embarrassed. I was the tough Goode sister, and never liked anyone to see me bothered whether it be mad or sad. Yet, here Canyon was, watching me cry like a little ass baby.

"Shorty, what happened?" His hand touched my bare thigh and

I jumped as if it were burning me. My vagina felt tampered with and I didn't like it. I was confused… scared… and I didn't like it.

Canyon squinted his eyes in confusion with a hint of anger. "Dree."

"Nothing happened to me, okay? I need you to go! Go be with Jodi like you want to! Or maybe your baby mama! Whatever bitch's week it is!" I shouted angrily. I didn't want him seeing me like this.

"Dree, tell me what the fuck is wrong with you, ma," he pleaded almost. His concern for me made me love him even more, but my pride meant more to me right now. I didn't want him seeing me so broken, dammit!

"Canyon, please go," I sobbed heavily into my pillow, barely able to see or breathe.

Instead of listening to me, he went and sat on the loveseat in my room. He knew I didn't want to be touched, which is why he'd distanced himself, but he didn't want to leave me. He sat there, in the dark, watching me until I dozed off.

CHAPTER FOUR

Jonaya

Leighton and I were out having lunch, just to catch up since I'd been pretty busy with school. We'd both kind of been dodging Wednesday because it was awkward as hell being around her. She acted as if nothing was wrong, and as if her lying to Waayil and getting him sent to prison wasn't a big damn deal.

It was hard to talk with her about other things because the whole time I would be asking myself how she could do such a thing. And it didn't help that she refused to explain herself. She just kept saying that she was young and dumb. Shit, I was too, but I never thought to lie on someone and get them murdered. The whole situation had me looking at her differently, because there was no telling what else she was capable of.

"How is Marquise?" Leighton inquired, making me sigh.

"He's good."

Marquise had been extra clingy lately, and it was driving me insane. All he wanted to do was be around me and I hated it. I needed space sometimes, especially now that my feelings for Nusef were starting to grow. It was almost like Marquise was sensing that I thought of someone else because he would say little things here and there. I didn't like it and it was a bit scary; like he was unhinged or something.

"That's it? You don't have more to say, Jo? This is the longest relationship that you've ever had, and he's just good?"

"Yeah, I mean, you know I'm not the relationship type, and Marquise is just overboard right now. Plus, ever since Nusef beat him up, I just don't see him the same."

Chuckling, Leighton said, "Damn, bitch, that's shady as fuck."

"No it's not. He shouldn't have tried to fight Nusef knowing that he couldn't take him. What makes it worse is that I think he was trying to show off for me."

"Why did he fight Nusef anyway?"

Her question caught me off guard because I didn't know what to say. If I told her the truth, she would know that Nusef had a thing for me, which would hurt her feelings. She seemed to really like him, and although I didn't want them together, I didn't want it to be because of me. Why couldn't they just naturally separate from one another?

"He umm, he… I think it was about something stupid like… a bet they made playing a video game. They both didn't think they should pay the other, and it just escalated."

"Niggas. They'll be ready to fight over the smallest things, but will be cool after having sex with the same girl."

"I know, right!" I laughed, happy as hell that she believed me.

"But speaking of Nusef, girl, I am in love!"

"What?"

"Not for real love, but, man. I can tell I'm gonna get there. He's a bit brash, not as bad as Waayil, but he's for sure related to him. However, he can be so nice when he wants to, and the sex? There are no words to explain it."

Jealous, I asked, "Did he finally, you know? Reciprocate?"

"No, he hasn't given me head yet, but it just doesn't happen. Like, we'll just end up fucking and…" She shrugged, cheesing widely as hell. "But we're getting really close. I'm excited. I've had a crush on him for years."

"You have?"

"Yes! I always thought he liked you, but then when you kept assuring me that he didn't, I decided to move in on him. And I'm happy I did. You should have tested that dick out while you had the chance."

Who says I still don't have the chance? Bitch.

"No, I'm perfectly fine."

"Well, we should go because I wanna take a nap before tonight." Leighton began to count out some cash for her portion of our lunch bill.

"Tonight? A party I don't know about?"

"No, I'm cooking dinner for Nusef. My mom and dad went to Seattle this morning, remember?"

"Oh yeah." I placed my debit card in the cardholder and retrieved her cash to stuff into my wallet.

"Yep, so Nusef is gonna come over. I have candles, lingerie, everything. So I'm thinking tonight we can make it official." She was grinning as she stared at me, but then it started to fade. "You okay, Jonaya?"

"Yeah, girl. I'm just happy for you, yet, surprised by how fast this is all going."

"Me too, but I have no plans to slow that shit down."

The waitress came over and took my card, then once she brought it back to me, I signed the receipt and Leighton and I were on our way.

I'd planned to go to the mall after this since my stepdad had broken me off nicely due to me getting three A's on my last three papers, but I was no longer in the mood. I drove all the way home, got in my bed, and just stared up at the ceiling with my hands lying flat on my stomach like I was in a casket.

Leighton sounded serious about Nusef. I didn't know how he felt because anytime I would ask him about her, he'd blow me off or say something slick. Then I could barely see him because Marquise was always breathing down my neck like some fire breathing dragon. And just as that thought crossed my mind, Marquise started calling my iPhone.

"Hey," I answered, voice drier than the Sahara.

"Sup, ma, where you at?"

"I'm writing a paper in the library."

"On a damn Friday?"

"I told you my dad is coming home in a couple weeks, and I need to stay on it if I want to keep getting money."

"Yeah, you right." He sighed. "Will I finally meet him?"

"Um, yeah, sure. He's a busy man, even when in Memphis, but I will talk to him for sure."

There was no way Marquise would be meeting my stepfather. Jasper, my stepdad, had high expectations for the men we dealt with, and I knew for sure Marquise didn't make the cut. And no, Jasper wasn't one of those dads that only wanted us with lawyers or doctors; he was actually pretty open when it came to these niggas' occupations.

What he didn't like was little boys trying to be men, because he felt like they couldn't do their job as a husband and provider in the long run. Hence the reason he couldn't stand Roscoe's ass. He always told us his biggest fear was for one of us to be married with kids and still calling him to help pay the bills because our husband couldn't.

"But hey, it's really quiet in here, Marquise, so I have to go."

"Aight, I love you. Hit me when you get out."

"Yep."

I hung up and turned my TV on to watch something on Netflix, but before I could even pick, I dozed off.

***

A couple hours later...

I woke up, still fully clothed with my shoes on and everything. Snatching my phone off the dresser, I checked the time and hopped out of my bed. I'd dreamt about Nusef and Leighton having dinner tonight, and it gave me the worst headache.

I brushed my teeth, and then grabbed my purse to leave. I realized my mom had gone somewhere with Buddy, and the only car here was Dree's, so I went to her room to see about it.

"Heeyyy, Dree." I smiled widely.

She was sitting on her bed with books and sheets of paper everywhere. Even though she was just in a t-shirt and shorts with her hair up in a messy bun, she was still so pretty. Something about her face and demeanor was different though. She didn't exude confidence, which was a rarity with someone like Dree.

"Yes, Jonaya?"

"Oh see, I umm, have this thing, and the only way I can get there is if I drive, but you see—"

"Take it." She pointed to her nightstand that had her keys sitting on it.

"Really?"

Dree hadn't let me use her car in the longest. And I for sure thought I'd have to do a bit more groveling to get it tonight. That was way too easy.

"Yes, take it before I change my mind."

"Is there gas in it?" I put my hand on my hip. It must have been on E, which was why she was allowing me to drive it.

"Yes, it's a little over half a tank." She kept her eyes on her papers and book, with a highlighter between her fingers.

"Great." I snatched the keys up. "Oh, Seeeaaan is calling," I sang when I saw her iPhone screen light up. Her phone was on silent though.

"Dree, did you hear me? Your boo is—"

"Jonaya, take the fucking keys and go before I change my mind."

"Damn, okay." I wanted to dig deeper, but I was on a time limit and I needed to use her car, so I jetted.

I left the house and drove right over to Nusef's place on Idlewild Street. I parked and rushed up, kicking myself for not looking for his car first. He could have already been over to Leighton's.

Slipping my key in, I turned it and let out a sigh of relief at the sound of Yo Gotti blasting from his bedroom. I gently closed the door and then went to the bedroom. I expected to see him getting dressed or something, but he was on the edge of his bed in gray sweats and socks, with no shirt on. He bobbed his head to "81" by Yo Gotti, as he rolled a blunt in the dimly lit room. His muscles seemed to flex every time he moved.

"Hey," I spoke to him, leaning in the doorway.

He looked up from what he was doing, honey eyes moving up and down my frame before he said, "What's good witchu?"

"Aren't you supposed to be getting dressed?" I came and sat next to him on the bed, kicking my shoes off. He smelled fresh, like he'd just taken a shower. I could still smell the soap on him.

"I will in a minute. You need something?"

"Nusef, I don't want you to go over to Leighton's."

He groaned out of frustration and replied, "Here we go with this shit. I thought I told you this wasn't up for discussion."

"She plans to try and make things official tonight!" I told him so he'd know it wasn't a good idea to go.

"And what's wrong with that?"

What the fuck?

"You don't want to be her boyfriend, that's what's wrong! You're gonna hurt her feelings when you say no."

"You don't know what I want."

"Stop being so nonchalant!"

In one motion, he got me onto my back and was in between my legs, pinning my hands to the bed.

"What you gon' do if I don't stop being so nonchalant, Jonaya?"

"I—I'm umm"

"You what?"

"Nusef," I whined when he started to kiss on my neck.

His big hands moved up my dress until he reached the top of my panties and started to pull them down. He was sucking on my neck so hard that I was getting wetter by the minute. I wanted to say stop, but it was feeling too good. I'd been dreaming about this ever since he'd given me head. He started to push my dress up, so I raised a little so that he could get it over my head. He crushed his lips against mine, and we began to tongue kiss hungrily and passionately. It was like an outer body experience right now. Feeling his strong hands on my naked body, as he kissed me like he loved me in this dim bedroom, had my heart beating way too quickly.

"I love you, Jonaya," he spoke lowly in between kisses.

Raising up off me, he climbed off the bed and removed his socks, sweats, and boxers, allowing me to take in his sexy chocolate body.

He was ripped and covered in tattoos. I, of course, couldn't help but notice that third leg hanging between his thighs. I had no idea my best friend was packing like that. I mean, I knew it wasn't little from small encounters, but damn. After rolling a condom down, he climbed between my legs and lowered himself onto me.

Looking down into my eyes, he demanded, "Tell me."

I could feel the head of his dick poking around at my opening, and I was salivating down below for him to get inside of me.

"Ah," I gasped lowly when he forced the head in. I dug my nails into his arms as we stared one another in the eyes.

"Fuck," he moaned, looking like he was about to nut just off the head being inside of me. "Tell me." He bit down on his lip, hazel eyes beaming down on me like a werewolf.

"Mmm," my voice trembled as he pushed more of himself inside of me.

"I wanna hear it."

"I love you, Nusef," I finally admitted, just as he thrust the rest of himself all the way in.

I was no virgin, but my pussy was not used to Nusef at all. I felt paralyzed at first as he stroked me slowly, breaking me in as if I'd never been touched. He laid down on top of me, making sure not to squish me, however, and held the sides of my face as he tongued me down slowly. His pumps sped up a little, but not too fast, as my body began to adjust to him. I couldn't say anything because of how good he felt; physically and emotionally, this was a different type of sex for me.

"Damn you feel so fucking good," he grunted into my mouth as we kissed.

My cries were soft and low, nails still digging deeply into his beautiful mocha skin, as he slid in and out of me. I hated slow strokes, but this felt good as hell, and plus, I needed to get used to him. Before I could wrap my mind around what was happening, I'd cum all over him.

"Mmm," he grumbled at the feeling of me gushing on his rod.

Grasping my hair and yanking my head back, he began to suck on my neck while beating it up. My moans were stuttered as he hammered me powerfully, bringing me to another orgasm. Our bodies clashed together, gliding off one another because of the sweat.

"Sef, mmm, ahhh," I called out, as he pounded me hard and fast.

"Oh fuck," he moaned against my face, and it was such a turn on hearing him being pleased.

Our bodies rocked harder together, our moans became louder, our skin crashed together, and soon enough, we'd both released, shivering hard.

"I love you, Nusef," I repeated again, feeling overwhelmed as he sucked on my lips.

I always hated missionary, but that was the best sex I'd ever had, hands down. I could only imagine what he could do in other positions.

"I love you, Nusef," I said again, almost like a recording. I couldn't stop saying it. It was like a revelation... an epiphany.

He chuckled, kissing down my collarbone and sucking my nipples.

Nobody mattered right now; not even Marquise and Leighton...

CHAPTER FOUR

Waayil

"Thank you, Waayil. It looks so good." My client, Elaina, smiled. She was a cute ass Puerto Rican bitch that had been trying to get on my schedule for the longest. What she wanted wasn't small—a big ass dragon on her hip—so there was no way I could squeeze her in prior.

"You're welcome, ma." I watched her as she admired my work in the mirror.

She then made eye contact with me through the mirror before turning to face me. Moving my way as I stayed seated, she lied back down so that I could wipe her down and cover it.

"So when are you gonna ask me out, Yil?"

"I'm not," I replied nonchalantly.

"Damn, so I have to ask you then." She turned a little because I gestured for her to do so.

"Nah, you don't. I have a girlfriend though."

"A girlfriend isn't a wife, boo. I don't give a fuck about no damn girlfriends. Now a wife, that's a different story."

"So if a bitch told your boyfriend that shit, what would you say?" I smirked. A hoe would come up with any muthafuckin' reason to still let a nigga smash.

"I would beat her ass."

"And what you think my girl would do if she found out you were trying to push up on me, ma?"

"I told you I don't care. You're worth that fight," she smiled.

Elaina's skin was a deep caramel, her brown hair was long as hell, and her body was nice as hell. I didn't just fuck anything though, especially not a bitch that was too damn dehydrated. That's how I got caught up with Alba's ass. Never trust a pretty ass bitch that's too eager to suck ya dick. It never ends well.

"You ain't my type, Elaina."

"What? I'm every man's type. What are you talking about?"

"You're too damn thirsty." I started to tidy up my area a bit, but I felt her eyes on my back.

"No you did not just call me thirsty, Waayil."

"You are though, and that shit ain't attractive at all, ma. I bet I could fuck you right now if I wanted to." I turned to face her.

Her mouth was ajar, and I guess she was waiting on me to crack a smile but I wasn't joking. I hated a thirsty hoe. In my opinion, women were to be chased, pursued, so a bitch that was too anxious to fuck with me was a turn off. There was a difference between wanting to be with a nigga versus doing the most to be with me, when I clearly wasn't interested. All my life women had done the most to get my attention, and it disgusted me. That's one reason I never wanted to sing professionally. The thought of having groupies made my muthafuckin' skin crawl because women just weren't supposed to behave that way. Hopefully, my harsh words were helping Elaina.

"I was just kidding." She half smiled.

Lying ass.

As Elaina gathered her shit, I got a text from my moms letting me know that Wednesday had left the house. Her birthday was tomorrow morning, and I wanted to slip her gift into her shoebox. My mama said she'd purchased some shoes she planned to wear tomorrow night, and when she opened the box, I wanted her to see this bracelet I had made for her.

It was covered in diamonds, and had her name engraved on the inside of it. The jeweler even placed these Chinese symbols on each side of her name that meant survivor. I thought that was dope, considering what she'd gone through at the hands of that buster ass Harry.

Me: On my way.

I hit my mom back, then escorted Elaina out, after assisting her in paying up at the front where Chiara was. Speaking of Chiara's stupid ass, I needed to talk to her about coming at my female clients sideways like I was her nigga. She had no muthafuckin' claim to me, but even if the bitch did, I still wouldn't tolerate that bullshit. This was my business, and her stupid ass needed to keep it fucking professional at all times.

"Remind me to get at you when I come back, aight?" I looked to Chiara who smiled for a moment until she saw the seriousness in my expression.

"Okay," she replied lowly, handing Elaina a receipt.

Elaina and I went our separate ways, and I headed straight to my parents' crib in Midtown.

"She only went to get something to eat from around the corner so be quick, Waayil," my mom explained once I walked into the house. I dapped my pops up and then went up the stairs so I could get to Wednesday's room.

Just a few more days, and all my furniture and shit would be moved into my new spot. Bitch ass Bradley had finally come out and approved it. Nigga was looking all up and through that bitch like he was a damn inspector. I knew he was looking for drugs or something like that. He was one of them muthafuckas that had no faith in the Black man. It was cool though. I could show him better than I could tell him by cashing these hefty ass checks.

As I tread down the hallway, my younger brother, Emil, was coming out of his bedroom. He nodded to say 'what's up,' before we dapped one another up.

"You good?" I asked him.

"Yeah, man. I'm still hot about what you did to Grant and Eddie," he scoffed, shaking his head.

"Get over it then."

"Yeah, aight."

He moved past me briskly, and I looked over my shoulder at him for a moment. Nigga was dumb as hell. He knew damn well I wasn't gon' let no shit like that go. And I understood him wanting to fight his own battles, but he clearly was trying to let them punk ass niggas slide. Fuck that bullshit.

Entering Wednesday's room, a smile spread across my face as I remembered what I was here for. My baby sister deserved this expensive ass gift. I wished I could see her face when she found it, but I'd rather her run across it than me giving it to her in person. That just seemed like it'd be more gratifying for me.

Opening her closet, I looked down at the plethora of fucking shoeboxes she had stacked up. I pulled out my phone to dial my mother, hoping she knew the brand or at least the damn color of the box.

"Hello?" she answered quickly, thankfully.

"Ma, what color box are the shoes in? Or what's the damn brand? She got all kinds of shit in here."

"The box is lavender, baby, but hurry up because she just pulled up and is walking in."

"Lavender? The fuck color is lavender?"

"Bless your soul. It's a light purple."

"Why you ain't just say purple then?"

"Because it's not— never mind. Hurry up."

I shoved my iPhone into my pocket, shaking my damn head at my mama and her particular ass.

"Fuck would I know what color lavender is?" I fussed lowly at her as I knelt down to scan the boxes. As soon as I found the right one, I heard Wednesday's voice, and the knob turning, so I quickly closed myself in the closet.

"Fuck," I mumbled. This bullshit reminded me of the time I had a threesome with these two bitches in tenth grade and had to hide when one of the girl's mamas came home.

"So you've been that damn busy, Jonaya? I don't think so." Wednesday sucked her teeth.

"Yeah, I have. If you haven't noticed, I'm back in school and I can't hang out all night or be available 24/7."

"No one asked you to. I'm in school as well."

"But your major isn't Chemistry, Wednesday."

I watched Jonaya plop down onto Wednesday's bed. It was hard to see through the slits of the closet door, but one of them were slightly slanted, giving me a better view.

As Jonaya removed her shoes, Wednesday did the same and then stood in front of her with her hand on her hip. I frowned at how short the dress was that she was wearing. As soon as I saw her tomorrow, I was gon' get in her ass about wearing that shit.

"I'm hungry, let's go make something to eat." Jonaya stood up, and now she was face to face with Wednesday.

Yes, please get the fuck out so I can too.

"Are you avoiding me?" Wednesday inquired, folding her arms and cocking her head.

"No, Wednesday. Why would I be avoiding you?"

"Because ever since I told you my little secret, it seems like you don't want to be around me. Both you and Leighton."

Secret?

140

Exhaling heavily, Jonaya replied, "I'm not gonna lie, Wednesday, it is weird being in your presence."

"Why!"

"Because what you did was fucked up! How could you do some shit like that and live with yourself! You need to tell Waayil!"

The fuck?

"Why does it matter so much to you? It's not like it's Nusef or something! And don't bring up Yikayla because this has nothing to do with her!"

"I know that, it's just... now, I'm burdened with this secret too and I don't like it."

"Ask yourself what would telling Waayil do, Jo? Huh? It's not gonna help anyone. It won't help him, me, and it damn sure won't bring whack ass Harry back from the dead, okay?"

My mind was going crazy right now. I didn't know what the hell was going on, but I had an inkling. If Wednesday and Jonaya were saying what I think they were, I was bound to strangle somebody with my bare fucking hands. Heat radiated from my body, and my blood boiled as I watched them go back and forth.

"It's not about that. It's about being honest. Your lie took years from Waayil's life, Wednesday. And it's best to tell him now then for him to find out somehow and hate you later."

"No! I said no! Are you deaf!" Wednesday yelled as I slowly walked out from the closet. If Jonaya's eyes had gotten any wider, her eyeballs would have rolled out onto the floor. "What?" Wednesday asked her since her back was to me.

Jonaya was too dumbfounded to answer, so Wednesday turned around with a confused expression. When she saw me though, she was just as perplexed as Jonaya.

"What you lie about, Wednesday?" I spoke slowly, trying to keep myself calm. My head was pounding and I felt like I was gon' have a muthafuckin' heart attack at any minute.

"No-nothing."

"Tell me what the fuck you lied about!" I roared, making both she and Jonaya jump back. I caught a glimpse of myself in the mirror, and the pure rage in my eyes even scared me a little.

"I didn't mean to! I was young and I didn't know! I—"

I walked up to her and brought my hands in the air, but landed them on my head. I locked my fingers on top of my head and closed my eyes. I almost choked the shit out of my little sister. When I opened my eyes, Wednesday and Jonaya were looking up at me as if I were Mike Myers or some shit and was about to slice their asses up.

"Jonaya, get out." I pulled my gun from my waist and removed the safety.

"Now, wait a minute, Waayil. Let's relax." Jonaya threw her shaky hands out, eyes locked on my gun as she slid her feet back into her shoes

"Waayil, please, I'm sorry," Wednesday begged.

"Waayil—"

"I said get the fuck out right muthafuckin' now before I push yo' shit back too!" I barked down at Jonaya who rushed out with tears in her eyes.

Turning my attention to Wednesday, I said, "What, you think my life is a game?"

"No, no, of course not." She shook her head repeatedly as I moved towards her. She backed up slowly as I kept coming, gun in hand and ready.

"Nah, you must think so, because why the fuck would you do that shit to me, huh? I'm yo' fucking brother and you played on my love for you like I don't even fucking matter! So why the hell should you matter to me?" I backed her all the way to the wall closest to her bedroom door. I quickly locked it when she reached for it, making her become even more frightened.

"Waayil, please let me explain! I didn't know you would react the way you did. I—"

"Why did you lie!!" I hollered in her face, making her wail loudly.

"Waayil Christian! Open this damn door now!" I heard my father shout as he banged on Wednesday's door, fumbling with the doorknob in between.

"Daddy!"

"Answer me before I crack yo' shit!" I gritted to Wednesday.

She wouldn't answer, she just kept shaking her head and crying hysterically. The shit was pissing me off.

BOOM!

I sent my fist through the wall, right next to her head, making her

143

scream and cry harder as she slid to the floor.

"Waayil! I don't want to have to call the police!" my dad yelled, still knocking.

Squatting down to Wednesday's face, I gritted lowly, "You gon' give me an explanation, ma. And if I don't get one in a timely manner, I'm sending you right where I sent Harry's broke ass. You got that?" I tapped her face with my loaded gun and then repeated, "You got that?"

"Ye—yes, Waayil," her lips trembled.

Pursing my lips, I prodded her forehead with my gun, beyond fucking tempted to just blow her shit open. It took the Holy Trinity and all the muscle I'd built in jail to pull me from her instead of sending one through her dome.

I stood up and unlocked Wednesday's bedroom door. When I yanked it open, there my parents were, along with Jonaya and Emil, staring at me like I'd just broken out of a psych ward. My mother rushed into Wednesday's room and cradled her, while my dad followed me, running his mouth.

Turning to face him, I pressed my gun to his forehead and spoke through clenched teeth, "Aye, look here, bruh. I'm gon' give you five seconds to back the fuck up off me before I murk yo' stupid ass. I ain't in my right mind, and I'm close as fuck to splitting yo' bitch ass wig. I love you, but it ain't nothing for me to kill you right about now."

Throwing his hands up in mock surrender, he backed away, eyes filled with fear and disappointment. I didn't give a fuck about what he thought of me. Shit, my mind was in shambles right now.

As I left the house and got into my car, Alba started calling my phone. I hit ignore, but she called back again… again… and again…

"You need to answer your damn phone when I call—" she started off before I could even say hello, but I cut that shit short.

"Bitch, you better pray to God that, that muthafuckin' baby is mine, or pay someone to alter the DNA results. Because if I even get a *whiff* of a hint that it ain't my baby in ya stomach, I'm charring yo' hoe ass and feeding you to the rats, bitch."

Click.

CHAPTER FIVE

Alba Micel

I stared at my phone in disbelief for a moment after Waayil hung up on me. He'd threatened me before, but this time was different. I felt his words deep in my chest and I was actually scared as fuck. The tone in his voice was murderous. The way he spoke lowly, while obviously clenching his teeth, was just eerie. I believed he would do exactly what he'd just said. That shit made me turn the lights on in my living room because I was afraid of the slight dimness right now, even though it was daytime.

I had a doctor's appointment in a couple hours, and I was calling that mean ass nigga to see if he wanted to come. I'm glad I didn't get the chance to ask, because now I wanted some alone time with my doctor to talk about some things.

I planned to get Waayil back on my side by the time the baby was due, hoping a DNA test would be the furthest thing from his mind. However, he was only getting worse as time went on. I was sure that by now he would have at least been warming up to me and our unborn, but shit, he was nicer to me *before* all this.

Picking up my phone, I dialed Ashley because I needed someone to talk to. Ashley could be stupid as hell sometimes, but occasionally, she gave me good ideas.

"Hello?" she answered, giggling.

Frowning at her happy mood, I asked, "Where the hell are you?"

"Oh, I just got off work." She chuckled again and then yelled 'bye' to some nigga in her background.

"Who the hell is that, Ashley?"

"Oh, my coworker, Edgar," she sighed. "So what's up?"

"I guess now that you have a car, you're trying to branch off and do your own thing, huh?" I spat. I didn't know why I was jealous of her seemingly being happy. Maybe because I was so damn miserable.

"What? No. Edgar just likes me and he flirts sometimes."

"If he works at Checkers with you, maybe you should leave that one alone. A man is supposed to make more than you, so unless you plan on, I don't know, selling ass for two bucks an hour, move on."

"Relax, Alba. I do not like Edgar. Plus, he's Mexican and I don't like men who can speak more languages than me," she joked, but I was still irritated, so I rolled my eyes. "How are you feel—"

"Look, I need your advice. Something crawled up Waayil's ass, and he's gone even crazier than he already is. He threatened me today and—"

"He always threatens you, Alba. Don't take it so seriously."

"No, bitch, it felt different. Like my bones shivered at the sound of his voice. It was almost like he wanted me to be lying about this baby just so he could kill me."

"I told you about fucking with his crazy ass. Nigga killed somebody, so of course he ain't all there. I mean, he's fine as hell and all, so I get it—"

"What should I do? I mean, this baby isn't his. It's Gavin's, and once Waayil finds that out, I'm gonna have to leave town to stay alive."

Ashley was about to get slapped in a minute. She was always talking about how sexy Waayil was and I hated it. She needed to focus on Nusef or something.

"What if you just tell him that it's Gavin's baby now? Maybe if he finds out before the baby even comes, and before he's invested time, he won't be as angry."

"Ashley, he threatened to barbecue my ass just ten minutes ago."

"Oooh, dang." I could tell she was driving because of the sound of her background. "Too bad you don't have any friends in the medical field that could falsify some documents for you."

I was laid back on the couch, but her sentence prompted me to sit up straight with a smile.

"Ashley, that's why I like you sometimes. You know, when you use your head for more than a wig holder. Talk to you in a bit." I hung up before she could respond.

I ran to the bathroom and started to do my makeup and hair since that was gonna take a while. I then started to put marks on myself using the makeup, so that it would look like some bruising. Once I had a few on my neck, shoulders, and forearms, I was good to go. By the time I was finished, I had about forty-five minutes left before my doctor's appointment.

I made it there with fifteen minutes to spare, and after signing in and waiting for about fifteen more damn minutes, I was called to the back.

My doctor had me undress and change into one of those backless gowns, and then she started to check me out to make sure I was okay. I was further along than I expected, meaning I was pregnant well before I took that pregnancy test. Gavin and I had probably hit the jackpot on the first try, and I just didn't know. This was even better because now it would be more believable to Waayil.

"So what did you want to talk about, Miss Micel?" my doctor quizzed once I entered and sat down in her office. I'd told her I needed to talk to her when she asked about the bruising on my body.

"Well, I wanted to ask a favor of you, but I don't know if I should," I replied meekly. It was so hard trying to play this soft-spoken, delicate role.

"Go ahead and ask. Does it have anything to do with the bruising on your body? If so, Miss Micel, you know you can talk to me about anything."

Exhaling dejectedly with my head hung low, I said, "Yes, it does have to do with the bruising. But, I feel that what I'm about to ask of you may be a bit unethical."

Dr. Blancher's eyebrows furrowed, and she turned a bit in her chair before lacing her fingers together on top of her desk.

"Why don't you ask me, and I will be the judge of that."

"You see, my boyfriend and I haven't been getting along for, oh well, about a year or so now. He works a lot, and he has a problem keeping his hands to himself." I picked my head up a little to make eye contact with her every so often.

"Uh huh." She nodded, brows still dipped between her eyes.

"A-and, he umm… well I…" I purposely stammered and took long pauses for a more dramatic effect.

"Take your time, sweetheart."

"I became close with another man who comforted me. And when I say close, I mean in ways that I shouldn't have been close with anyone but my man. However, I couldn't help it because he treated me so nicely. I haven't been treated like anything but trash in years, so it was hard to resist." I sniffled, trying to bring on the tears.

"Hey, that's understandable, Miss Micel. We as women need attention, so there was nothing wrong with you falling for someone who showed you that." She yanked a couple tissues from the box on her cherry wood desk.

Nodding, I accepted the tissue she reached out to me and dabbed at my dry ass eyes as if I were really broken up.

"Anyhow." I sniffled again. "I became pregnant by this other man, which is with the baby I'm carrying now. And you see, my boyfriend had his suspicions about me and is threatening to do something really bad if this baby doesn't turn out to be his."

By now, I was looking deeply into her eyes, hoping that she was catching onto what I was saying to her.

"What exactly are you trying to get at, Miss Micel?"

"I need the DNA test that my boyfriend will request, to come out saying he is the father. If it doesn't, I'm not sure me or my baby won't make it, Dr. Blancher."

"Miss Micel, I sympathize with your situation, honey, but I cannot do that. I—"

"So how are you gonna feel when you find out I've been murdered? Both my unborn child and I? Because that's exactly what's going to happen once he reads the results."

"Sweetheart, we can involve the authorities and have you protected from all of that. If you would just give me his name, I can make sure that nothing happens to you." She grabbed a pen and Post-It pad.

I literally wanted to slap the shit out of this bitch. Involve the authorities? I wish I had recorded her so she could hear how stupid she sounded when I played it back. If what I was saying were true, I was sure Waayil would have no problem making this hoe disappear. She knew nothing about the hood and how hood niggas made moves, because if she did, she would have agreed to my request.

"You know what, I shouldn't have asked. Forget everything I said, okay?"

"Miss Micel! Miss Micel!"

I left that bitch's office fuming. If I stayed any longer, I might have whooped her ass and I didn't want to do that. She had fucked up my whole plan. I needed to figure out a way to get that DNA test to read what I needed it to. But in the meantime, I wanted to make nice with my actual baby daddy, because I may need him to step up if shit continues to go left with Waayil.

Once I was inside my car, I called Gavin to see what he was up to. He'd been calling me non-stop since the day I found I was pregnant, but a couple weeks ago, he stopped. It was like his ass died or something.

"What's up?" he answered rather unenthusiastically. He usually had this happy ass tone whenever he answered my calls, almost like he felt blessed to be hearing from me. I liked that about him, because he knew and appreciated what was in front of him, unlike Waayil.

"Hey, how are you?"

"Good, Alba. What do you need? I'm working."

"Nigga, you sell dope, quit acting like you're on a schedule."

"Stop running yo' mouth about shit that you have no idea about, shorty. Fuck do you need, and make it quick, before I hang up."

Words failed to come out of my mouth because I was baffled at his tone and his choice of words. Gavin was always sweet to me and so mild mannered in my presence. I didn't know who this nigga was. Not liking that both of my men were being rude to me in the same day, my pregnancy hormones got the best of me.

"Why are you talking to me like that?" I whimpered, on the verge of crying.

Gavin sighed like he was annoyed with me, which made me sob harder.

"My bad, ma. I just think we should end this shit. I'm working on sticking with my girl, and to do that, I can't be in contact with you."

My tears dried up immediately at the sound of his plan. Some weeks back, I would have been jumping for joy, but now that it was very possible that I'd lose Waayil, I needed Gavin as backup.

"What? I thought you loved me!"

"I do, ma, I do, but when it comes down to it, I love Rori more."

"Rori? Rori Goode?"

That name wasn't too popular in Memphis, but I was hoping he was talking about another bitch.

"Don't worry about it."

Yep, it was her. His voice was a bit panicky, letting me know he was afraid that we knew one another. No wonder he'd never said her name to me, but thank God he'd just slipped. Of course I would know her, because I was dating Waayil who was very close to that Goode family. I swear all of those Goode bitches just needed to die. Niggas needed to realize that there were more women in the world other than them four bitches.

"Well, you'd better hope Rori is fond of being a stepmom, you asshole, because I'm pregnant."

"What—"

I hung up on him and fell back against my driver's seat. What the fuck had I done with my life?

CHAPTER FIVE

Rori

The next afternoon…

$\mathcal{I}$ was sweeping the porch because I hated when it got real dirty. I didn't have any homework to do, class had gotten cancelled, and it was an okay day, so I decided to get out there and fix it up.

As I swept and straightened up the porch furniture, I heard loud rap music coming from a car that was speeding down the street. It was an expensive car for sure, all black and clean as ever. I stopped what I was doing when it parked right in front of my house, and placed my hand over my eyes to shield them from the sun.

"Hey, baby." Gavin got out, grinning like a complete fool. I hadn't seen him in a couple weeks and he looked… good.

"Gavin, what the hell is that?"

"A Tesla." He shrugged as if he had plenty of nice cars and a mansion or something.

"You bought a Tesla? How?" I came down the steps and walked

closer to him.

"Nah, I rented it." He pulled some flowers from behind his back and extended them out to me. "What, man?" He laughed when I stared down at the bouquet suspiciously before taking them. I was still holding onto the top of the broom, with it pressed firmly into the cement of the driveway.

"Why are you bringing me flowers, and rolling up on me in this rental car, Gavin?"

His smile dropped into a more serious expression before saying, "Because I miss you and I have a big day planned for us… well, night."

"What makes you think I want to go anywhere with you? We aren't together anymore, Gavin." I frowned, annoyed that he *still* didn't get it.

"Right, but this is my way of trying to change your mind. Like I said, baby, I'm really trying to do right this time. Being without you made me realize that I need to get my shit right."

"Well, the first part of becoming a changed man is admission. So whose earrings were those in your bedroom?"

He blew out hot air and dropped his head before shaking it. Slapping his fist into his open hand, he said, "Aight, look, they belonged to another female that I messed around with."

"I knew it!"

"Yeah, but I'm sorry though, Rori." He palmed his chest, but then placed his hands on my waist as he stared down at me. "Just give me this one night, and if you enjoy yourself, then we can work towards getting back where we were but better."

"And if I don't enjoy myself?"

I don't even know why I was even contemplating going out with this man. I guess I just missed how we used to be and wanted that again. Not to mention, I felt like shit for fucking his best friend, even though it was the best dick I'd ever encountered. I found myself nibbling on my lip at the thought, so I cleared my throat out of embarrassment. I didn't even hear Gavin's response.

"So what do you say? Just tonight."

"Fine, Gavin, but you'd better take me somewhere nice."

"Aight, cool."

I'd never seen this nigga grin so widely before, so I guess he was happy as hell that I'd said yes. I didn't know why I was going, but for now, I wasn't going to turn down free food at a nice place.

"See you tonight then." I turned to walk back up to my house but he stopped me.

"Here." He peeled off some money from a knot of cash. "Go buy yourself something nice to wear for me."

"Really, Gavin?" I took the three hundred dollars into my hand and stared at it as if it were foreign.

"Yeah."

I watched him as he backed away smiling like he'd just heard the greatest news ever. Shaking my head, I stuffed the money into my pocket and rushed back into the house. I was done sweeping, and wanted to get some shopping in. I wasn't hurting for money, but it was a pain asking my step dad for cash when you didn't have a good grade to show him.

"Hey, have you seen Waayil?" Yikayla cocked her head.

Chuckling a little, I replied, "Umm, isn't he your boyfriend? Just call him."

"I have called him, Rori. I even went by the shop. His parents said he hasn't been home. I think they knew something though because they were like rushing me off."

"Hmm." I squinted my eyes, remembering he wasn't at Wednesday's birthday party. "That's not like him."

"I know, which worries me."

"Maybe he told his parents where he was going so they don't feel the need to worry about anything."

When I said that, Yikayla looked saddened. And I guess I'd be hurt too, if the man I loved didn't feel the need to disclose his location with me.

"Yeah, maybe." She adjusted Lonan on her hip, and as we walked past one another, I kissed his fat cheek, which made him smile.

"Are those the Pure Money Jordans?" I looked at Lonan's fresh ass kicks.

"Courtesy of Waayil." Yikayla shook her head and chuckled as she adjusted him on her hip. Waayil loved him some Lonan.

"Byyyye!" Lonan sang to me in his cute little voice. That was his new word in addition to 'Mommy.'

"Byyyee!" I replied giggling.

I put the broom back, put the flowers in some water, washed my hands, and grabbed my mom's keys up before she decided to go anywhere. I ended up at my favorite mall, Oak Court, and bought a few things from a couple stores. As I walked by Foot Locker, I saw these Nikes that Eko had just bought when we were still hot and heavy. I smiled thinking about him, and wondered what he was up to. Maybe I did actually like him, and not because he had been a shoulder to lean on or a dick to ride.

Once I was done shopping, I was a bit famished, so I went to Chick-Fil-A, another one of Eko's favorites. I never went there much before I started hanging with him, because they were so damn expensive to be fast food. But he had me damn near addicted like him. I ordered the spicy chicken sandwich, his favorite, and then sat down at one of the empty tables.

"Rori." Someone called my name just as I bit into my sandwich. I looked up to see none other than Jenni, holding a bag from Banana Republic and then another from Finish Line.

"Oh, hey, Jenni." I covered my mouth since I was chewing. I expected her to keep walking, but she sat down across from me.

"How are you?"

"I'm… great, Jenni. What's up?"

"So you and Eko are really close." She nodded repeatedly with a smile. The more I looked at her, the prettier she was. She reminded me of Megan Fox, just with bigger lips.

"Uh, yeah, we're good friends."

"Yeah, I… wanted to talk to you about that. You know, you guys being close and all."

Girl, if you're about to come at me about being with your man, you need to be a bit more aggressive.

"Oh?" I bit my sandwich because I was too hungry to stop for this seemingly meaningless conversation.

"Yeah, see, Eko and I haven't really been seeing eye to eye lately. I mean, you witnessed that the couple times you dropped by his home unannounced."

Was that shade?

"I dropped by unannounced because he made me feel like I could," I subtly snapped.

"Oh no, girl," she laughed. "I'm not saying it like it's a bad thing! I was just trying to remind you."

"Jenni, what's going on? I mean, get to the point. Why are you sitting across from me trying to be my friend when—"

"I need your help." Her expression was serious. She was begging me with her eyes and her words.

"Help with what?"

"Help getting things back on track with Eko and I. I love him, but ever since… well, I'm sure he told you."

"No. Ever since what?" I folded my arms and sat back. Now I was curious.

I never realized that when Eko and I were together, we never talked about his past trysts. We were always either fucking or talking about what a future together would be like, and our goals.

"I made a bad decision, and that's all I'm going to say. But look, you know Eko well and I need you to tell me what to do. I need you to guide me back to his heart. He is so closed off with me, but he doesn't seem that way with you. So maybe you could talk to him or give me some tips."

After staring at this bitch like she was a fool for a few seconds, I burst into laughter. She couldn't have been serious. I mean, was she honestly asking the woman who had fucked her man, to help her get back on his good side? This couldn't be life. I'd seen a lot of unbelievable shit go down in Memphis, but this took the cake.

"Are you joking?" I quizzed honestly, after sipping some of my iced tea to calm my laughter.

"I know it sounds insane, but I've run out of options."

"Jenni, has Eko ever talked about me to you?"

"No. When I was suspicious of you and questioned him, he just..." She shook her head and sighed. "He just blew me off. You know how rude and evil Eko can be."

No, not to me.

She was there when he chased after me when I caught them fucking. But hey, maybe she was stupider than she looked.

"Look, Jenni, I'm sorry you've had to come to this, but I can't help you, okay? I have my own problems." I packed my food up as I spoke, and then stood up.

"Wait, I will even pay you if that's what you need." She then began digging into the Finish Line bag, before retrieving a box. "You won't

161

even have to do much. Just advise me on small things; like these shoes for instance. I bought them for him, do you think he will love them?" She cheesed as if she knew I was gonna say 'yes.'

"Jenni, Eko only wears Nikes."

"Oh." Her smile dropped as she looked down into the open box. She quickly closed it, and then chuckled awkwardly before shoving them back into the bag. "Guess I will return those."

"Well, I have to be somewhere later. But good luck, Jenni."

"Wait, Rori!" She called after me but I kept walking. That bitch was crazy as hell for asking me to do some shit like that. It probably was a damn set up. She couldn't be that dumb to think all Eko and I did was bake cookies together and talk.

That bitch was dickmatized…

***

That night…

Gavin had surprised the hell out of me by taking me to this nice French restaurant. My stepfather had taken us here before, but I didn't expect Gavin to be able to.

We'd just finished eating our entrees, and were waiting on our dessert. The conversation had been nice, and I guess it was because Gavin and I rarely just talked. The only alone or couple time we had together was in the bedroom. And for the past year, we barely got in there.

"So can this shit happen again or what?" Gavin smiled, looking very nice in his button up shirt. He'd gotten his hair cut and everything.

"Yeah, I guess so." I smirked, stirring my drink. I didn't know what I was saying. As nice as this was, the spark we'd once had was just… gone. And I couldn't get Eko out of my head.

"Can I ask you something, Rori? You know, since we're putting everything on the table and shit."

"Okay."

"When you and Eko were chilling and shit after we broke up, did you sleep with him?"

"What?" I frowned, trying to appear offended.

"Did you fuck him?"

"Are you serious right now, Gavin?"

"Deadass serious, ma. I feel like I need to know. I can't stop thinking about that shit. Ever since the homie said he saw y'all out together, I've been buggin.'"

"I have two—"

"Can you give me mine to go? Excuse me," I said to the waitress as she set our desserts down. I quickly hopped up and started towards the bathroom, ignoring Gavin calling my name lowly.

I used the bathroom, and as I washed my hands, I took a couple deep breaths so that I'd calm down. I didn't want to lie to Gavin, but I didn't want to tell him either. Fuck.

By the time I came out, the bill had been paid and Gavin was outside in the grass, on his cellphone. He was pacing a little, and his body was tense, showing he was in a heated conversation. As I neared him from behind, his words became clearer.

"And how the fuck do I know that's my damn baby? … Because!

163

You've been MI-fucking-A for the longest, ma! … Get the fuck outta here! … Yeah, yeah aight. Don't call my phone no more!" He hung up and turned around to see me standing there… frozen. "Rori—"

"You stupid ass nigga!" I swung on him, but he ducked and grabbed my midsection.

I rained blows down on his head and back, as he called my name loudly, while bear hugging my waist.

"Rori! Let me explain!"

"Fuck you! Get off of me!" I grunted, kneeing his stupid ass in the nuts. He let me go, and with tears in my eyes, I panted, "Don't you ever fucking talk to me again, Gavin Peace. Ever."

"Rori," he breathed heavily, cupping his knees.

"Ever," I repeated before walking off.

"Rori! Rori, bring yo' ass back here!"

I didn't know how I was gonna get home, but I'd rather walk than ride back with that lying ass nigga.

CHAPTER FIVE

Canyon

That same evening...

"Aye, it's time to clean up so you can eat, lil' man," I told my son Cade as I stood up from the floor.

Little nigga had his Legos all over my damn living room. I had a mind not to buy him that bullshit, but he'd been doing so well in preschool that I promised him I'd get him whatever toy he wanted. Of course, he chose the biggest muthafuckin' Lego shit they had in that bitch. I shook my head at the thought as I watched him scoop up the Legos with his little ass hands. That shit was gon' take forever, but it'd give me some time to figure out what the hell we were gon' eat for dinner.

I walked to my kitchen and opened my fridge and freezer to see what the hell I could put together. I'd bought a lot of shit like chicken, steaks, pork chops, and a bunch of other shit you had to cook, knowing damn well I wasn't about that life. I was trying not to eat out, so I went ham at the grocery store, but that shit wasn't doing me any good in times like these.

"Almost done!" Cade shouted from my living room. I looked to my left to check the scene, and he definitely wasn't almost done. I chuckled lightly at his ass.

"Fuck," I mumbled, closing the fridge doors.

My phone chimed, letting me know I had a Facebook message, so with a confused frown, I pulled my iPhone from my jean pocket.

I didn't get on Facebook at all because it was a work page, meaning my boss and co-workers were a part of my friends list. I couldn't post what the fuck I wanted like I could on Instagram, so I strayed from Facebook unless it was something PG like family stuff. By saying that, no one messaged me on Facebook, because everyone who would had my phone number.

Looking at the screen, I let my head fall back and groaned after seeing it was from Jodi. I had to block that bitch's number in my phone, and I guess she found another way to contact me. Bitch was way too pretty to be stalking my ass like this. Her pussy was A1 too, so I didn't know why she hadn't given up on the nigga that clearly didn't want her crazy ass.

Jodi Hembry: Hey

And she sent a 'hey' like we'd been keeping in contact. I smashed that bitch one damn time, and she'd gon' off the damn rails.

Me: Stop hitting me up, Jodi. For real.

I stared down at my phone as them three little dots moved around on the screen. I was praying she took what I'd said and kept it moving, but if she'd gone this far already, I had a feeling a simple message wouldn't do the trick.

Jodi Hembry: Wow, why so hostile?

Jodi Hembry: I thought we had a good time?

Jodi Hembry: Did you block me in your phone?

Jodi Hembry: Hello!

My phone blew up with back-to-back messages, but I just shoved that shit into my pocket so I could help my son hurry up. As I helped Cade scoop his Legos back into its container, my doorbell rang. My damn stomach dropped thinking it was Jodi's crazy ass on the other side of it.

"Don't move, Cade. Aight?"

He nodded in response with his eyes locked on the front door of my apartment. I walked to the door, face angry as hell, and then yanked it open. I expected to see Jodi holding a cake with a knife in it like old girl from *Thin Line*... but it was Dree. She was wearing a dress, but it wasn't anything fancy, and her hair was in one braid going straight down her back.

"Is this a bad time?" she questioned softly.

"Nah, come in." I stepped back.

My days of being an asshole ended the night she came home going crazy damn near. I stayed with her all night, watching her sleep peacefully after a while. In the morning, I tried to ask her what happened, but typical Dree pretended like everything was fine and that she was just panicking under the influence. I loved a lot of things about Dree, but her unwillingness to show vulnerability was irritating as hell.

"Hi, sweetie, I'm Dree." She walked right over to Cade, who stood up to shake her hand. That sly smile he wore made me chuckle because I knew he had a crush already.

"I'm Cade. I'm four now!" he told her.

"What? So this is your home?" Dree smiled and Cade nodded his head 'yes' with his lying ass. "Wow, well then maybe we should kick your daddy out, huh?"

"Yeah, okay!"

"Cade, how you gon' do Daddy like that?" I picked him up and clawed playfully at his stomach, making him laugh and beg for mercy. I placed him back to his feet, and he fell to the floor dramatically, trying to catch his breath. "I was just about to make us something to eat, but it looks like it's pizza for the night."

"Pizza!" Cade shouted with his arms in the air.

"I can make you guys something if you'd like. What do you have available?" Dree placed her purse on the seat cushion next to her and stood up.

"Nah, baby, you don't have to. He likes pizza anyway."

"Yes, but that's because he hasn't had any of my cooking. Do you have chicken? Rice? Anything green?"

"Most of that in the fridge."

"Good." Dree walked to my kitchen and immediately started pulling what she needed from the fridge, the cabinet, and the pantry.

I watched her for a minute, liking how beautiful she looked even when she dressed down. Not to mention, it made my dick hard seeing Dree cater to me, especially because she was usually acting tough as fuck.

I put a movie in for Cade to watch while Dree cooked, then I went into the kitchen to join her. I kept hearing the notification tone that meant I had a Facebook message, so I put my shit on silent before slipping it back into my pocket. I wasn't scared of many things, but Jodi had me a little worried.

"What's all this for, ma?" I asked Dree as soon as I sat down at the table.

"I always cook for you." Dree seasoned the chicken with her back to me.

"Yeah, but what's been going on with you? One minute you don't want shit to do with me, then all of sudden, it's like you've changed your mind. Then, that night—"

"I told you I had too much to drink that night, and that I had smoked some weed for the first time. People can have bad reactions to weed, Canyon."

"Who did you smoke with?"

That shit bothered me. I always told Dree back in the day that if she wanted to smoke, it needed to be with me. And even when we linked back up and she told me she still hadn't done it, I reiterated that. So to know she was out getting high, and then reacted badly to it pissed me off. That was exactly why I didn't want her hardheaded ass doing it with anyone else. No way I would have let her drive home in that state.

"With umm… Sean."

"Is that your nigga that you stopped fucking with me for?"

"It wasn't like that, Canyon."

"It wasn't? Let's see, we were on our way to being in a relationship, and then all of a sudden, you didn't want it anymore."

"No, your drama with Luna scared me off and you know it."

I let it go, and just changed the subject to something lighter while she cooked. It was done pretty quickly, and she made a plate for all three of us. While we ate, Dree and Cade interacted the whole time, and that shit caught me off guard. For a minute, I thought she was put off by the fact that I had a kid, but right now, it was almost like she loved that I had a son.

After Cade had his bath and brushed his teeth, I put him to bed and then Dree and I laid out in my bedroom to relax.

"You staying the night?" I inquired as I pulled my shirt off.

"You want me to?"

"Up to you."

She laid down on my bed after taking her shoes off, and I sat on the other side. I couldn't help but to brush my hand up and down her smooth deep chocolate thigh. She was so fucking sexy to a nigga that it made no damn sense. I bit my lip, thinking about the times I was stroking between her hips, as I caressed her thigh. She caught me, and smiled widely, which made me chuckle.

I climbed on top of her, getting in between her legs, before kissing her soft full lips slowly. My dick was hard in under two seconds as it pressed against her pussy. She locked her arms around my neck as I parted her lips with my tongue, while groping her soft ass. Pushing her dress up, I yanked that shit over her head, then cupped her perfectly round breasts in my hands.

"Ahh," she moaned softly as I sucked her nipples.

Once I'd had enough, I trailed my lips down her stomach, while tugging on her panties. As I planted kisses on her inner thighs, I heard light sniffles, which made me look up at her.

"Dree?" I frowned.

"No, it's fine." She forced a smile.

"Are you crying? Baby, what the fuck is wrong?" I came back up and towered over her as she lied on her back.

"Nothing is wrong, Canyon. Come on." She reached to start unbuckling my jeans, but I knocked her hands away.

"I'm not about to fuck you while you're crying and shit. My damn dick not even hard no more," I hissed.

I was about to move from hovering over her, but she grabbed my wrist and said, "Canyon, I need you to do this."

"Do what?" I scowled. I was getting angrier and angrier as this shit went on.

"I need us to have sex, please. Canyon!" She called my name when I rolled off of her and off the bed. "Please, Canyon."

"Dree, tell me what's wrong with you, ma."

Suddenly, she started sobbing with her face in her hands. She turned on her side so that her bare back was to me, and just cried. I realized she still didn't want to talk about whatever the fuck was wrong with her, and as badly as I wanted to shake her ass up and make her say

171

it, I couldn't.

Removing my jeans, I got back onto the bed and hugged her body from behind. She turned to face me, and buried her head into my chest as I pulled the covers over us.

I didn't know what the fuck was wrong with my baby girl, but if it had something to do with that Sean character, on God it was about to be some shit.

CHAPTER FIVE

Yusef

Jonaya: I'm gonna bring you something to eat.

Me: Good. I got a taste for you.

Jonaya: No, real food, lol.

Me: Aight.

$\mathcal{I}$ set my phone down on my desk, grinning hard as hell. Ever since I'd broken Jonaya's ass down and made her admit her feelings, shit had been real good for me. I was beating that pussy up every chance I got. I'm talking in between clients, in between her classes, late at night when she would roll through; just all the damn time. Jonaya stayed wet, and the way her pussy hugged my dick... shit should have been a crime. I was hard as fuck just from thinking about the shit.

The only slight problem was that Leighton was still hitting me up and shit like I was still rocking with her. I thought Jonaya would have told her the deal, but I guess she hadn't done so. It probably was my part to take care of, but damn, I needed a break from letting bitches down. Rebecca was already giving me enough shit.

KNOCK! KNOCK!

"Yeah!" I called out to whomever was knocking on my office door.

Rebecca entered and closed the door behind herself. Shit was awkward because we hadn't talked much outside of work since that shit popped off in the parking lot of Sax's party. She was back to moping around, but she still handled her business, so I wasn't tripping.

"Hey, so everyone paid their rent except Moses."

"Why?" I was leaning back in my chair, but when she said that shit, it made me sit up.

"He said things were slow for him this month, and he wants to know if he can pay in a couple weeks."

"Rebecca, you know the deal. Why are you even bringing this to me? You know I don't give any extensions."

"I mean, you have in the past. Remember Arianna? Or was that just because you were fucking her behind my back."

I chuckled angrily at Rebecca's words.

"Okay." I laced my fingers together. "Rebecca, anything I ever did with another woman was never behind ya back. You know why? Because we weren't exclusive. You knew that shit the whole time I was fucking you, so kill that woman scorned act, ma. Please. I got enough shit to deal with."

"Yeah, see, you said we weren't exclusive, but you did everything a boyfriend would do. Telling me you loved me, not using protection sometimes, hell, what was I supposed to think!"

"You weren't supposed to think shit but what was coming out of my mouth every time you asked what we were! Yeah, I loved you, but I didn't want to be with yo' ass like that!"

"You did me so wrong all the fucking time!"

"Then why did you keep fucking with me, huh? I was fucking bitches behind ya back 24/7, so why were you still in my bed when I wanted you to be? Be mad at ya damn self for playing the muthafuckin' fool, ma, not me."

Swiping the tears from her eyes, she whimpered. "So you don't want to be with me?"

This bitch was out of her monkey ass mind.

"No. I don't," I stated calmly but sternly. Fuck being sympathetic.

"Oh, but you want Jonaya? Just like a nigga to pick a been around the block ass bitch, instead of one that has respect for herself."

I rolled my chair back and stood up, before coming around the desk and getting in her face. She moved back some, blinking repeatedly.

"So look, no matter how many times you've sucked my dick or spread your legs for me, ma, what you need to remember is that I'm ya fucking boss. This is my shop you working in! I sign yo' checks," I hissed, still moving towards her until I had her backed into a wall. I was waiting for a smell to hit me, because from the look on her face, I was sure she'd shit on herself. "By saying that, from now on, don't come at me on work hours trying to discuss no personal shit. And secondly, don't you ever disrespect Jonaya Goode in my fuckin' presence, or not only will I terminate yo' ass, but I may put hands on you. You got it?" I gritted, teeth clenched so tightly that I was waiting for them to crack. I

175

was wishing she were a nigga right now so I could deck her dumb ass.

"Ye-yes, I'm… I apologize."

"Get the fuck out. And when Moses comes in, make sure you pull that nigga to the side to get my damn money."

"Yes, sure. Okay," she replied frantically, before yanking my office door open and damn near running out.

I closed it behind her and let out a deep exhale.

"Where is this nigga, Waayil?" I frowned.

Muthafucka had gon' MIA the day before Wednesday's birthday and the shit was starting to worry me. I felt deep down like something was wrong, and when I questioned my parents at Wednesday's party, they were acting all weird and like shit was no big deal. I loved Wednesday, but Waayil worshipped the ground she walked on, so for him to not come to her birthday, was beyond strange.

As I dialed his number for the hundredth time, my door came open and in walked Jonaya. She came at the right time, because had she arrived not but five minutes earlier, it probably would have been some shit. I no longer put it past Rebecca to fight at work after the way she dragged Leighton's ass out of here.

"Where you bring me food from?" I asked, grinning at how pretty her ass looked.

She had on some tights and one of them tops that showed her stomach. Her hair was hanging down, and I could tell that she didn't have on any makeup. Biting my lip, I admired the way my office lights made her smooth cinnamon complexion appear even more vibrant than it already was.

"I cooked for you."

She placed the plastic bag in front of me, before untying it and removing a plate covered in the foil. The strong smell of some good ass fucking seasoning hit me like a ton of bricks, and I knew it was my favorite somewhere under that silver cover; hush puppies. My stomach did somersaults at the sight of the hush puppies, macaroni and cheese, greens, and fried chicken. That was another thing about Jonaya and her sisters; they could cook their fine asses off.

"Damn, baby," I mumbled, not even able to take my eyes off it as she set my bottled drink down and unwrapped my silverware.

I prayed and when I opened my eyes, she was sitting across from me, cheesing.

"You're welcome," she smirked.

"You ain't bring none for yourself?" I frowned. Ain't no way I was sharing this plate, even though it was a lot.

"No, I had a little bit already. I was at the gym earlier, and all that would defeat the purpose."

"You spending the night, right? It's Thursday, your weekend."

"Umm, I wanted to, but I have to type this paper so I can't. My professor just assigned it this morning, and it's due a week from today."

"Bring yo' laptop. I can help you."

"Nusef, no. I can tell by the lustful way you're looking at me that you will not be interested in my paper."

I was about to respond but her phone started ringing and moving around on my desk. I saw Marquise's name, and when she went to grab it, I snatched that shit up.

"Hello?" I answered, frowning so hard I could feel it.

"Aye, who the fuck is this?" he spat.

"Ya old bitch's new nigga. Who the fuck is this, bruh?"

"Nusef!" Jonaya shouted in a whisper. She'd come around my desk to try and take her phone from me, so I stood up. She was way shorter than me, so she gave up.

"Mane, if you don't put my girl on the phone—"

"You gon' do what? This is Nusef, nigga, and if you got a problem with anything I just said, come down to the shop. Come get fucked up again." He was silent as hell once he heard who the fuck it was. "That's what I thought. Save yo'self the embarrassment and don't call this line no more, bruh. On God, I'll crack yo' face."

"Man." He sucked his teeth and hung up just like the fake, fraud, bitch ass nigga that he was.

"Nusef!" Jonaya shouted and snatched her phone when I reached it out to her.

"Fuck you calling my damn name for, huh? You my girl ain't you? Or am I wrong?"

"No, I am, I just—"

"And why the fuck he don't know that, Jo?" I barked as she sat back across from me. "I swear you gon' put another Christian in jail, woman. I bet not find out he's still checking for you, or it's over with for that nigga and you."

"Fuck you, Sef." She pouted like a little ass kid, arms folded and everything. I chuckled a little when she stared off to the side, since she didn't want to look at me.

"Come here."

"No."

"Jonaya. Come here."

Rolling her damn eyes so hard that I low-key wanted to smack her, she got up and walked over to me. I pulled her between my legs since I was sitting, and placed a kiss on her stomach.

"What, nigga?" She turned her lip up.

"You mad?"

"Nusef."

I laughed a little bit and then hugged her waist.

"Aye, I'm sorry for threatening you, but I'm dead serious, ma. If that nigga contacts you again or tries to carry on y'all relationship, we gon' have a problem. And you'd better let him know that if he comes at you." I kissed her stomach again as she stared right over my head at the wall. "Nah, don't even talk to him if he comes at you. Play Helen Keller on that nigga."

A smile tugged at her lips.

"Can I go now? I have stuff to do."

"Yeah. Get a start on that paper so you can sit on it tonight." I watched as she started to walk off.

"See—"

"And give me a kiss."

Smiling, she tied her hair up and then came back around to peck me. I held her there though and tongued her down nastily, while squeezing on her small, round, fat booty. I couldn't get hitting that shit from the back out of my mind, especially while pulling on that hair.

I let her go, and locked my eyes on her ass until she was out of my office. She'd left the door open, so I could see Rebecca in the front looking over paperwork. When Jonaya walked by, Rebecca gave her a look on the low that even gave me a few chills. Jonaya didn't notice though as she left.

"Bitch is crazy," I mumbled as I got up to close my door.

I sat back down to enjoy my food, and even the slice of strawberry pie Jonaya made. I hadn't been to the gym all week because my workout had been fucking, but I needed to ASAP. I had to stay in shape, and that was gon' be hard with a girlfriend who cooked like Jonaya did.

I hadn't let my food settle for a good ten minutes before I heard female screams and a bit of ruckus up front. I knew the women's voices belonged to Rebecca and Chiara, so I hopped up and snatched my door open.

When I stormed to the front, I saw Waayil choking the shit out of Moses. I mean that nigga was red as a damn tomato, and I was waiting for his head to burst. Chiara and Rebecca were begging Waayil to let Moses go, as Moses stared at Waayil with wide eyes. I could tell Moses thought this would be his final moments.

"Waayil, what the fuck!" I shouted, trying to pry his hands from Moses's neck. Waayil's face was calm, but his eyes were murderous. I didn't even recognize this nigga right now. It was like something had taken over his damn body. "Waayil!" I hollered even louder, shoving the shit out of him so that his hands came from around Moses's neck.

Moses collapsed to the floor, passing the fuck out.

"Oh my gosh!" Rebecca whimpered, dropping down to feel for Moses's pulse. "What do I do?"

Chiara was frozen, eyes locked on Waayil in horror. I was holding him by his biceps, but he snatched from me and walked off outside.

"Rebecca, stay by him! Chiara, give me two minutes before you call 911 so I can send this nigga home! Remember, the story is some dude came up in here mad about a tattoo Moses had done and choked him."

Chiara nodded.

If Moses made it, I prayed he wouldn't snitch and tell the truth. If he did, it'd be a price on his head for sure. And not just from Waayil. We didn't do the snitching shit 'round here. If Moses wanted to get back at Waayil, he needed to do it without the police.

"What the fuck, man!" I barked at Waayil once I was outside with him.

"He didn't have his money ready," he replied nonchalantly as if I'd asked him what the fuck he'd had for breakfast.

"So you gon' kill him!" I yelled. I was confused as a muthafucka right now.

Chuckling like a maniac, he responded, "Maybe. Tell that bitch ass nigga that if he don't die, to have my damn money or I'm gon' make sure he spends the rest of his life with a shit bag attached to him."

"Waayil!"

He yanked his car door open, hopped in, and sped out with his music blasting. This was too fucking much, bruh.

CHAPTER SIX

Yikayla

I was feeding Lonan his last little bits of dinner, trying to hold myself together in his presence. We were in Waayil's house, and had been staying there ever since he'd given me a key. Waayil hadn't been here in a little over a week now, and I believe his parents lied to me when they said they contacted the police about it. They were just too calm to have a missing son. Plus, Mrs. Samuels loved her some Waayil, so I knew if she were really worried, she'd be panicking like me.

"All done!" I smiled at my baby.

"All done!" he repeated, banging his little hands on his high chair.

"You are so adorable, Lonan!" I squealed as I scooped him up and kissed his cheeks.

I went to give him a bath, and then we brushed his few teeth a little since he liked to do that now. He was passed out after sucking on his pacifier for only a few minutes, so I put him in the bed with me.

As I laid down on my side, attempting to fall asleep, I heard the front door open and close. I was scared for a moment, thinking someone had broken in, until I heard Waayil's sexy singing voice. He was singing lowly, but I still knew his tone well.

BAM!

By the time I got out of the bed, the bathroom door slammed closed, before the sink came on. When I got to it, it sounded like he was brushing his teeth.

"Waayil!" I called out, knocking hard.

I got no answer as he continued to sing softly to himself just before gargling the mouthwash.

"Waayil!" I shouted more angrily this time, fumbling with the knob, which was obviously locked.

The shower came on, and I knew by then he wouldn't be able to hear me, so I went to sit on the couch. I waited for what seemed like hours before the water cut off. Then another decade seemed to pass before the door came open and steam flowed from it. I was lying down on the couch, but at the sight of sexy chocolate Waayil, I sat up. The towel was wrapped around his waist, and his six-pack and pecks were protruding something serious. Water droplets flowed down his perfectly built body, seemingly tracing his many tattoos on his chest and arms.

"Waayil," I spoke again, but much calmer than before.

Again, he ignored me and just went into the bedroom. Irritated, I got up and followed him in there. By the time I made it to him, he was placing his gun into the drawer, which stopped me in my tracks. I didn't know what to say as he turned to face me, looking crazy but fine as ever. I missed him and I didn't know if I should kiss him or slap the shit out of him for not being around.

"Waay—"

Before I could finish, he began kissing me roughly, reaching under my nightshirt and ripping my panties off like they were nothing.

"Stop!" I shouted in a whisper so I wouldn't wake Lonan, as I pushed his hands from under my clothing. "How dare you go missing then try to come up in here to sleep with me?"

"Yikayla, I promise I will explain myself to you but please..." he spoke in between planting kisses on my neck. "Let me be close to you."

I allowed him to pull my nightgown over my head, and he let his towel drop before picking me up and carrying me into the room where Lonan usually slept. Pressing my back into the wall, he positioned his head against my opening and began forcing himself inside. I'd gone a week without him, and my pussy definitely needed time to adjust.

"Shit," he grumbled against my collarbone as I whimpered softly. "I missed you." He sucked on my bottom lip as he pounded me nice and slowly first, so I could open up. The way he looked me in my eyes as he invaded my body was something else.

"Mmm," I whined, hugging his neck. He was plunging so deeply inside of me with precision, that I was already on the verge of cumming.

He leaned his head back for a kiss, and I slipped my tongue into his mouth as he gripped my ass cheeks roughly, while holding me up and drilling me. I could barely keep up with the kiss because I was releasing back to back. I guess it was a combination of me not seeing him, and his sex game that had my body reacting like it never had before.

185

"Oh my go-gosh," I cried as Waayil beat it up against the wall.

Hearing his subtle groans was so damn sexy. I felt myself gushing on his pole, and he cheered me on lowly every time I came.

"That's right. Cum for daddy," he whispered against my collarbone before sucking it.

Suddenly, he pulled out of me, bent me over the dresser in the room, and fucked me hard from behind. The sound of him moving in and out of me powerfully, along with our sweaty skin coming together, almost drowned out my stuttered moans. My nails scraped against the wooden dresser top as Waayil yanked my head back by my hair. Again, my clit tingled just before I released on his pole.

"Fuck, Kay." He slowed down his strokes, still holding tightly onto my hair.

He spanked and groped my left ass cheek, before speeding back up, pounding me so hard that I could barely get one full moan to pass through my lips.

"Uhhh," was all I got out as he slammed into me, filling me up and tapping my spot perfectly every time.

Taking himself out again, he turned me to face him abruptly, and then went down, putting my legs over his shoulders. My chest heaved up and down rapidly as he feasted between my legs. Waayil was insatiable, and after a while, I would simply become a rag doll due to being worn out. But I loved when he pulled out and ate it.

"Oh shit," I whimpered, feeling myself about to reach my peak. He was sucking and teasing my clit passionately as hell, while caressing my thighs and moaning the way I liked. "Waayil." My voice trembled as he pushed my leg outward for more access to me.

My body froze as he attacked my center viciously, and soon after, I was exploding yet again. Rising to his feet, he placed one of my legs over his shoulder, and locked the other around his waist as he entered me slowly. His beautiful honey eyes stared me down hard, as he started off slowly. He bent down to tend to my nipples for a little bit, then gripped my waist with his large strong hands before pummeling me into another orgasm. He delivered a few more long, hard pumps, then exploded himself.

"Shit." He panted against my neck, dick still inside of me. "Been way too long," he added.

Finally, he pulled out of me, and carried me to the bathroom so we could clean ourselves up. I was sweating hard as hell though, so I decided to just take a shower. Waayil climbed in with me, and as I faced the showerhead, he planted soft kisses on my shoulders. My euphoria from our sex session began to disappear though, and anger came back.

"Where were you, Waayil?"

The thought of him being laid up with some woman, namely Alba, made me sick to my stomach.

"I'd been in Nashville, but I got back two days ago." He lathered up the face towel and began to wash my back.

"Why did you shower when you came back?"

"Was at the shake junt." He smirked as he turned me to face him so he could wash the front of my body. As cute as he was, I didn't have a smile anywhere on my face, however.

"Explain yourself. I'm tired of asking questions. And if I don't like what you have to say, I'm leaving you."

Tossing his head back to laugh, he brought it back up and shook his head with a beautiful smile. I couldn't help but to admire the depth of his dimples.

"No you're not."

"Excuse me?" My eyes followed him as he lowered a little bit to clean my bottom half.

"I'm not saying you wouldn't, baby. What I mean is I'm in this shower washing you off like a damn servant or some shit. Clearly, I'm in love with yo' ass and because of that, I ain't letting you go no muthafuckin' where. You can try, but it'll be a waste of your time." He lightly pushed me towards the showerhead after cleaning between my legs, and I let the water rinse the soap off.

I helped him give himself a quick wash, then he got out of the shower. He opened a big warm towel for me, and I stepped into it.

"Wednesday lied."

"About what?" I quizzed, spritzing on some of my homemade body oil. When he didn't respond, I looked up at him. He was just staring at me somberly like he was waiting for me to catch on. "What did she lie—" I stopped mid-sentence when it hit me. "No, not about..."

He nodded and groaned, before running his hand down his face. Water was still cascading down his tall, muscular frame as he stared off, shaking his head.

"When I found out, the shit fucked me up. I'm still a little fucked up, and I needed time away from everybody before I did some crazy shit. I still feel like I will, but I couldn't be away from you and Lonan for too much longer, baby. I'm sorry for leaving." He sat on the closed toilet top.

I was still baffled, so it took me a minute to respond.

"Wait, when did you find out? How do you even know she lied, Waayil? Did someone tell you that?"

"I heard it come out of her mouth, Yikayla." He looked to me hard so I nodded. "And I found out the day before her birthday."

All I kept thinking was how could she do that to him? And why would she? Waayil treated Wednesday like a queen, so how could she betray him like that?

We left the bathroom and put on something for bed, before going into the living room. The heater was on, so we just relaxed.

"Did you know?" he questioned lowly as the TV lit up the dark room.

"Know what?" I frowned as I stared at the side of his handsome face.

"That she lied, Yikayla."

"How the hell would I know?"

"Your sister knew. Jonaya knew she lied and didn't say shit to me, but maybe she told you."

"And you think I wouldn't tell you?"

He shrugged as he focused back on the TV.

I couldn't believe Jonaya right now. That wasn't even like her,

189

especially with her sisters. She told us everything. A part of me didn't want to believe Waayil, but he wasn't the lying type.

"Well I would have told you, stupid, so don't ever ask me something like that again. You're the only one who keeps secrets in this relationship."

Typical Waayil didn't respond. He just ate one of the tortilla chips from the big family-sized bag he had, as he focused on the TV.

"Fuck you, Waayil, and goodnight." I hopped up and walked towards the back. I discreetly looked over my shoulder at him, but he paid me no mind as he continued to eat and watch television on the couch.

"Yikayla." He called my name just before I'd gotten into the bedroom. I came back to the living room and he said, "Sit down. Didn't I say I missed you?" He gave me a look like I'd better not try to refuse.

I rolled my eyes and plopped down, wanting him to think I didn't wanna be in here with him when really, I was turned on by his command and happy to stay in the living room.

As soon as I sat down, he laid his head in my lap, kissing one of my thighs before focusing on the television. I just caressed his head and kissed his temple.

I wanted to be angry with him, but instead I was worried. Waayil loved Wednesday more than anything, and what she did wasn't only wrong because she lied, it was wrong because of how much he cared for her.

Lord, help my baby.

CHAPTER SIX

Wednesday Samuels

The next night... Around midnight...

"What are you doing!" I shouted to my uncle Harry, when I caught him in my room reading pages of my diary.

With a conniving smirk plastered on his face, he shut my diary with one hand and said, "A crush? On your own brother?" He chuckled and ran his tongue across the few gold-plated teeth he had in his top row. "I wonder what he would think if I showed him this."

"Stop!" I reached for my precious diary, but Harry just stuck his arm straight up in the air to keep me out of its reach. "Please give it back," I whined, feeling the tears well up and the fear in my heart intensify.

"What will I get out of it?"

"Huh?"

"If you want me to keep your little secret, Wednesday, I'm gonna need something in return. Otherwise, Waayil is gonna see you for what you are; a fast, little hoe, lusting after him."

"I will give you my full allowance! It's $200!"

Harry let out a crazed laugh, clearly seeing my pathetic offer as comical.

"Nah, baby girl, I need something a little more precious." He moved closer to me, running his rough ashy pointer finger down my delicate cheek. I was surprised he hadn't sliced it open. *"Tomorrow night, be up waiting for me... naked."*

"Uncle Harry, please—"

"Do we have a deal or do we not? I know how much Waayil loves you, and to see the things you put in this here diary, it will make him see you very differently." With a smirk, he added, *"Hell, I see you differently."*

As much as I didn't want to comply with Harry, I couldn't risk Waayil finding out about my feelings. He was so nice to me, and he treated me like I was a precious gem to him. I just couldn't let him become aware of my true feelings because it would ruin everything.

I watched Harry leave my bedroom, diary clutched in his hands. I tried to think of a way out of this, but I got nothing. Unless he somehow died, I was fucked either way.

I'd barely been getting any sleep lately ever since Waayil found out my secret. I thought about calling him or texting him, but honestly, I was too afraid. I never planned for him to find out, but if he had, I never imagined he would react as badly as he did. He'd actually pulled a gun on me, and looked at me like I was the enemy. I'd never been so scared in my life like I was that day. I had nightmares about it for three days straight.

I'd finally drifted off to sleep a couple hours ago, but now I felt myself waking up. An eerie feeling had come over my body for some reason. I opened my eyes, and when I saw Waayil sitting in the chair at my desk, watching me with his gun in hand, I almost peed on myself.

"Waayil," I whimpered, praying like hell he wasn't here to murder me.

If you had have asked me if Waayil would kill me some weeks back, I would have laughed your question off. But these days, I looked over my shoulder constantly, wondering if he was gonna run up on me and murk me. For the first time, outside of him murdering Harry, I was seeing the other side of Waayil that people used to talk about and fear. He usually only showed me his sweet side, and I was missing that already. But it was my fault that I was seeing this side of him.

"Why did you lie?" He took a large gulp from the biggest bottle of Hennessy that I'd ever seen. His eyes shined brightly in my dark bedroom, as he kept them on me hard.

Sitting up slowly, I peeled my covers back, and threw my feet off the edge of the bed. I didn't know where to start, or how I would tell Waayil why I did what I did without sounding like a complete fool. I was young and thinking that my life would be over had Waayil found out about the contents of my diary. And I honestly, truthfully, assumed Waayil was just gonna beat Uncle Harry up. I had no idea he was going to kill him.

I didn't even get the idea to lie, until I burst into his room to see he and Yikayla laid up, naked in the bed. That infuriated me, because I was coming to lie down with him like I always did some nights. I knew the next day I'd be in bed with Uncle Harry, being violated, and

I needed one more night with my brother before it happened. But to see him and Yikayla like that, it pissed me off and I concocted a plan. I came up with a story, roughed up my hair, and put some tea tree oil near my eyes to make them watery and red.

I wanted Waayil to beat Harry's ass to the point where he'd be too scared to tell, and then I wanted Waayil to be reprimanded for doing such a thing; which at the time I assumed would be getting grounded by my parents, causing him to stay away from Yikayla. Had I known what would have transpired, I would have never—

"Talk!" Waayil barked, making me jump. I swear the house shook.

"Ha-Harry had threatened me the night before, and—"

"Threatened you how?"

Swallowing a big ass lump, because even now at age nineteen, I was still afraid to tell Waayil that I'd crushed on him. I still kind of did have one, but I was old enough to realize that we would never be. And in the end, he *was* my brother and the thought of being with him was a bit disturbing, even to me.

"He found some things that I wrote about you, and he told me he would tell you what it said. Well, he was gonna show you what it said, and I knew if you saw, you would hate me!"

"Wait, wait." He laughed maniacally. "You did all of this shit because of some bullshit you wrote in a damn diary?" The scowl that appeared on his face was frightening to say the least. And him using his gun to express himself instead of his hand, didn't make shit better.

"I'd written that I was in love with you and wanted to be with you!" As I pleaded, he laughed harder, scaring me. I couldn't tell him that seeing him in bed with Yikayla was *also* what ultimately made me do what I did.

"You'd better be joking right now, ma." He chuckled, dimples appearing.

"It wasn't like that, Waayil! I was afraid that our relationship would be ruined, so I—"

"So you lied to me, causing me to do some shit that sent me to jail." He laughed again, taking another big gulp of the Hennessy. "I should shoot you," he added, voice deep, low, and serious.

"Waayil, please don't. I swear I didn't mean it. But look on the bright side, you're out of jail now—"

"Bright side? What fucking bright side, Wednesday! I lost six fucking years of my life over some shit you wanted to keep a secret in ya damn diary! Do you hear that shit, ma? I murdered a muthafucka because of a crush!" He was standing up now, going 9,000. "If Nusef hadn't have opened the tattoo shop for us, do you know I would be struggling to get a job right now? Do you know how it feels for people to look at me when they find out I'm an ex-con? Or all the damn hoops I had to jump through to get my own spot?"

"Ah!" I screamed when he tossed my big, heavy bookshelf to the floor. "Waayil!" I cried, afraid for my damn life.

Stepping over the collapsed bookshelf like a serial killer, he walked up on me as I stayed seated on my bed, paralyzed. He pushed the gun into my mouth forcefully, as I whimpered, letting tears cascade down my face. His mouth was twisted, and his honey colored eyes burned with fire, as his chest heaved up and down.

"Quit all that fucking crying!" he gritted, gun still planted in my mouth.

I tried to stop, but I was panicking, so it didn't work. I felt my heart beating out of my chest, and warm urine seeping through my underwear and onto my bed.

Almost like he turned into someone else, his face softened and he slowly removed the gun from my mouth.

"I ain't decided if I wanna kill you yet." He spoke calmly as if what he'd just said wasn't anything much. "And shut that shit up!" he roared about me sniveling. I covered my mouth quickly, in hopes it would calm me down and ease the crying.

As if nothing happened, he yanked my bedroom door open and left the room. As soon as I heard him hit the stairs, I buried my face into my pillow and cried loudly. I didn't know if I was just scared of what was to come, or if losing my relationship with Waayil just hurt this much.

***

The next afternoon...

I woke up feeling disgusting because I'd cried myself to sleep, not even caring that Waayil had caused me to pee on myself. But as nasty as I felt, I didn't even want to get out of my bed. I just wanted to lie there and die. My brother was my world and without him talking to me, I felt like there was really nothing for me to live for. I wasn't doing well in college and I didn't have a job, so honestly, me just disappearing wouldn't really matter.

Sitting up, I slowly climbed out of bed and turned up my lip to see my sheets. Snatching everything off, I balled it up and sat it in the middle of my floor, before yanking my nightshirt over my head, and tossing it along with my panties into the pile. I went into my bathroom that was located within my room, and brushed my teeth before hopping into the shower. I stayed in there way too long because after a while, the water started to get cold as hell.

"Honey, would you like some waffles?" My mother had come into my room just as I was leaving my bathroom, and she was holding my pile of pissy sheets and clothes. I hadn't noticed before, but my bookshelf was back up.

"No," I responded somberly.

Dropping what was in her hand, she came all the way into my bedroom and closed the door behind her.

"Baby, yes, you should feel bad for what you did, but thankfully, God didn't have Waayil spend the rest of his life in jail." She rubbed my hair back. Why did she always rub my hair back? Who likes getting their hair rubbed back?

"You don't hate me? Uncle Harry was your brother."

"He was, but..." she nibbled on her lip. "He was my brother, but I am sure you had good reason to want him gone."

"Beat up, maybe, but not completely dead." I started to sob a little, and she pulled me into her, pressing her chin into the top of my head.

"He wasn't a good person, and sometimes when you go through life mistreating people, bad things happen to you. And in Harry's case, if he wasn't stealing, scheming, or blackmailing someone, then he was probably asleep."

I chuckled a little at her humor because it was true. Only time Uncle Harry wasn't making someone's life miserable, was if he was knocked out on the couch with his mouth wide open. However, I just wished maybe someone else had killed him and not my beloved brother.

"And hey," she pulled away to look me in the eyes. "Waayil will get over this. I will make sure of it. And if I can't do it alone, your father will help." She half smiled and I nodded. "Now do you want waffles?"

"Sure, I guess."

I watched my mom leave, with a small beam on my face. I still felt like shit, but I appreciated her efforts. Blood doesn't make you closer to someone, because I swear, she was my real mother. I never, ever felt like she was an adoptive mother.

Picking up my phone, I called Jonaya. She'd been hitting me up to hang out and stuff, but I always declined.

"Hey!" she answered.

"You owe me for not keeping your mouth shut," I spoke angrily.

"What? I don't owe you shit, Wednesday. If anything, you owe me for trying to make me keep that damn secret!"

"No! If you hadn't have come here trying to—"

"No, bitch, you're the one who yanked the shit out of me! I tried to tell you I wasn't being distant, but you kept prying, not knowing your brother was in the damn closet! Stop looking for someone to blame!"

Before I could respond, she'd hung up in my face. I dialed Leighton, so damn mad about what Jonaya had just said that my hands were shaking. Of course, like always, Leighton's shady ass didn't answer. At that point, I just decided to contact Waayil, but through text.

Me: I'm sorry.

He never responded.

CHAPTER SIX

Eko

I was deep into playing 2k17, when someone started ringing my doorbell. Too many muthafuckas didn't know where I laid my head except Gavin, Rori, and Jenni. A few other hoes I'd busted down at random times too, but it wasn't likely that they'd be popping back up at my shit, especially in the middle of the day. Pausing my game, I got up to look through the peephole and saw annoying ass Jenni cheesing hard as hell.

"What?" I hissed.

Her ass had been doing the most lately, and I'd told her stupid ass multiple times that nothing she did would make her my bitch again. She would never be shit to me other than something to help me bust a nut. Period.

"Hey, baby, I—" She tried to hug me, but I put my hand out to stop her ass.

"Fuck you doing here, Jenni? I'm busy."

"You are?" She pointed to the paused video game on my living room TV screen.

"Yeah, I'm playing that muthafuckin' game you're looking at right now, so make this shit quick, ma."

Stomping her feet and whining, she yelled, "Eko! Stop being this way! I did what I did so long ago, and you're telling me you stopped loving me that quickly?"

"Stopped loving you? When the fuck did I ever tell yo' ass I loved you, Jenni? See, that's what the fucking problem is. This whole time you thought I loved you but I didn't."

Plopping down on my couch, Jenni dropped her face into her hands and began sobbing. I swear I'll never hit a woman, but Jenni was a bitch; a bitch asking to get knocked the shit out of.

"Come on, man, you gotta go." I yanked her up by her arm as she cried like a newborn baby.

"Eko, please don't!"

"Get the fuck out! Damn! You gon' have my neighbors calling the police on a nigga! And once the police see it's a white bitch I'm having problems with, they gon' toss my ass *under* the jail."

"Okay! Okay!" she shouted, snatching her arm from me.

She stared at me panting, and then moved towards me, grabbing at the belt on my jeans. I wanted to stop her, but when I saw her squatting down to give me some of that good ass head, I let her do her thing. As soon as my dick got in her mouth, I let my head fall back. Her shit was already filled with saliva as she deep throated my shit with no damn problem.

"Damn, Jenni," I panted, cupping the back of her head as I watched the way she took my whole damn dick into her mouth like it was nothing. Shit was like a damn magic trick, because ya boy was not packing lightly at all.

Jenni slurped and sucked my dick, damn near trying to tug my nut out. She then pulled me out and took my balls into her mouth, sucking them softly as fuck before switching back to my dick. You see why it was so hard for me to get rid of this girl? She had me on the verge of crying out like a bitch right now.

Grasping her hair, I began humping her face feverishly until I busted hard as hell. Without even batting a damn eye, she swallowed that shit up and gave me a sexy ass smile.

"Bend over the couch," I demanded, reaching in my pocket for a condom. As I did that, my phone started to ring in my pocket. I pulled it out to see the homie, Tic, calling, which prompted a frown to appear on my face. "Hold up," I told Jenni who was bent over the couch with her panties around her ankles. "Hello?"

"Aye, mane, they're raiding the trap!"

"What? And they let you make a damn call?" I frowned, rushing to the bathroom to piss and clean my dick, as I held the phone between my shoulder and ear.

"Nah, I was coming up the street to park and saw a gang of fucking police cars outside. Shit! They got Gavin in cuffs right now!" he shouted as I washed my hands.

"Fuck. Aight, I'm on my way."

I hung up before darting out the bathroom. Jenni's stupid ass was in the same position I left her in, texting on her phone.

Shaking my head, I said, "Aye, Jenni, I gotta go somewhere so you gotta get up outta here, ma."

"Okay, where are we going?" She followed me out of my crib and pulled her thong back up. Why would she wait until we were outside to do that? Hoe shit.

"I don't know where the fuck you going."

"Well, then I can wait until you—"

"Jenni! Stop! Take yo' ass home!" I barked, making her jump a little bit.

"Fine. I love you! Drive safe!"

I ignored her as I hopped into my whip and peeled off towards the trap on the Southside. When I pulled up, one police car was driving off the street, and I saw Tic getting out of his whip. I got out as well, making my way over to the house, and when he turned to face me, I yoked his ass up.

"How the fuck I know you ain't set this shit up?" I glared at him.

"Because I need my money too, mane! Why would I do this!" he pleaded, eyes full of fear.

I had a mind to blow his muthafuckin' head open, but I wasn't too sure if he had anything to do with this raid. Not to mention, I was trying to steer away from this lifestyle, and adding to my body count wasn't the way to do that shit.

Slamming him into the wall one good time, I let him go and he slid to the ground of the porch. Making my way into the house, I saw the shit was ransacked. I tugged on the heater that we hid a lot of shit behind, and out crawled Bryan, one of the trap workers. Nigga looked like he'd shit on himself, and low-key smelled like it too.

Snatching his ass out, I threw him to the couch and asked, "What happened? And I want details, nigga."

"I don't know. The shit happened so damn fast. Gavin, Day, and I were in here chopping it up about certain moves, when we heard sirens all of a sudden. Them niggas started scrambling to hide shit, and I hopped behind the heater."

"So while they protected the product, you hid like a bitch?" I quizzed, pulling my piece from my waist as Tic walked in and closed the front door behind him.

With his eyes on my gun, Bryan stammered, "Nah— nah, Eko, it wasn't even like that! I just did what I had to do because—"

"Because you's a muthafuckin' bitch and I don't need that shit on my team!"

"Nah—"

POP! POP!

Tic's eyes widened as Bryan's body dropped to the floor, making the ground shake a bit. Nigga was looking uneasy as fuck and I ain't like that shit.

"You got a problem with what the fuck I just did, bruh?" I started towards Tic slowly and he shook his head repeatedly with his hands up in mock surrender.

"Nah, I swear I don't!"

"I think you do."

"Eko—"

POP!

I sent a bullet through his head, and watched blood pour from the back of it as he laid out on the living room floor by Bryan. I was pissed as hell that not only did the traps get raided, but also, I had killed two muthafuckas. This was not a part of my damn plan. Today was my kick back day, especially since I'd been putting in work to fuck over Gavin every day damn near.

"Stupid ass niggas. Now why the fuck y'all make me murk y'all?" I spoke to Bryan and Tic while dialing the cleanup crew.

I waited, pacing the living room floor trying to figure out who the hell had dropped the dime on us. Not to mention, I would have to answer to Neo about this shit. I had just started building a relationship with his ass outside of Gavin for reasons already explained. Now this shit happened. Fuck!

Once the cleanup crew came by to handle shit, I contemplated calling Neo but decided I would do that shit tomorrow. I'd dealt with enough for the damn day. I made it home after stopping to get something to eat, and was happy to know Jenni's ass had listened and taken her stupid ass home. She wasn't good for shit but head and pussy, but even that was something I was gon' have to stop indulging in if I wanted her ass gone for good.

I ate my food, then brushed my teeth before hopping into the shower. Once I was dried off and had on a fresh pair of boxers, I powered my game back up to ease my mind.

I wasn't playing that shit for very long before someone started to attack my damn doorbell though. If this was Jenni, she'd better have a good ass reason for this shit because she was about to become my third body tonight.

I opened the door to see Rori standing there, frowning hard and with her arms folded.

"You aight, baby?" I stepped back to let her in, and she switched passed me with her cute ass, but still scowling.

"Did you do this to him?" she inquired as I closed the door behind her.

"Do what to who?"

"Gavin. Did you set him up and get him sent to jail, Eko? Don't lie to me either. I can tell when you lie."

"Look, ma. I know I said I wanted to do that nigga dirty, but I don't fuck with the police. My only plan was to leave him begging like a bitch for a dollar on the corner, not to have his ass behind bars."

Shaking her head while chuckling, she began pacing my living room.

"Really? You did all this just to be with me?"

Frowning hard, I stared at her ass for a moment. I was trying to tell myself she didn't just say what I'd heard.

"Rori, you can take yo' ass home with all that bullshit. Yeah, I wanna fuck with you, but a nigga ain't that hard up to be putting muthafuckas in jail just to smash their bitch."

"That's not what it seems like."

207

"I don't give a fuck what it seems like. Plus, I've *been* smashing you while he was out of jail, so what would be the point in me sending him, huh? So I can fuck? I already did that."

She furrowed her brows, deepening her frown at my words. I ain't wanna talk to her ass like that, but she was asking for that shit.

"I just think it's funny how I went on a date with him and now he's—"

"Wait, so you back fucking with this nigga?"

"Don't act like you didn't know. And now, no I'm not, but I thought about it when he took me out. The date just ended badly." I knew she was just talking to make me jealous, but I was still mad she even went out with him.

"Wow, so you told me you needed to be alone, when really, yo' stupid ass wanted to be ready and willing when he came back for you, huh?"

"No, Eko—"

"Get out." I yanked my front door open.

"Eko, no! It wasn't like that! I felt bad for what you and I had done, so I agreed to have dinner with him! And I'm sorry for accusing you, I just… I just thought you did this because…"

"Yeah, you don't even know why. But look, you need to step, ma."

"Eko."

"Rori. Get out my crib."

She stared at me with them puppy dog eyes, and as badly as I wanted to kiss on her and put her legs over my shoulders while pounding that pussy, I couldn't. Rori needed to learn the fucking game. I wasn't gon' be here when she wanted and then not here when she didn't want me to be. If she wanted to fuck with me, she would have to do that shit the long way. I didn't have time for the bullshit. I needed a bitch that was gon' ride for me 'til the end, and Rori clearly wasn't about that life yet.

Realizing I wasn't gon' change my mind, she stormed her sexy ass out my spot. I slammed the door behind her, and looked down to shake my head at my hardening dick. That shit was always on some hoe shit.

CHAPTER SIX

Dree

A few days later...

I was lying on the examination table at the gynecologist's office, hoping she didn't confirm my suspicions. This was not what I needed right now, and the way it happened wasn't how I had expected it to. I kept praying to God to spare me this once, and promised I would be a changed person from now on.

"Okay, sorry about that, Miss Goode." My doctor returned, smiling, and holding a manila folder.

"It's no problem." I sat up, crossing my ankles.

"Okay." She sighed, sifting through the paperwork and reading. "Alright, Miss Goode, so you are definitely pregnant." The smile on her face faded when she saw my expression. "Is this not good news? You're at a great age."

"No, I just... I'm surprised, I guess."

"Oh yeah, I know. I felt the same way when I got pregnant with my fourth," she joked. I gave her a fake laugh because I wasn't really in the mood to play around with anyone.

"Well thank you. I'd better go."

"Oh wait, honey. We need to have a look at you, and then get you some prenatal pills. Trust me, you want to be very careful in these first few stages of pregnancy, Miss Goode."

"Right, but I have to get to class. The professor is really strict, and he—"

"Honey, I can write you a note to give to him."

"I—" I stared into her eyes and saw she wasn't going to give up. I truly did have to be in class, but the teacher wasn't strict when it came to tardiness, so I knew I'd be okay.

I let Dr. Orphan check me out, and make sure everything was going okay with the baby. She told me how far along I was, which matched up perfectly to the night I'd woken up naked in Sean's bed.

I still hadn't told anyone about what happened, because for one, I was embarrassed, and two, shit, *I* didn't know what happened myself. I was always the responsible one, so it wouldn't look good on my end, admitting that I'd drank too much and couldn't remember sleeping with Sean.

After getting some breakfast food, I headed straight to school because I wanted to get at least a part of the class I was missing. Thankfully, Sean wasn't in this one. I did need to speak with him about the child, but I didn't think I was ready yet. I wanted an abortion, but I was too old, I felt, and people would judge me for that. I always only saw abortions as options for reckless teenagers, so I couldn't get one, even though this child came about totally wrong!

With abortion not being an option, this baby did make me wonder if I should maybe try being with Sean again. I'd been enjoying Canyon's company, but he wasn't the father of my child. Sean and I were the child's parents, so I felt that maybe I should at least give us a go as badly as I didn't want to. Yeah, I wanted to be with Canyon, but people made sacrifices like this for their children every day.

And I loved my stepdad, but I always used to wish my mother could have somehow made things work with my real dad, whoever he was. By saying that, I didn't want to completely write off my child's father just because I didn't want him. Plus, I felt kind of bad for cutting Sean off without telling him why. It just seemed like I was making a somewhat bad situation seem terrible.

"Hey, Dree!" my classmate, Monroe, called after me. When I turned to look her way, she was waving her notes in the air.

"Oh shit, I forgot I texted you about those. Thanks so much." I smiled as I shoved them into my messenger bag.

"No worries. So how are you holding up? Tyson's study group has really helped me a lot. I thought you were gonna join us."

"Uh, well yeah, I was, but then I realized the times you guys get together didn't really work for me."

"Oh." She cocked her head wearing a worried expression. "Well maybe you should move some things around, Dree. I'm telling you, it will be worth it."

"Maybe I will." I exhaled heavily and gave a faint smile to another classmate walking by. "So hey, thank you for this."

"Sure."

I walked off, and when I glanced over my shoulder, Monroe was still watching me. I'd been so wrapped up in wanting to be alone, that I'd completely forgotten about the study groups. And any time I did crawl out of my room, I was in class or with Canyon and his adorable son, Cade. I smiled at the thought of them.

That smile quickly dissipated upon seeing Sean walk by with his arm draped around some girl. Oddly, I wasn't jealous at all. Crazy enough, I wanted to be jealous so that I would know that I still had some sort of attraction to him, but I guess I didn't. However, seeing him did give me the courage to talk with him.

Rushing over to them, I said, "Excuse me, Sean, can I speak with you for a moment?"

"Why don't you go get us a table, baby." Sean smirked down at the girl, pecking her lips before removing his arm from being around her.

"Is everything okay, Sean?" The girl eyed me before looking back up at him.

"Perfect." He winked. He kept his smile on until she was pretty much in the student union, before dropping it and looking at me. "What, Dree?"

"I know you're angry about me kind of cutting you off—"

"Kind of? Kind of cutting me off? You crept out of my bed and haven't talked to me since. In classes, you act like I have the plague or something."

"I know and I'm sorry. I was just confused when I woke up in your bed because… because I don't really remember doing anything with you, or at least agreeing to it." I whispered the last part since people were walking by.

"Well maybe you shouldn't drink more than you can handle, Dree."

"But see, I didn't."

"And?" He frowned hard. I'd never seen Sean act like this, ever. "What are you implying? That I put something in your drink?"

That *had* been what I was thinking, but looking at him, I remembered who he was. Sean would never do anything like that. I guess my cocktail at the restaurant was stronger than I thought, and then with the champagne, it must have taken me out.

"No, no, of course not," I giggled. "But hey, that's not really what I wanted to talk to you about." I watched as he folded his arms and waited. "I'm pregnant, Sean."

Letting out a loud laugh, he scoffed before saying, "And?"

If he said 'and' one more time, I was kicking him in the nuts.

"What do you mean *and?* Why do you think I'm telling you, nigga?" He was pissing me off now, because I had a feeling he was insinuating something that would get him smacked in the mouth.

"You disappear on me, probably because you were with some other guy, and now you come to me saying you're pregnant? Come on, Dree. How do I know that kid is mine?"

"You're the only person I've been with lately, Sean. And the time frame matches up to how far along I am. Why would I lie to you?"

"Because I'm an aspiring lawyer with a hefty trust fund, and the real father is probably some lowlife with no means to an end."

WHAM!

After slapping Sean across the face, he grabbed me by the neck, catching us both off guard I guess, because when he realized what he was doing, he let me go and straightened his clothes.

"Dree, that is not my kid. And if it is mine, I want you to get rid of it as soon as possible. I have my life planned out and it doesn't include having a child before my first courtroom case, okay?"

"Well you should have thought about that before you slept with me!"

"It was one time! I slept with you one time, and I'm sorry, that's not enough to convince me. However, I like you, so I'm willing to assist you in getting rid of your problem. I can find the doctor so that this will be done correctly and discreetly, and then I can pay for it."

Without another word, I turned around and started towards the parking lot so I could leave. I had another class, but today's agenda wasn't anything I couldn't handle on my own. We were just gonna go over some chapter section questions, and I was sure I could answer them myself. Right now, I just needed to get out of here and away from Sean. He had the same class as me later, so that was another reason I didn't want to attend. The way he'd talked to me had me fuming and wanting to whoop his ass.

I felt really hungry and I didn't know if it was because of the baby, or if I was just assuming I was hungry because I knew a baby was in there.

I remembered that Rori said she was making spaghetti tonight, so I just went straight home because that sounded perfect.

Walking into the house, the smell of the sauce on the pasta immediately hit my nose. I heard my sisters, my mom, and Buddy in the dining room already, along with the sound of clinking silverware.

"Hey, sweetie. Don't you have a class in like fifteen minutes?" My mother rose to her feet, collecting her empty plate as well as Buddy's.

"It was cancelled."

"Oh, okay. Well would you like me to make your plate before I leave?"

"No, it's okay."

I felt everyone staring at me because I usually wasn't such a glum person. These days I'd covered it up pretty well, but after confirming my pregnancy, and then having Sean treat me like a street whore, I no longer had the strength to put on a fake smile.

After washing my hands, I made my plate, and then joined my sisters at the dinner table to eat.

"You okay, Dree?" Yikayla questioned as she cut up her meatballs.

"Yep."

"I told y'all she's been acting like a rape victim for the past weeks!" Jonaya joked, and even though I knew she had no idea, what she'd said stung. Dree and victim didn't belong in the same sentence.

"You really shouldn't talk like that, Jo." I sucked my teeth. "Question." I set my fork down. "Let's say you got really drunk one night with your boo, and then you woke up in his bed naked with your clothes on the floor, and you could tell you'd been penetrated. What would you say?" I smiled to lighten the mood so it wouldn't seem like I was digging for advice.

"Do I remember the sex?" Rori inquired.

"If not, then he doesn't need to be your boo anymore," Jonaya scoffed.

"No, you don't remember because you were too drunk. The last thing you remember is sipping your drink on the couch, and nothing else after."

"Umm, so my boo is a rapist?" Yikayla chuckled but with a slight frown.

"Well no, because he's your man and you just drank too much," I corrected her.

"Okay, but if I don't remember anything, then how did I tell him it was okay to fuck me?" Rori asked, wearing the same frown as Yikayla.

"Exactly," Yikayla agreed. "And if I was passed out, what kind of creep is he to still fuck my limp body?"

"You don't even know if you were passed out and limp! But why does it matter if you were probably gonna have sex with him anyway!" I hollered.

"Calm down, Dree, damn. That's their opinion." Jonaya touched my shoulder.

"Well what's your opinion?"

"I mean, I don't know. That is kind of weird. To be drinking one minute and then wake up in the bed naked. I don't know if it's rape, but

I definitely wouldn't like that."

"So it's his fault that you drank too much?" I shook my head and rolled my eyes.

"No, but as my man or *boo*, I would want him to see that I'm pissy drunk and put me to sleep, not have sex with me," Yikayla replied.

"Why?" Rori cocked her head.

"I— umm… it was a topic in class today. I'm on the defense side, so I was just trying to figure out my argument," I quickly and perfectly lied.

They all nodded, and we resumed eating, changing the subject to something lighter.

CHAPTER SEVEN

Jonaya

Yikayla and I hadn't really been talking like we used to ever since she found out I'd kept Wednesday's secret. The only time we'd talk would be if it was a multi-person conversation, and even then, she would only speak to everyone at the table, and not me directly. I wanted to blame Wednesday for this, but it was my fault for choosing not to say anything. I had my reasons though, and for the past week, Yikayla didn't want to hear it, but I was gonna make her. I'd given her space, and now she needed to come the hell around.

I knocked on her door and entered upon hearing her yell 'come in.' I noticed she and Lonan had been sleeping at home and not at Waayil's house, for a minute now. I wanted to see what was up, but we weren't on the best terms for me to be asking some shit like that. However, deep down I prayed they weren't having problems because of what I'd done.

"Hey, what are you doing?" I sat down on the edge of her large California King bed.

"Just straightening up my things."

That was the most she'd said to me in a week, but her tone was still dry as ever, and she wouldn't stop what she was doing to look at me. I was gonna ask another question just to test the waters some more, but I decided to get to the damn point.

"Yikayla, you cannot still be mad at me." I picked my adorable nephew up, who was moving everywhere in his little white onesie.

"Oh, I can't?" she chuckled. "I can be as mad as long as I want."

"Okay, yes, I was wrong for not saying anything, but you're acting like you're Waayil! He's the one that went to jail, so I can understand him being mad as hell, but you?"

Dropping the clothes she was folding, she looked at me and said, "First of all, Jonaya, that is my nigga, meaning anything that happens to him is going to bother me, especially him being shipped off to jail because he did something that he thought was protecting someone he loved. Secondly, you witnessed firsthand, how broken up I was when he went away, and then when he told me to leave him alone. So excuse me if I'm a little upset about the fact that all the time he and I lost, all the heartbreak I experienced, all the time I spent hating a man that I really loved, was all over a lie. And you as my sister, didn't even have the decency to let me know. All the shit we share, not to mention blood, yet, you felt the need to be loyal to Wednesday and not me."

"Kay, I'm sorry, I didn't look at it that way. The way Wednesday explained it to me just made sense and I..." I sighed before letting my nephew back down to the floor since he was starting to talk loudly in his baby language. "I just thought if I said anything it wouldn't help anyone."

"I know, and I guess I shouldn't be so hard on you. I'm sure it was difficult for you to have to choose between a best friend and your sister. But Jonaya, that secret was not something to be taken lightly. Wednesday cheating on a test, or sneaking out at night, those are secrets best friends keep, not shit like that."

Nodding my head, I replied, "Yeah, I agree. If it makes you feel better, I barely got any sleep thinking about it."

"Not really, but I appreciate knowing you have a conscious," she half smiled.

"So why are you back sleeping here?"

"What? You want me to leave again? I'm looking for a place to move to now. I found a few spots that I'm gonna look at tomorrow."

"What I mean is, why aren't you staying with Waayil anymore?"

"He needs to be alone right now. He's still very messed up about finding out that Wednesday lied, and he's not himself. So I think it's best he and I live apart for some time. Plus, we kind of rushed right into a relationship as soon as he got out."

"Rushed? You guys have wanted to be together for years. If anything, it was overdue for you to be in a relationship."

"Maybe so, but right now we need to be just boyfriend and girlfriend, not living together or anything like that."

I nodded.

"Well I have to go get ready for dinner." I rolled my eyes, making Yikayla laugh as she placed busy ass Lonan in the middle of the bed.

"Nusef has you doing things you wouldn't usually do, I see."

"Yeah," I sighed.

"That's what happens when you fall in love. I like seeing you that way though. No more worrying whenever you leave the house to meet some new no good nigga."

"Whatever." I chuckled.

I was about to leave, but Yikayla called me back to give me a hug and a kiss. Like a little ass baby, I was jumping for joy on the inside from receiving attention from my big sister.

I went to take a nice hot bath with the new bath bomb I got from LUSH, and then I brushed my teeth before putting on my tan skirt and top set. I threw on some nude sandal stilettos to match, and then took down the braids in my hair so it'd have some curl. My press job was done for about three days ago, so I had to work it out until I could get in the salon on Monday afternoon.

By the time I was done applying my makeup, Nusef was banging on the damn front door loudly as hell like he was the SWAT team. Matter fact, I would have thought it was the damn SWAT team had he not been blowing my phone up at the same time.

"I got it!" I yelled to my mom when I saw her open her bedroom door. A thick cloud of smoke came through, so I knew she and Buddy were getting high. My stepdad would be home very soon, so she needed to gradually start cutting that nigga off.

I opened the front door, and Nusef's deeply embedded frown faded instantly. His lips were slightly parted as he scanned me from head to toe.

"Damn, Jo." I watched him lick his thick lips, before he bit down on the bottom one with his perfect teeth.

He was wearing navy blue tonight, which looked so good against his deep chocolate skin. His shirt was quarter sleeved, so you could see his muscular arms, covered in tattoos.

"Thanks," I finally said after stopping the drool trying to come from my mouth.

I don't know how I went so long just being this man's friend. Nusef was that gangsta nigga fine, and his personality was even better. And now that I knew what his sex game was like, I was a little beyond sprung. I was high key kicking myself for waiting so long to tell him I loved him.

I slipped my hand into his big strong one, and then checked his nails to make sure they were clean as we descended the porch steps. He just laughed at me. His nails were never dirty, but after being with so many guys who didn't take care of themselves, I'd developed a habit.

"You know them niggas fingernails were dirty because they didn't wash their fucking hands, right?" He opened his passenger door for me.

"Nu unh!"

"Niggas do not wash their hands, ma,." He chuckled. "I mean, I do, but I'm a rare breed."

He closed the door and I just kept my lip turned up at his statement. All them times I let niggas finger me. I felt like I needed to get a vagina cleanse. On the bright side, if them nails were dirty, I always made them clean them with soap, water, and alcohol before doing anything with me. However, the thought was still stomach churning.

Nusef got in on the driver's side, and once he had on the music I liked, we were on our way. I didn't know where we were going to eat, but he just told me he was taking me on a date. I despised dates, but for some reason, I was excited. I always got anxious and excited when I was about to spend time with Nusef, and that was very new to me.

We ended up at this restaurant named Flight, and we'd only ordered drinks, yet, I was very pleased with the waitress already. She acted like she loved this job, and that she was here to serve us completely. I didn't go to many restaurants unless my stepdad took the family, and usually, I paid no attention to the staff; only my food and the menu.

"Are you comfortable, baby?" Nusef asked since we chose to dine outside.

I nodded with a smile. I loved when he did that. He treated me like a porcelain doll or something. It sounded like something I would hate, but I adored it. Really.

"So what's the budget?" I joked, scanning the food choices.

"Nah, get what you want."

"Oh, I forgot you got a little money on you, baby." I batted my eyelashes and he flashed his sexy smile. He smelled so good and looked even better. For a moment, I just stared at him, basking in the bliss. "Well, I'm gonna get the Louisiana Redfish."

"I'm gon' get the Bourbon Stuffed Filet."

"I want that too. Yeah, I think I'm gonna get that."

"You always do that shit." He laughed. "You'll have yo' whole damn meal planned out until I say what I want, and then you change."

"You don't like me copying you?" I cheesed.

"Nah, I love you and everything you do. Even that annoying shit."

"Aww, I love you too, baby."

We both stared at one another for a moment before bursting into loud laughter. A few people seated near us looked our way as I covered my mouth in embarrassment.

"Who knew we'd be on that mushy shit, ma."

"I know." I exhaled, still chuckling lightly.

We ordered our dishes, and as we ate, we had good conversation like always. I didn't know why I thought getting into a relationship with Nusef would ruin our friendship, but it did the opposite. Our friendship was stronger now, and him being my boyfriend was the greatest shit ever. If you've got a fine best friend who you click with, date his ass. I'm telling you, it's the shit.

The only problem with this date was that when I checked my phone once to show Nusef a picture, I saw I had forty missed calls from Marquise. I simply showed Nusef the picture I was looking for, and placed my phone back into my purse. Thankfully, I'd had it on silent.

After dinner, we shared the Lava Cake for dessert, and then Nusef paid the pretty hefty bill. Valet brought the car around, and Nusef tipped him before opening the passenger door for me. The night was perfect, and all I wanted to do now was get fucked and I knew Nusef would handle that.

We pulled up to Nusef's spot after jamming to the Aaliyah station on Pandora the whole way. After he parked, he leaned over to kiss me a couple times. My clit was throbbing already just from feeling his big hand on my thigh.

"Get down, baby," he said suddenly, making me chuckle.

"Baby, we can just go in the house and—"

Before I could finish my sentence, Nusef damn near hopped into my seat to cover me.

POP! POP! POP! POP!

Bullets shattered the car windows, as I screamed for what felt like forever. It seemed like the bullets would never stop. Finally, they did, and Nusef was still covering me, but he wasn't moving.

"No, no," I whimpered, nudging him back so that I could look at him. He had bullet holes everywhere, and blood was pouring out of his mouth. "Baby, wake up! You have to wake up!"

I dug into my small purse for my phone, not caring that I was covered in glass, Nusef's blood, and him damn near smashing me.

Lord, please don't let him die, I prayed silently as I dialed 911.

CHAPTER SEVEN

Waayil

The next morning...

Staring at my brother hooked up to all these fucking machines only infuriated me more. Hearing he got shot was enough to make me go on a damn Ted Bundy killing spree, and now looking at him, I was ready to tear Tennessee apart.

It was crazy to me how all these doctors felt like they knew why he'd gotten shot. They assumed because he had a little money on him, that he must have been involved in drugs, or a gang; shit that normally got black men shot, according to them.

Like me, my brother wasn't into none of that shit, and I wasn't gon' sleep until I found out who came for him. Little did that hating ass muthafucka know, he was dead already. Whoever was the culprit had better enjoy their life, because I was taking that shit with my bare fucking hands.

"Did you want some tea, Waayil?" Jonaya entered the room.

She looked a damn mess and rightfully so. I might have not been feeling her secretive ass at the moment, but she loved the fuck out of my brother. If Nusef was ever gon' settle down, it was best to do it with Jonaya.

"Nah, I'm good."

"Waayil, I'm sorry. I know I never really apologized for what I kept from you."

"You good."

"No, I'm not. I can tell by how cold you're being to me. Look, I know you need time and that's fine, but I don't want you to be mad at me forever."

"I won't, ma. And this shit is Wednesday's fault, not yours. I don't fuck with the fact that you didn't say shit, but ultimately, that was Wednesday's job to do."

She nodded and then said, "Thank you for not telling your brother."

"Don't thank me. Only reason I haven't is because I haven't had time to talk to him about what Wednesday did. But as soon as he wakes up, I will."

"Me too." She exhaled and rubbed his head.

I couldn't stand looking at Nusef with that shit shoved down his throat and all these damn machines beeping, so it was best I get the fuck out of here. Watching him only made me angrier, and in a minute, I was gon' be murkin' muthafuckas just to release some of this tension.

"Aight. Well, I'll be back tomorrow morning. You know you can go home for a minute, Jonaya."

"No, I don't want to. And Rori is bringing me some clothes and stuff. I can just shower in there. Plus, I'm gonna be away from him enough when I go to class."

I smirked at her response, because it just solidified the fact that she was the one for my brother. Before Nusef told me he loved her, I never saw them together, but now I don't understand how I didn't see it. Them niggas were just a-fucking-like.

I left the hospital, keeping my eyes steady and on what was in front of me. My hands were aching, and I knew that shit meant that they wanted to strangle a muthafucka. I had to keep my eyes off these doctors, nurses, annoying ass patients, and their family members before I indulged.

When I got down to my car, I let out a heavy breath. I'd been feeling empty as fuck lately, and I knew why; Yikayla wasn't around me as much. I was too wrapped up in my own damn thoughts and problems to really pay attention to our shit. She'd told me she was gon' get her own spot, and at that moment, I didn't really care. I was moping around over the fact that I'd lost six damn years of my life; six years that I could have spent helping my brother build Monarch, and being with Yikayla. But shit, I was wasting more time that I could spend with her, bullshitting and being angry.

Picking up my phone, I dialed her number and prayed she answered. We weren't broken up because a nigga would never let that shit happen, ever, but I knew she wasn't fucking with me like that. I would text her small shit saying goodnight and that I loved her, and she'd be dry as hell. I didn't care enough before, but right now, just thinking about that shit was killing me.

"Hello?" she picked up, voice monotone as hell.

"Where you at? Work?"

"Yes, Waayil."

"Don't say my name like that, Kay. Only time I want you calling my name is when I'm inside you."

"What do you want? I'm busy."

"Meet me at the Marriott Downtown."

"The one on Monroe? For what?"

"Because I asked yo' lil ass too, that's why."

"What time? I have to drop Lonan off to his father's house, but I have to make sure he's asleep first."

That was a damn shame that this man's son wouldn't stay with him unless he was tricked into it. I hated that shit because I couldn't imagine Lonan waking up in unfamiliar territory and having to stay there for a couple days. I didn't like that shit at all, but at the end of the day, he wasn't my kid and he did need to know his dad. Even if that nigga was an old dried up ass bitch with no ambition and empty pockets.

"Whenever you're done, come. Just let me know when you're on your way. Don't forget that part."

"Why, so you can get the other bitch you're fucking out of the room before I get there?" I was silent as fuck, because it was the only way to keep from gettin' out of pocket and hurting her feelings. I guess she knew that because she added, "I'm sorry, baby. I was kidding."

I would *never* fuck around on Yikayla, ever, and she knew that.

"Aight."

***

That evening… Around 6:45 p.m.…

A little bit ago, Yikayla texted me that she'd dropped Lonan off and was on her way to me. I waited for some time, then I started lighting a few candles that Rori told me she liked from Bath and Body Works.

I felt like a damn fish out of water in that fucking store. I had to damn near curse one of them hoes out for trying to sell me them damn lotions and shit. Yikayla only wore natural shit anyway. Not to mention, I'd specifically told that bitch I was there for the candles written in my notes app, and not a damn thing else. Instead, I just ignored her whenever she tried to sell me on something. I scoffed and shook my head thinking about that shit, as I lit up one candle that smelled like flowers and sugar and coconuts and all the bullshit females liked.

As the bathwater in the tub ran, I used this bubble bath I'd gotten from Family Dollar, and poured some of that in there. I'd never done shit like this for any woman, but I was hoping Yikayla liked it.

I left the bathroom once the tub was full to my liking, and called downstairs for room service. I ordered what I wanted for us, and told that nigga it'd better arrive at the time I gave him, or when I was done whooping his ass, he'd be the same gender as his mama. By that time, Yikayla was knocking, so I rushed to answer the door.

"Hi." She smiled shyly and came in.

I hugged her body from behind, groping her a little bit and kissing on her neck. I missed her scent, and touching that soft cocoa skin. I'd worked hard getting that bath together, but right now, I wanted to fuck.

"Waayil." She nudged me back, chuckling.

"Look what I did for you." I took her hand and led her to the bathroom.

"No wonder it smells so good in here! How did you know I liked these candles, baby?"

"Because I know you, that's why." I shrugged with a closed mouth smile when she beamed at my response. As she tossed her arms around my neck and kissed me, I said, "Nah, Rori told me."

She sucked her teeth and rolled her eyes, before sitting down on the closed toilet top to remove her shoes. I moved her way and helped her out of her shirt and jeans. I couldn't help but to plant kisses on her toned stomach and her pussy as I tugged her panties down.

"Waayil, let me get in the bath first."

"Yeah, get in that damn bath. Shit had me sweating like a Hebrew slave puttin' that shit together."

Laughing, she submerged her body in the hot water after removing her bra and tying her hair up. I planned to leave her in the bathroom alone, but I had to just watch her for a moment. She was already starting to sweat from the heat of the water, and that shit was sexy as hell. After kissing her a few times, I left her to relax.

I made a few phone calls, a couple to the homies to keep their ears to the streets, and then I handled some business shit. By that time,

Yikayla came out in one of the robes, smiling and glowing. I hadn't seen her smile that much in a minute, and it felt good as hell.

"Thank you, I needed that. But why all this?"

I pulled her into my lap and kissed her neck. Rori had given me one of her natural soaps to bring over here, and that shit smelled like candied yams or something.

"Because I ain't been on my shit. I ain't been handling business on the home front, and I wanted to do this to show you that, that ain't gon' be the case no more. It's also my way of saying sorry, baby."

"You didn't have to."

"Yeah I did. And I wanted to. You deserve shit like this just because, but especially because I've been acting an ass. All that muthafuckin' time we spent apart, missing one another, we shouldn't be wasting a damn minute of the day."

"Yeah." She nodded, cupping my face and pressing her lips against mine. "I don't wanna live somewhere else."

"I don't want you to either."

"Sing something to me."

"What you wanna hear?"

"Anything from Eric Bellinger," she cheesed. I didn't say anything back because I wanted to take in her beauty for a moment.

"You love that nigga. Don't tell me I gotta whoop Bellinger's ass."

"You better not!" She laughed hard as hell when I bucked my eyes at her response.

Placing her onto her back, I started to tickle her midsection because I knew she couldn't take it. When I finally stopped, she was panting heavily and smiling.

"I love you so much, baby," I whispered as I stared down at her.

"I love you too. Now sing me something."

I kissed her a few times as I thought of a song.

"My love is year round, our family's year round. In 365 days, there ain't one I ain't holding you down. Watch, they gon' hate all year round. 'Cause we celebrate all year round. Won't catch me out there looking thirsty..." I sang Eric Bellinger's "Year Round" mainly because that was exactly how I felt about her. About us.

"In the wintertime, we cuffing," she finished my line.

We continued to sing the hook together in between kisses, before we were interrupted.

KNOCK! KNOCK!

"Who is that?"

"Food." I grinned and got off the bed.

The room service attendant brought in the steaks I'd ordered, along with the expensive ass champagne. I tipped his ass, and then Yikayla and I set everything out so we could eat and drink. She was all over me the whole damn time with her little horny ass, but aye, wasn't shit better than eating a good ass steak while getting yo' dick rubbed on.

Once we were done with the food, we polished off that champagne, ordered another, and then I laid her in the middle of the bed so I could give her a full body massage with this oil. Once she relaxed and shit, I got off the bed to remove my clothes, and then got back in. Lifting her hips a little, so that she was still lying kind of flat, I pressed the head of my dick at her opening.

"Fuck, baby," I mumbled, seeing how fucking tight she was.

Her soft whimpers as I barged my way inside of her tight walls, had me on one already. Gripping her hips tighter, I forced the rest of my dick into her body, and just sat in it for a moment, enjoying how gushy, warm, and snug she was. I stroked her slowly, opening her pussy up some more, and once I was able to slide in and out with ease, I began pounding her pussy hard.

"Mmm, ahhh." Her voice shook as she grabbed at the sheets.

That oil spread all over her plump round ass as it bounced against me, had me ready to bust that quickly. I was gon' have to incorporate that oil shit some more. I felt like I was in a porno or some shit, watching her shiny ass jiggle crazily.

"Baby, I'm sorry," I apologized. It wasn't for what y'all are thinking though. I was saying sorry because I was about to bust this nut way faster than I'd planned.

Clenching my teeth together, I tried to hold out by thinking about something else. That was working until Yikayla came hard on my dick, while moaning all sexily and shit. I looked down at her, staring at me over her shoulder with her pretty ass. Grasping her ass cheeks, I spread them to watch my dick invade her pussy some more as I beat that shit up feverishly.

"Tell me who this pussy belongs to, ma."

Truthfully, I should have shut my ass up, because all that dirty talk was gon' do, was make me nut.

"It's your pussy, daddy," Yikayla sniveled right before coating my dick again. Her pussy was messy wet, and I was in muthafuckin' heaven right now.

Fuck.

Our skin was smacking together so harshly, that I was sure we'd both have some bruising. She was sopping wet, and sounding like macaroni and cheese every time I plunged in it. Not able to take it anymore, I gripped her shoulder and pounded her hard until I busted. I kissed down her back for a minute, then slid out. After we cleaned up, we got back in the bed.

"Have you talked to Wednesday?" Yikayla inquired as she lied on my chest, tracing my tattoos with her soft fingers.

"A little, not really. I can't even look at her ass without my trigger finger itching."

"Damn. She's your little sister, Waayil."

"I know, but… I'm trying not to see her ass differently, but I do."

After a few moments of silence, Yikayla picked her head up to look at me. "Don't shut me out like that anymore, Waayil."

"I won't." I kissed her lips and she blushed. That shit was cute as hell when she did it. "I still make yo' ass blush, huh?"

"I don't know!" She squealed and laughed, making me smile.

Yikayla and I talked for a little more until we dozed off. Around 3 a.m., I woke up to the sound of my damn phone ringing. Looking at the number, I saw it wasn't stored in my phone so I answered, assuming it was business and not remembering how late it fucking was. A nigga was half sleep.

"Hello?" I answered.

"Hey, Waayil, it's Zia," she replied wickedly.

I hung that shit up so fast, I had to make sure I actually did it. After putting my phone on silent, I laid back down and stared off. The bullshit seemed to only keep coming.

CHAPTER SEVEN

Yikayla

*W*aayil had to be at the shop early this morning, so I took this time to sleep in at this hotel. Lonan was with his father, and I didn't have to be in to work today, so that extra sleep time was needed. Especially after Waayil kept me up all night with his horny ass. Every time I thought about how insatiable he was, it made me a little jealous of whatever bitch he had coming up to the jail to get sex from. All that time she was getting prime rib dick, and I was back home getting McRib dick.

Speaking of Roscoe, I wanted to FaceTime my baby before I went out, so after brushing my teeth and showering, I dialed his number. He quickly picked up, smiling in the screen with his face all close like an old person does.

"Can you back up some?" I rolled my eyes. "And where is Lonan?" Speaking his name made me smile immediately.

"Damn, you can't talk to me for a little bit, Yikayla?"

"No, for what? I can talk to you after I see my baby."

"Nah, you can talk to me right now, or you ain't seeing no damn body. I got the upper hand right now, so if you wanna see Lonan, talk to his daddy for a minute."

"Let me see him first, to make sure he isn't off in the corner somewhere crying because he's hungry."

Grinning hard with his stupid ass, Roscoe got up from wherever he was sitting, and walked a little bit. Finally, he showed me my baby, strapped in his kiddie chair, watching TV and eating baby cereal all by himself like a big boy. His grandmother must have set him up like that because Roscoe didn't care enough.

"Hi, Lon—"

"Nah, you saw him, now it's my time."

See, this was the exact reason why I didn't like letting Lonan go with his father. Roscoe was spiteful like this, and like Waayil said, he enjoyed using the fact that we shared a baby to his advantage.

"Oh my gosh," I sighed.

I wanted to just hang up, but the last time I did that, Roscoe wouldn't answer the phone for hours and I had to drop by his mom's, only to realize they'd all gone out somewhere. And to make matters worse, I found out Roscoe was off in Nashville, while Lonan was with his grandmother at the grocery store. I was currently making a mental note to get Miss Laughton's cell number the next time I picked up Lonan. She swore she didn't use it much, but she was about to start.

"You naked?" Roscoe bit his lip as he looked into the camera. He was so not sexy to me anymore.

"I have a towel on, pervert."

"Drop it."

"Roscoe, what the fuck do you think this is? Do you honestly want my nigga to whoop your ass? Because that's what's gonna happen if I tell him you're not letting me talk to my son, and telling me to drop my towel."

"I don't give a fuck what that nigga thinks. Plus, you ain't his only one. He been getting at hella junts when you ain't around."

Tossing my head back, I let out a loud ass laugh, before looking back down at the phone.

"No, that's you, Roscoe. Please don't ever mix yourself up with my man. He's mature enough to stick with one woman."

"That's what he tells you," he smirked.

I chuckled again.

"Like I would believe anything you say. Nigga, please let me see my child, I do not want to talk to you."

"I love you, Kay."

"That's too bad, Roscoe. Love the mother of your four-year-old, because I'm sure she still holds a torch for you. What's her name, Shamaria?"

"Don't worry about her. And I don' told you Shamaria is not my damn baby mama. Quit saying that shit."

He finally let me see Lonan, who was smiling and grinning at the camera every time I did. Miss Loughton got him to say bye, and I legit almost melted. Everything he did was so cute to me.

243

I got dressed, then stopped by Waayil's house to take a look at his fridge. I saw he had next to nothing, so I made a list of things to get, along with some foods for Lonan since he was almost out back at my house anyway. After shopping, I decided to pick some food up for Waayil since he told me he usually went to break or lunch at this time.

Pulling up in front of Monarch Tattoo, I turned down my music and got out of the car, carrying Waayil's food. Of course, a couple of niggas were standing outside since a liquor store was in this same shopping center. I pretended not to hear a few of them calling out to me, and entered the shop.

One question, what respectable woman would answer to some dirty nigga in a yellow tinged wife beater, who is calling her chocolate drop?

When I walked into the shop, no one was at the front desk, which I found odd. That bitch who had a staring problem was usually there, and on other days, Rebecca would be. With my brows furrowed, I scanned the clean ass lobby, before the sound of a female laughing caught my attention.

Making my way back there, I saw it was coming from one of the offices that belonged to the twins. When I saw Nusef's was closed, my skin became hot because that meant some bitch was in Waayil's.

Entering his office, knocking lightly, I spotted him sitting behind his desk eating, and that bitch from the front, on the opposite side, sitting on the edge. She was talking her own head off, and Waayil wasn't paying her any mind as he ate his food and wrote down some stuff. How desperate for his attention could she be?

"Hey, baby." Waayil grinned, showing off his deep dimples. He looked good as hell right now, and I didn't want this hoe in here. I admit I was feeling myself seeing him light up at the sight of me.

"Hey. Can you excuse us?" I looked to Kiana, Chiara, or whatever the hell her name was.

"Umm..." She looked to Waayil who nodded with a frown like she was stupid for even contemplating. "Okay. Nice to see you again, Yika—"

I slammed the door on her before she was even all the way out. Waayil laughed when she yelped, because I was sure the door hit her somewhere.

"What is she doing back here and not upfront?"

"Damn, boss lady." Waayil chuckled with his fine ass like some shit was funny. He munched on his sandwich as he eyed my body.

"Hello, nigga? Why is she back here with you? What if I was a customer? And where the fuck is everybody else?"

"Venus is in her room tattooing, and so is Moses. Yo' ass was so busy trying to get back here and start some shit with shorty that you didn't notice."

"Whatever. Who bought you food?"

Waayil stared at me, and then grinned widely because he knew his answer was about to piss me off.

"Why does that matter, baby? As long as I eat, right?"

"No! If that bitch is the only way for you to get food, you need to starve." I sat down in the chair in his office.

"Relax, I'm fucking with you. Venus's mama brought a platter of sandwiches for everybody." He was laughing hard, and I was trying not to as well. I felt stupid for letting him get me so mad.

"Anyway," I smirked, "What the fuck were y'all laughing about? I don't like that bitch."

"That's obvious, baby." He balled up the sandwich paper. "She was just telling me how Moses be scared to ask me the simplest shit ever since I choked his ass."

His phone lit up and Alba's name flashed across, showing she'd sent him a text message. Bitches every damn where. I suddenly started thinking about Roscoe's words earlier.

Yikayla, don't let bum ass Roscoe get to you.

I watched Waayil check the message and respond, before setting the phone down.

"Baby, please don't be mad. I swear I didn't know she was in here for like the first two minutes." He looked to me smirking with his wannabe comedian ass. I couldn't help to smile as well, so I rolled my eyes to balance it out. "You brought me food?" He waved for me to come around his desk to him.

"Yeah, but it's no point now," I whined as he pulled me down into his lap.

"That small ass sandwich did not fill me up, I promise." He kissed my neck. "What you got for me?"

Just that easily, I was cheesing as I looked into his beautiful eyes. Waayil was a charmer, and I didn't know if that was a good thing.

CHAPTER SEVEN

Alba

"Wait, you did what?" Ashley chuckled as she held the big ass wine glass to her face.

We were chilling and drinking, since today was my wine day. I was regretting this baby thing more and more each day, and contemplated seeing if I could get it terminated. But then I remembered there was a greater goal to be achieved.

"I tipped off the police on Gavin's ass, and made sure he got arrested. Now his ass is rotting in jail. Well hopefully the charges will stick so he can rot in jail." I gulped down my red wine and refilled my glass.

"Girl, there are no limits to what you will do."

Things seemed to be going the opposite of well for me lately. Waayil went from being mean to me to falling off the face of the damn Earth for some reason, but now he'd resurfaced.

For a minute, I had given up on being with Waayil, and decided to tell Gavin the truth about me being pregnant with his baby. At first, he didn't want to believe it, and talked to me as if he hadn't been purposely trying to get me pregnant awhile back.

Suddenly though, he came around and wanted to be a father to my child. I think it was because his plans of rekindling things with Rori Goode had gone awry. Funny enough, when he came knocking, wanting to play father, I had changed my mind about letting Waayil go. I'd come up with a plan that I was sure would work in securing Waayil as my man and as my child's father. When I told Gavin to get lost, and stupidly let him know that I was gonna be with Waayil, he threatened to tell Waayil the truth. I couldn't have that shit, so I did what I had to do to get him out of the damn way.

"So what now?" Ashley inquired.

"The same plan is in effect, of course. I've already called Waayil and he said I could meet him at his place."

"But didn't Sax say Yikayla lived there with him?"

"So what? He's *my* baby daddy and if he says I can come over there then I damn sure will!"

"No, I know. I just don't think you should be dealing with any confrontations while pregnant, Alba."

"You needn't worry about me, Ashley. If there is a confrontation to be had, I assure you that Yikayla will be the one getting the business."

"I just don't know, Alba. Didn't you say Waayil threatened you last time? Maybe you should just let this go while you still can."

"Get out."

"Huh?"

"Get the hell out of my house right now! I don't need this type of negative ass energy around my unborn and me! If you don't support what I'm doing, you can get your anorexic ass out of my place!" I stood up and shouted over her.

"No, Alba, it's not like that! I'm just… I love you and I don't want anything happening to you. It's not like Waayil hasn't committed heinous crimes before. He blew his uncle's head off, and he wasn't even remorseful in court."

"How do you know that!"

"Because you told me."

Sighing heavily, I fell back onto the couch. No one told me that I would have memory problems while being pregnant. I hated that shit so much.

"Look, Ashley, I appreciate you worrying about me and all, but Waayil was just talking when he threatened me. That man loves me. He wouldn't have stuck around for almost ten years if he didn't. He had plenty of chances to be with Yikayla, but he chose me! And I put too much time into that man to just let him go!" I shouted, crying even though I didn't want to. "I refuse to just let that bitch have him after I did all the fucking work!"

"Yes, okay. It's okay, I understand, Alba." Ashley scooted closer to me on the couch and hugged me.

Ashley ended up cooking a late lunch for me, and after we ate, she went home so I could take a nap before tonight. I was a bit nervous, like always, when I had to discuss this baby with Waayil.

I woke up a couple hours later and saw it was almost time to meet

249

him, so I quickly brushed my teeth, grabbed a snack and some water, then rushed out the door. All the other times I'd spoken to Waayil, I didn't know what to expect, but this time I knew for sure that things were gonna go my way. He just needed proof, and today I was gonna provide him with that.

I made it to his place in Midtown, and once I found a park, I texted him to let him know I was there. The sun had already set and now that the season was changing, the nights were very chilly. I kept my car running with the heat on until I saw his fine ass walking to the car. He looked so sexy with his bowlegged ass, gliding to my car in the typical hood nigga attire: a hoodie, sweats, socks, and Nike slides.

"What you getting out for?" He frowned when I opened my car door and stood out. Why was his screw face so sexy? Especially when he tucked those lips and made them dimples come out.

"I thought—"

"Nah, ma. We can talk in the car. My girl is inside and I ain't about to let yo' ass come in."

My blood boiled high hearing him tell me I couldn't come in because of stupid ass Yikayla.

"Waayil—"

"Get back in the car," he stated sternly but calmly.

We both got back into my vehicle, and for a minute, I stayed silent so I could calm myself down. Every damn time I thought Waayil would show me some respect and love, he spit in my damn face. I was tired of it, but not too tired to give up on him. Trust me, I'd thought about it, and even called myself doing so, but when I laid down at night and thought about how Yikayla would reap all the benefits of the man I'd spent almost a decade with, I couldn't do it. I just could not. I refused to come out of this relationship with nothing to show for it.

"You said you had some shit to show me, Alba."

I wasn't even in the mood anymore, but I reached into my purse, which was in the back seat, and pulled out the envelope. Taking a deep breath, I handed it over to Waayil so he could take a look.

I was all too ready to try to make things work with Gavin's stupid ass until I came up with a foolproof idea.

I found someone on this site where people do all kinds of shit for a minimum of $20. The ad that stuck out to me was the guy who could fake medical documents, including DNA tests and sonograms. I was skeptical at first because he wanted $100 for what I needed, but after I saw some samples that he'd done, I was all for it. Homeboy was the new aged Frank Abagnale. His turnaround time was longer than I liked, but it was well worth it when I got my 'DNA test' in the mail, saying Waayil was 99.99% the father of my child.

A smirk crept across my face as I watched Waayil eye the already open envelope, and then reach inside to unfold the paper in it. He read it, and when I saw the sorrowful look appear on his face, a bittersweet feeling took over me. In a sense, I was happy that he believed what he'd read, but a bit hurt that such news could make him look so damn miserable.

"How you even get this shit done without my DNA?" He looked to me with a scowl. It was a worried one though, like he was hoping he found a loophole in my story.

Had I *not* ran this by Tammy and Ashley already, he would have caught me up, but they told me he'd ask so we came up with something. Thankfully, when Waayil got out of jail, he stayed with me for a minute. When he did, he left things there like a hairbrush, toiletries, and my best friend: his toothbrush.

"I gave them your hair and toothbrush, Waayil."

He turned away from me and looked out the window at his place.

"Why you didn't tell me you were getting this shit done? You act like I've been dodging you or some shit. You ain't have to use my shit I left at yo' crib to get this done, Alba. You do the dumbest shit sometimes."

"Look, with the way you were treating me, namely threatening my life, I didn't want to have shit to do with you. I wasn't about to come to you for DNA just for you to slit my throat." I held my mouth open as another rant came to mind. "Plus, no one has seen you for a minute, Waayil!"

"I was going through some shit. But aye, I'm gon' get my own shit done and I'm gon' do it the right way just to be sure, so you're invited obviously."

Feeling infuriated beyond belief, I yelled, "Why! I gave you proof! Stop denying this baby so you can keep playing daddy to some bastard!"

As soon as the last words left my lips, Waayil had my hand in his, doing something that made it seem like my bones were cracking. I was sure my hand was breaking as he continued to do a massaging motion with my hand that hurt like hell. Only a crazy nigga would learn a move like that; so simple, yet, so devastatingly painful.

"What I tell you about getting smart and talking shit about my bitch, huh?" His voice was raspy, scary, and cold as ice.

"Please, Waayil. I'm sorry. I'm pregnant and this hurts!" I cried, eyes darting back and forth between him and my poor hand. That was the most truthful thing I'd said this evening.

Upon hearing my plea, he softened his grip and let go of my hand.

"Alba, I don't like hurting you, ma, but you make me. Don't talk about my fucking girl. I don't know how many muthafuckin' times I gotta tell you that shit. I don't play about my girl, and any muthafucka that wants to talk shit about her is bound to get fucked up, including yo' ass."

His eyes stayed on mine as he spoke. I don't even think he blinked.

"I understand." I wiped the tears that had fallen from my eyes. My hand was throbbing right now as I held it still as if it were in a cast.

"Come here." He kissed the top of my head and then my forehead. Feeling his lips against my skin again, made me feel better than I felt when my direct deposit hit. "I'm sorry for squeezing ya hand, aight? But keep Yikayla and Lonan's name out ya mouth."

I nodded and then asked, "Will you come to my next appointment in two weeks?"

He looked at me for a minute and said, "Yeah, I can, but only because this could be my baby. I'm gon' find out for sure with my own test. And we both gon' be there so no funny shit." He started to get out, but stopped and turned to me before saying, "And if this child ain't mine, Alba, you better run for ya life."

Even though I was sweating bullets at the thought, I smiled and shook my head as if I was perfectly fine with everything he'd just said.

He gave me a hug as if he didn't just threaten me, allowing me to inhale his cologne and enjoy the feeling of his strong arms, and then he got out. I watched until he disappeared, and then pulled off, praying somehow God got me through this with my desired results.

CHAPTER EIGHT

Rori

A few days later...

*G*avin had been locked up for almost a week now, and during that week, he called me nonstop. I'd only answered once to speak with him because I felt bad, but after talking with my sisters, I stopped taking the calls. I needed to stop feeling bad for Gavin because it was keeping me attached to him when I didn't want to be anymore.

And it's not like I felt bad because of his life choices that had gotten him thrown in jail. I felt terrible because I was falling for his best friend; his brother damn near. I was repeatedly blaming and punishing myself for sleeping with Eko, which had to end as well. I wanted to be with him, and I realized now that there isn't anything wrong with that.

How is it my fault that Gavin treated me more like a flunky than a girlfriend? How is it my fault that he allowed his best friend to pay more attention to me than he did? Had Gavin been doing what he was supposed to do, I wouldn't have had time to sleep around with Eko.

Also, in my defense, what Eko and I had wasn't some lustful affair like I thought it was. At first, I thought my attraction to him was purely based on the fact that I was feeling neglected by Gavin, in combination with Eko being fine as ever. But as I thought about it, I'd always been close with Eko and always liked him. I never saw it as a romance because of his position in my man's life, but it definitely was. We had a real ass connection, and us sleeping together was well past due. I was just allowing Gavin to blind me from what my heart was trying to help me see.

I was here at visitation to see Gavin, because I felt the least I could do was tell him the truth in person. I was too much of a coward to let him know the deal when he was free, so the least I could do was be brave now.

When he saw me, he smiled hard as hell, like I was the love of his life. I wished he'd looked at me like that some time ago, because maybe we would have had a chance. But this thing with Gavin was something I should have let go a long ass time ago. The comfort factor, amongst other small things, kept me here.

We both picked up the phone as we locked eyes through the glass. I expected to be able to touch him, at least hold his hand in mine while breaking his manly ego, but that plan had gone out the window.

"How you doing, baby?" Gavin smirked, licking his lips at me.

"I'm doing okay, actually."

I'd be doing better if Eko answered my numerous calls and texts, but Gavin didn't need to know that... yet.

"I hate being away from you, Rori. My people are working on getting me out of here so I can be home to you soon."

"Gavin..." I half smiled and he returned the gesture. "We had a lot of good times together, but for the past year or so, I haven't been happy."

To see the smile on his face drop like a New Year's ball, was slightly saddening, but I already felt a weight being lifted just from the few words I'd already spoken.

"You ain't been happy? You sure and the fuck acted like you were happy!"

"How would you know?" I chuckled angrily. "When was the last time you paid any attention to me, Gavin? When was the last time, not counting that night I found out you possibly have a baby on the way, that you took me out?"

"Because I..." He looked around and then lowered his voice. "Because I work, Rori. Any nigga that spends all his fucking time with you, ain't got no damn money."

Shaking my head with a smile because Eko had crossed my mind, I replied, "That's not true, and you know it."

"Baby, I know what this shit is about. That baby is not mine, and if it is, I promise I made it while we were broken up for that little time."

I knew he was lying but I didn't care.

"This isn't because of that baby; this isn't even because of the earrings I found on your nightstand, or you threatening to kill me a few moments after that. I'm not in love with you, Gavin. I haven't been happy with you in over a year." I took a deep breath, preparing myself for his reaction once hearing about Eko and me. "I have found someone that's made me happy though."

"Wh—" He was about to ask who, but when his eyes slightly

widened, I knew he was aware of exactly who I was speaking of. "You fucking Eko?" His lips tightened as he spoke through clenched teeth. I saw him gripping the shit out of the phone he was holding.

"Yes, I have been, and I want to be with him. We wanna be with each other. Being with him made me feel like my life was more than just going to school or being some trap nigga's girl."

"No! No!" He slammed his palm against the thick ass glass, making me jump and the guards start towards him. "You better stop right fucking now, Rori! I swear to God I will fucking kill you!" he roared as the guards began dragging him through some door. "I will kill yo' hoe ass, bitch! I swear on my life!" he hollered out just before the door slammed.

Still sitting there with the phone in my hand, I admit I was shocked. I knew he would call me names and try to make me feel like shit, but I didn't think he'd threaten to kill me. And shit, I don't know why I felt that way when he'd threatened to harm me before. The demonic look in his eyes let me know that if he ever got within two inches of me, he would do just what he said he would.

"What?" I hissed at the bitch sitting at the next stall. She was watching me, along with a few other people. I don't know if they heard what I was saying to Gavin, and honestly, I didn't care. I'd never be back here.

I left my visit, and once I got near my neighborhood, I stopped to get some food. I planned to go home and eat it, but I decided to stop by Eko's house. I don't know who he called himself ignoring, but he had me fucked up.

When I got to his place, his car wasn't in the driveway, which made me suck my teeth. Just as I was about to leave, loud rap music started booming down the street, and I saw Eko's car coming down through my rearview mirror. Smiling, I checked myself out to make sure I looked good still, and then watched as he swooped into his driveway.

I watched Eko step his fine ass out, dressed simply in a white t-shirt, navy basketball shorts, socks, and some matching navy colored Nikes. He adjusted his hat as he checked the time on his nice watch, and then closed his door. I stepped out of my car as he rounded the back of his, opening his passenger side door. I paused for a moment, waiting to see Jenni get out, but instead some light-skinned black girl with a short haircut and a body that bitches had in music videos stepped out. I had to clutch my chest, because I was close as hell to having palpitations.

I was gonna leave, but fuck that shit. I just possibly got a price on my head from a crazy nigga in jail over Eko, so I wasn't about to scurry off.

"Eko!" I yelled, crossing the street. I was in jeans, a halter-top, and heels. I could walk well in heels though, so I wasn't worried.

He had his hand on the small of her back as he escorted her to his door, but when I called his name, he turned to me and sighed.

"What you doing here, Rori?" He slid his hands into his shorts pockets.

"Can we get some privacy, tip drill?" I looked to that bitch.

"Excuse me?" She stepped up, so I stepped closer, but Eko got in between us.

"Here, go in the house. I'll be there in a second." Eko handed her his keys, holding his house key between his fingertips.

That bitch glared at me for a moment and then did as she was told.

"Eko, really? You've moved on already?"

"I ain't moved on to shit. I'm smashing who I want since you was on that bullshit."

"Eko—"

"Rori, I told you I don't have time for no damn games. And you, you're on that dumb shit. I need a woman, not a little girl who can't stop chasing after a nigga who don't give a fuck about her."

"Eko, I was never chasing him! I haven't wanted him for the longest! I told Gavin today that you and I—"

"Oh, and so because now you're ready, I'm just supposed to hop up and say, 'yes massah, Rori!'. Nah it don't work like that."

"So you still let Jenni and other hoes come around, but you're cutting me off for good?" I raised a brow.

"Yep." He stared down at me with his fine ass.

"Fine. Fuck you, Eko." I punched his stomach, which was hard as a brick wall, and he just looked at me like I was stupid. I felt stupid for that move too.

Trying to shake the pain out, I walked to my car.

I pretended to look at something to the side of me, and saw Eko still watching. Yeah, he wanted me, but I needed to get these other bitches out of the way.

Getting into my car, I sat there trying to relax. I was used to Eko putting me on a pedestal, so him treating me like I was nothing definitely hurt.

Picking my phone up, I went onto my Instagram since I remembered Jenni's weird ass followed me a couple days ago. After scrolling down and locating her follow, I followed her back and then slid in them DM's.

Me: Hey I can help you.

Bitch answered so quick I had to blink a couple times to make sure I wasn't seeing shit.

JenniStarr: With Eko?

Me: Yep!

JenniStarr: Thank you so much, Rori!

I smiled before asking her to send me her phone number. Once I sabotaged what she had with Eko for good, I would be the only woman in his life. As much as Eko liked to shrug Jenni off, she was a constant in his life and I didn't like that shit. Plus, unlike before, Jenni was a bigger priority than me right now, since I had burned Eko too many times. But once she was gone, Eko would see who was really for him.

CHAPTER EIGHT

Canyon

Later that night...

Today I was off, and it was a weekday, which meant a lot to a nigga who only had weekends off. Shit sounded like heaven when I first got my job, but when you need to handle business, an off day during the week was like a blessing.

Although I did have some shit to do, I'd spent the whole day with my son, taking him wherever he wanted to go since I wouldn't see him again until Friday. He was going to Mississippi with Luna to visit her parents for a couple of days. He was supposed to be in school and shit, but his instructor assured me that he was ahead and could stand to miss.

It was around 9 p.m. right now and I'd finally finished some work I'd taken home. After hopping in the shower and then brushing my teeth, I was able to lie my ass down so I could soon drift off. Today had been tiring as hell.

Luckily for me though, I hadn't even had my eyes closed for longer than a damn minute before someone was at my door. And they were using that stupid ass doorknocker that I should have been ripped the fuck off.

Throwing my damn covers off, I went to peer through the peephole and saw Dree. She was crying, hard too, which made me hurry the fuck up and open the door.

Ever since she came over that last time and cooked for Cade and me, we'd been pretty cool. We weren't fucking around or anything like that because some shit was wrong with her, and I refused to go back to what we were until she could tell me what the fuck was up.

"I'm so sorry, Canyon." She sniffled upon seeing me. "I didn't mean to just drop by but I called and you didn't answer. I need someone to talk to and I—"

"Dree, it's aight, baby." I nodded for her to come in, and when she did, I closed and locked the door before hugging her into my chest. "You want some water?"

"Yes, please."

I let her go and she went to sit down on the couch in my dark living room. After getting a bottle of water for her from my fridge, I returned to the living room and reached it out to her.

"Dree, you gotta tell me something, baby." I rubbed her leg.

She was sexy as hell to me, even right now with a tear-stained face, and dressed in jeans and a white t-shirt. Her smooth dark complexion looked like it had glitter on it or something because of how she glowed. I hadn't fucked shorty in a minute, and damn was I missing that already.

She drank the bottle down halfway, before securing the top back on it and placing it on the coffee table. She took a deep breath, and then shifted her body a little so that she was somewhat facing me.

"Canyon, I'm a terrible person," she sobbed, running her fingers through her hair. "I don't like who I am right now and I don't know what to do."

"Dree, you gotta be more specific."

"I had sex with Sean…" She saw my facial expression and placed her small hand on top of my knee. I mean I figured she was fucking the new nigga she dissed me for, but damn, hearing that shit still fucked with my ass. "But I didn't want to, Canyon, I didn't. I didn't want anyone to touch me after you, even though I'd convinced myself that you weren't the one for me," she sobbed.

"What do you mean you didn't want to? He raped you?" My fists balled up out of reflex, but I didn't notice until Dree unfolded one of them to hold my hand.

"Well, no, not really. He—"

"It's a yes or no question, Dree. If you didn't want the nigga to fuck you and he did, then how is that shit not rape? Tell me something, ma, because this shit is about to go left."

"I had a lot to drink and I don't remember if I told him it was okay to sleep with me, Canyon."

"How much to drink?"

"I had a cocktail at dinner, two glasses of champagne, and then it was like I blacked out."

I laughed angrily and shook my head.

"Dree, I've known you for years, and I ain't never seen you get drunk off no one weak ass cocktail and two glasses of champagne. We used to take down whole bottles of Hennessy together, and you would still be able to remember certain shit the next day."

"I know, but maybe my tolerance has died down some. I don't know, but my point is that now I'm... I'm pregnant, Canyon." Tears began to pool her perfect brown eyes again. "But I don't want to have this baby. Am I a terrible person?"

Hearing that nigga got her pregnant was like a dagger to the chest, but I had to stay strong right now for her.

"Nah, ma, you're not."

"Really? Or are you just saying that to make me feel better?"

"I'm being honest. You have plans for your life, and a baby wasn't a part of that plan right at this moment."

"I mean, yeah, that's the obvious, but how it came about is what bothers me most. I can't help but think that every time I look at this baby, I'm gonna remember how I woke up next to its father with no clothes on and no recollection of what happened."

The more she kept mentioning that shit, the angrier I got. She could think what she wanted, but I knew exactly what that nigga did. Sucker ass rich niggas like him always drugged bitches to get shit they wanted because they felt like they were untouchable. Dree obviously was turning this nigga down from what it sounds like, so he took matters into his own damn hands. But little did he know, I would be doing the same shit.

"So what we gon' do?"

"We?" she sniffled and chuckled. "You still want to be with me? Even though I left you for some bougie trust fund baby and got pregnant?"

"I mean, now that you put it like that, not really." I grinned when she hit me in the chest. "Dree, that's what the fuck I've been trying to get you to understand, and that's how much a nigga loves you and cares for you. Yeah, I wanna choke yo' ass a little bit right now, but I'd rather hold you, comfort you, and help you, ma. I may not be able to give you all the shit you want as far as material things, but emotionally, and definitely physically, I got you."

She locked her arms around my neck and hugged me so damn tightly, I could barely breathe. When she loosened her grip, I kissed her soft neck, while caressing her back.

"I made an appointment for tomorrow. I don't have to stay really long or anything because it's just a pill, but I'm gonna be sick and I will need someone."

"I have to work, but I can call out."

The school year had started already so I didn't have as many appointments as I used to. They were a few times a week, but most of the shit I did was just paperwork. I could afford to miss, but for good reason only. I was a perfect attendance type of nigga otherwise.

"Oh shit. No, Canyon, you don't—"

"I already decided, Dree." She smiled shyly with her pretty ass, and then cupped my face to kiss my lips. "Aye, but if you pull that shit you pulled awhile back, I'm fucking yo' ass up, on God."

267

"I believe you, but I won't."

I wasn't playing with Dree's ass. She was gon' find her name on the missing person's list fucking around with me.

***

The next afternoon...

I'd driven Dree to her appointment, which they explained would last a couple hours. I didn't know how the fuck swallowing a damn pill caused for her to be there for a couple hours, but shit, the only thing I knew about women's bodies was how to make 'em cum.

Anyway, I'd just picked her up, and I admit I was caught off guard when they rolled her ass out in a wheelchair. I guess I expected for her to be walking like shit was normal, but then again, I'm sure they told her not to drive herself for a reason. I didn't take that shit seriously, them telling us that she would need someone to look after her for the rest of the day, but I'm glad I did a little bit of stuff back at my crib for her.

"Canyon," Dree whispered as I helped her into my apartment. "You didn't have to do all of this."

I'd pulled the sofa bed out, and had it covered with fresh blankets. I even bought some new thick ass pillows for her to lay that big ass head on. I had some of her favorite movies on DVD, along with everything hooked up, so all she had to do was press a button.

"I know I didn't," I replied, making her chuckle softly.

I helped Dree to the bed and carefully laid her down. She winced in pain a little bit, and honestly, I was curious as hell about all of this.

But I was gon' wait until a later time to ask all them fucking questions.

Once Dree was relaxing and eating that soup I hope I'd made correctly, she passed out in the middle of watching *Hustle and Flow*. I hated that damn movie so I was thanking God right now that I could cut that shit off.

As I covered her up, my phone buzzed and I saw it was a text message from my co-worker, Roselle. She sent me Sean's class schedule, so I would be able to catch his ass. After replying with a 'thank you,' I put my shoes on and left the crib.

I got to the school about thirty minutes before his second to last class was over, so I just chilled, trying to calm down a little bit. I was definitely gon' be on some bullshit with his whack ass, but I didn't want to go too far because for one, I worked here, and secondly, with my type of temper, I was bound to kill his ass in broad daylight if he got to slick by the mouth. People forget the old Canyon still lingered within me.

Once it was closer to the time his class would let out, I climbed out the car and started over that way. I knew it was risky showing up here since I'd called off, but I worked on the undergrad side, so the chances of me being seen by my boss or a hating ass co-worker weren't as likely as you'd think, but it could definitely happen.

Sean's class ended, and about eight or so minutes later, I saw him crossing the area I was seated in. He had his arm draped around some bitch, and he was smiling down at her. He was so busy looking at her, and she at him, that neither of them noticed me cut their path off.

When they did though, Sean's smile faded quickly as hell.

"Let me talk to you for a second, Sean."

"And what is this in regards to, sir?"

His high-pitched ass voice caught me off guard for a moment, because that really wasn't how I'd expected his ass to talk. I'd seen him before, only once, and I knew he was the muthafucka Dree was rocking with because I'd seen them together.

I was extremely fucking offended that she'd kicked me to the curb for some square with a voice softer than Michael Jackson's. I even looked at the bitch under his arm with a frown, wondering how in the hell he'd convinced her to do anything with him with that feminine ass bitch-boy voice. She was looking at me too, but like she wanted me to put her face in the pillow and show her some things this adolescent ass nigga couldn't.

Gaining back my train of thought, I said, "Dree."

Chuckling, he looked off before whispering in the girl's ear. She walked off and sat down at a table a little ways away.

"What about Dree?"

"The fact that you fucked her after slipping some shit into her drink, and then got her pregnant but didn't want to address the situation."

"Look, sir, I didn't do anything Dree didn't want me to."

"Say that shit again and I'll knock yo' ass into next week," I gritted, stepping up closer and towering over him.

He cleared his throat, eyes darting to his girl as if he was asking her for help.

"I'm sorry, okay? Maybe Dree and I had a—" He stopped when I raised my brow. "I apologize. Uh, is there anything I can do to help? I can write you a check for any amount, sir."

This nigga's voice was trembling like Ray J's on that "One Wish" track. Any other time, it'd be funny as fuck, but I wasn't in a laughing mood.

"Nah, I don't want yo' money, bruh. I came to let you know to stay the fuck away from Dree, *after* you deliver an apology. If you don't apologize, I'm gon' fuck you up."

"Yes, no problem at all. There is no need to get violent…" His last word trailed off as his brows furrowed.

"What, little nigga?" I snarled.

"Don't you work here? I know I've seen you before." He then gave a conniving smile before saying, "Yeah, you do. You work as a loan officer in financial aid or an academic advisor or something like that."

"So."

"So, if you come near me, I will definitely let the right person know. You will lose your job, and won't be able to work in a school that isn't in Mississippi."

"You threatening me, muthafucka?" I admit, he had me a teeny bit, but I wasn't no bitch.

"No, I'm simply explaining the potential consequences of your actions. You decide if Dree is worth it or not." He adjusted his backpack strap and walked off, joining old girl at the table.

If he thought he won, he was sadly fucking mistaken. He'd only made shit worse for himself.

CHAPTER EIGHT

Nusef

$\mathcal{I}$'d woken up last night, finding myself hooked up to a bunch of shit like I was an experiment. For a moment, I was dazed and confused as hell, as Jonaya and the medical staff made a huge ass fuss over a nigga. I didn't understand how I'd ended up here, and what the fuck was going on until about an hour after they removed all the shit lodged in my throat, and had me drink countless cups of water that was way too damn warm.

Remembering that someone had shot my ass was crazy. According to Jonaya and my doctors, I was hit ten times, but I only remember about the first three before completely passing the fuck out. My only goal at that time was to protect my girl and make sure that she made it out alive. I didn't really care too much about what happened to me, as long as she was good. If I wasn't mistaken, it even looked like the shooter was coming at her, which led me to think Marquise was behind it.

Nigga had gone coo-coo for cocoa puffs over Jonaya, even while he was still with her, and according to a few of the homies in the streets, he was extra salty that I'd snatched her from him. And unlike me, Marquise was into that street shit, thinking he was actually hard when really he only hung with niggas that did his dirty work.

I may not be into selling drugs or gang banging, but I learned more in the eight years I spent with my real parents, than Marquise had probably learned in all his life. Midtown, where I grew up, was a pretty good neighborhood, but it had its areas that weren't so nice.

Plus, growing up, my brother, friends, and I mainly stayed out in Orange Mound and the Southside more than anything. Midtown, on most days, was just a place to lay our heads.

By saying that, niggas didn't need to let this legit money making fool their asses. No fucking way was Marquise about to get away with trying to ice me, and that was on everything I loved. I was coming for that nigga and I wouldn't stop until the people who loved him were boo-muthafuckin-hooing over his body being lowered into the ground. And shit, who knows, I may even show up at the services.

"Excuse me, Mr. Christian." My pretty ass nurse, Tyra, walked into my room.

Bitch knew damn well she needed to go up *three* sizes in them damn scrubs. But shit, I didn't mind. I loved Jonaya, but I wasn't dead or blind. A nigga still liked to look. And as long as I kept my dick in my pants, kept the conversation to a minimum and extremely platonic, I didn't see shit wrong with it. Not to mention, as hard as I worked to get Jonaya to even admit she had feelings for me, I wasn't about to fuck that up.

"How are you feeling, Mr. Christian?" she asked, smiling as she checked my vitals for the hundredth time today. The way she was acting, I thought my ass was gon' croak at any minute.

"I'm good, and Nusef is fine."

"Okay, Nusef. Have you had a chance to look over the menu and see what you want for dinner?"

"Yeah, and all of this shit looks nasty as hell. Why don't y'all serve steak, or ribs, or something a nigga likes to eat?"

"Well, for one, that's not really good for the patient's diet usually." She smiled. "But if that's what'd you'd like, I guess I could maybe go out and get something for you."

"You can do that?"

"Well, I'm not supposed to, but for you I can. You deserve it after all that you've been through."

"Thank you, but I already asked my girlfriend to bring me something. She's cooking me a big meal and will bring it by later." Looking at the clock I replied, "Actually, pretty soon."

"Oh, the young light-skinned girl?" Tyra clutched the clipboard and placed it flat against her thighs.

"Jonaya."

"Oh that reminds me. You have someone here to see you. She said her name is Rebecca Chase. Is it okay if I let her in?"

"Umm…" I stared hard at the clock, trying to calculate if she and Jonaya would run into one another. "Yeah, but just for a minute."

"You're a very popular man, Mr. Chris— Nusef."

I watched Tyra's ass as she switched out my room, and shook my head. I hope they weren't letting her thick ass work around muthafuckas with heart problems, because that ass was bound to give these grandpa ass niggas a heart attack.

My mind quickly drifted to Rebecca. I honestly didn't know why she was here to see me after our last few encounters. Even at work, ever since I barked her stupid ass up out of my office, we didn't say much to one another. She kept shit short with me, which I preferred, and I barely looked her way unless we were having a conversation.

"Hey," Rebecca's voice traveled through the room.

I looked to my left at her, and she was holding a big ass bouquet of flowers, which made me frown. The smell was loud as hell. She was looking right as hell tough.

"What's up? Everything aight at the shop?" I tried to sit up a little but my body felt too stiff and taut from all the bullet holes they'd bandaged up.

"No... I mean yes, everything is perfect." She chuckled breathily. "I just heard you got shot and was worried. Then when I found out from Chiara that you'd woken up, I decided to come see you."

"Thanks."

"I see your little girlfriend decided not to stick around."

"She was in class, ma. And don't start that bullshit. We may be outside of work, but when I said to stay out of my personal, I meant in every location."

Rebecca nodded and sat down in one of the chairs as I sipped on some of the water to calm my loud ass stomach. I was hungry as fuck.

"I did come here for more than just to make sure you were okay."

"Oh yeah? What for?"

"To give you a heads up that I'm dating someone now. I didn't want you to be blindsided or anything."

Chuckling, I said, "I'd have to care to be blindsided. I'm happy for you though. You deserve somebody who's into you, and you only."

"So you weren't into me? It sure seemed like it."

"Did I say I wasn't into you? And I said you need someone who wants you and you only, ma. I wanted you, but I wanted someone else more."

"I'm dating Sax."

Now that shit did blindside me. It wasn't like I wanted to be with Rebecca, but that revelation made me wonder if he'd been watching her the whole time I was fucking her. But then again, the shit was kind of funny so I laughed a little bit.

"Oh word? I'm happy for you."

"Are you? Then what's so funny?"

"That's just crazy. I never even knew y'all were close or anything like that, but hey. Do you, ma."

"Well, we weren't close until you broke my heart. He was there for me, and things just developed from there."

Before I could open my mouth to respond, Jonaya walked in, holding a plastic bag that contained my food, and a duffle bag over her shoulder since she refused to sleep at home.

"What's going on here?" Jonaya's brows dipped a little bit as she carried her things, along with the plastic bag to the chair.

"I'm just having a conversation with my ex man, if that's okay with you," Rebecca spat, rolling her damn eyes.

"Aight, Rebecca, you can go now, ma."

Getting up, Rebecca responded, "Call me if you need anything, Nusef."

"You know what, bitch, say one more slick thing and I'm gonna whoop your ass," Jonaya stated calmly, so I knew her ass was serious. I was too tired, hungry, and weak to witness Rebecca in another fight, especially with crazy ass Jonaya.

"Is that a threat?" Rebecca raised her brow.

"Nope, a 100% guarantee, bitch."

"Ladies, please. Rebecca, you got to get up outta here before I have to fire yo' ass. I'm not fucking around."

"You'd fire me for this?"

"Hell yeah! You ain't got no business coming down here anyway, ma. Get out of here while you still have a job."

Shooting daggers through me, Rebecca turned on her heels and left the room. Jonaya went to close the door, before giving me a look and then going into the bathroom. I waited until she was done, before she finally maneuvered my table in front of me, and placed my plate on top of it.

After we prayed and both started eating, she said, "I wanted to talk to you about your sister."

"Which sister?"

"Well, Midori is miles away and I'm only really close with Wednesday anyway," she replied nervously.

"Talk then."

"So, I know you've noticed that Waayil and Wednesday have been kind of distant, right?"

"I mean, no. I've noticed that Waayil's been acting like he can't control himself, and Wednesday has been acting like her dog died. That's about it."

I didn't know where she was going with this, but if it had something to do with my fucking siblings, why weren't they the ones to tell me?

"Nusef." She placed her plate of food to the side, and nervously rubbed her hands up and down her thighs. "Wednesday... she umm... she did something really bad and I knew about it. Well, I didn't know about it like when it happened, I only recently—"

"What the fuck did she do?"

"Waayil can talk to you about that, but I just want you to know that I didn't keep her secret for malicious reasons. So when he tells you what it is, don't get mad at me for not saying anything."

"Jonaya, what the fuck did she do!" I yelled.

Shaking her head slowly, she replied, "I have to let your brother, or even Wednesday tell you, but it's not my place to."

"You my damn girl. How is it not yo' muthafuckin' place to tell me some shit like this, huh?"

I loved Wednesday, just like I loved Midori and Emil, but I couldn't deny the fact that Waayil and Wednesday had a closer relationship than she and I did. So whatever she did to make Waayil distance himself from her had to be horrible as fuck. I racked my damn brain trying to think of something... anything she could have done to make Waayil back off, and have Jonaya sitting in front of me looking like she'd seen a ghost. Nothing came to mind though.

"It's just not, Nusef. And please don't—"

"Then why the fuck you bring it up?"

"Because I didn't want Waayil to tell you how I knew and never said anything! I wanted you to hear that part from me! So when he does explain, you're not as mad. At least I hope you won't be."

The more Jonaya talked, the harder my brain pumped trying to think of some shit that could have popped off between Waayil and Wednesday. My shit wasn't working right though, I guess, because again, nothing came to mind. Not even a damn hint. I just hoped when I found out, it wouldn't make me change feelings towards anybody in my life.

CHAPTER EIGHT

Yikayla

Thursday morning…

I was getting the last few things out of my closet to take over to Waayil's house, when my mother came in the door. She wasn't smiling like usual, which was strange, but I just kept putting my clothes in the tall ass box in the middle of my floor. Packing was so much easier with Lonan being out of my way and with his dad, but I missed him so much already.

"Yikayla, Freya came to speak with me today and she asked me to talk to you about something." My mother sat down on my bed, after refolding one of Lonan's onesies.

Freya was Waayil's mother, and she and I were pretty close, so I didn't know why she was sending my mother to talk to me about anything. I mean, unless it was something so terrible that she couldn't bear to say it herself. Then again, ever since Wednesday's lie was exposed, I hadn't been over there much to see her.

"What did she want you to talk to me about? You know Freya and I talk all the time; I mean, usually."

"Yeah, but she wanted me to get you to talk to Waayil, and convince him to sit down with Wednesday. Maybe take her to lunch or something."

"No. Waayil will sit down with her when he's ready. What she did, I'm not sure if you're aware of it, but it was despicable, Mama."

"Yes, Freya updated me, Yikayla. And yes, I agree that what she did was pretty bad, but she was a young girl and she was afraid. She didn't even expect Waayil to react so viciously."

"I've been young and afraid before, but I've never thought to lie about something like that. Especially to someone who I know cares about me more than anything. Waayil loved Wednesday a lot, so I'm not too sure what she thought he was gonna do to someone he believed was raping her."

"Yikayla, you seem very hostile."

"Yeah, I am, because I love Waayil! I'm angry for him, because he was manipulated in a sense! And then for myself a little bit because he was taken away from me!"

"But you got to see him every couple of months while he was in jail, Kay!"

"No I did not! Stop saying that! When he got home from jail the night of his party, Mama, that was the first time I'd seen him in six years! That was the first time I'd talked to him in five years!"

"But I thought you said you'd visited him a couple months before he got out—"

"No I didn't, Mama. I never said that. The only time I mentioned visiting him was during the first year he'd gotten locked up, when we were still communicating. But Jasper told me I couldn't go, and eventually, Waayil cut me off."

"I'm sorry, honey. I just assumed you guys had been seeing one another and communicating the whole time." She blinked repeatedly as she looked off, obviously floored.

"No, Mama. We were ripped apart. And do you honestly think I would have started anything with Roscoe, had I been still communicating with Waayil?"

"You and Waayil were only best friends before he went to jail, so yes."

"Ugh!" I growled. "What do you pay attention to, Mama? Other than Buddy and Jasper's money? You don't even go down to the waffle house anymore, and you need to! You have no idea what's going on with anybody!"

"Yes I do!"

"Then where am I going today after I'm done with this?" I pointed to the box of clothes. "I go there four times a week so this should be easy."

"I... umm... you were on the schedule for the waffle house, right?"

I chuckled angrily because she was ridiculous. I never cared too much that my mom didn't pay attention to my sisters and me like that, but at this moment, it was driving me insane. I could never imagine myself just living life and not wondering what the hell was going on with Lonan. I couldn't imagine him walking out the door fully dressed, and me not feeling inclined to ask where he was going or what he was doing for money.

"No, Mama, I got a job at a fashion house. I work there four days a week."

"I'm sorry, Kay. I don't mean to be neglectful, I just…"

"Have your own shit going on." I began angrily taping the box closed. "Look, Mama, I love you and I've known what type of person you were since I was a little kid. However, the next time you want to put in your opinion on my life, please make sure you have all the facts. Wednesday selfishly took Waayil from me, his family, and his friends, all because she was scared that he'd find out about a damn crush. I don't hate her because I just can't, but right now, I'm really not in the mood to go campaigning for her."

"I understand." She got up to leave, but stopped with her hand on my doorknob. "What's the name of the fashion house?"

"Jerica Rose."

"Mmm, black girl, huh?" She half smiled.

"Yeah."

She nodded and stared at my hardwood floors for a moment, before leaving my bedroom.

Once I was done packing up, I FaceTimed Roscoe so I could see Lonan, but he didn't answer. I tried him once more, then called his mother, and of course, she had my baby anyway, so I hung up and FaceTimed her so I could see him.

I was happy to know that he was okay and playful. I loved him so much, so even though he couldn't talk to me on FaceTime, and all he did was eat seedless cherries in the screen, it was the best 'conversation.'

I took the box down to my car and after dropping it off at Waayil's place and locking up, I headed to work. When I got there, I was happy to see I only had two racks today because I swear my arms were getting buff from steaming four and five damn racks a day.

"Hey, girl." Brynn walked in smiling.

Ever since we went out that night, she'd been pretty cool. I actually liked having someone to talk to while at work. Not to mention, she was always offering to bring me teas, water, or food from some of the places around. I always tried to pay her back, considering I knew I made more than her, and because she shouldn't have been buying me stuff, but she always declined.

"Hey, how are you?"

"I'm pretty good." She closed the door and sat down to the side of me as I started to steam the next dress. "So are you busy tonight?"

"Well, my man and I are going out to dinner and to see a movie. Then we may go have a drink at a lounge or something. Some friend of his is rapping during an open mic and asked him to swing through."

"What's your boyfriend's name again?"

"Waayil."

"Oh yeah, you know, I remembered his tattoo shop name. I drove

285

by it the other day and almost went inside."

"Why? For a tattoo?"

"I mean, no, just to say hi to him."

"Oh." I furrowed my brows in confusion. I had no problem with Brynn speaking to Waayil, but her stopping by his shop just to speak was a bit much. That was shit you did when you had a crush on a guy.

"Oh, girl, no! Okay, it is nothing like that! It's just you talk so much about him that I kind of wanted to meet him in person since I've only seen him the night we went out, which was from afar. He sounds so great."

"Yeah, well, he is. I can't help but to talk about him." I hung the dress back up and grabbed the next. "You never talk much about your child's father."

"Not much to talk about really. And to be honest, I'm thinking about leaving him anyway. I met someone nice that night at the club."

"Really?" I grinned. "Now I feel bad that I yanked you and Rori out of there after getting into it with that guy!"

"No, don't! We'd exchanged numbers after I put it on his ass on the dance floor, so by the time you were ready to leave, it'd been signed, sealed, and delivered."

"Good. Good to hear. So this new guy, what's his name?"

"Jerrod, but I don't want to jinx anything. Right now, he's just someone for me to talk to and stuff. Keep my mind off baby daddy."

"I'm so sorry, Brynn. All this time, I've never asked you if you had a son or daughter and how old. I feel like such a bad person." I chuckled.

"I have a daughter, and she's three. Her name is Haven."

"That is so pretty. I can't wait to have a daughter one day. My baby boy is so rough sometimes. Waayil gets on me about being too soft with him, and I just cringe whenever he body slams my baby onto the bed, but Lonan laughs hard like it's the best thing ever." I laughed along with Brynn.

"Yeah, that's how my nephew is. He loves to play fight and everything, but he's only two so it's hard to watch sometimes, but he has a ball."

Suddenly, Jerica walked into my office area, dressed to the nines like always. Her eyes were hard on Brynn, as she clutched two of her cellphones in her hand.

"Brynn, my phone out there has been ringing off the hook for the past five minutes. If you want to sit and talk with Yikayla, you need to wait until you have a break, or even better, just do it once you're off."

Now, I wasn't scared of any bitch ever, but you know how some people just instilled a teeny bit of fear in you? That was Jerica. Don't get it twisted, if we ran into one another at the club and she came at me, I would definitely whoop her ass. But here at work, she just gave me chills and not the good kind per se.

The way she carried herself and how she spoke so perfectly, was inspiring yet intimidating as hell. It was like when she told you to do something, you nodded repeatedly like a servant. And when she spoke to you, it seemed like you were paralyzed until she was finished. I couldn't wait to have that much quiet power.

287

"Yes. I apologize, Jerica." Brynn hopped her ass right up and slipped past Jerica.

"Yikayla, I have one more rack coming. I don't need it done until tomorrow though, so don't panic." She was talking to me but staring down at her phone, before walking out, not waiting for my response.

A couple hours later, and I was finally off work. Jerica's Fashion House was downtown, and next door to her was this newly built fast food spot named Green Bean. They were like a coffee and teahouse, but they had organic food, to-go salads, sandwiches, and pastries too. They'd just opened this past Monday, and I'd already been there five times. Keep in mind, I only came to Jerica's four times a week.

When I walked out of Jerica's, waving bye to Brynn, I saw a car parked across the way. It'd been there all damn day. I only noticed because pretty much the same cars parked over here, since it was a working street that I was on. But this bright orange-red Lexus stood out to me.

I ordered my tea latte, along with a salad I'd come to love, and then stepped to the side to wait. I looked to the door when the bell rung, to see some girl walk through. She looked familiar as hell, but not familiar to the point where I'd hung out with her. I'd seen her somewhere in passing, but just didn't know where; maybe when I was up over in Nashville for school. As she ordered, she kept glancing at me and I could have sworn she was giving me attitude.

Walking my way, which was in the waiting area, she stopped right next to me, allowing me to smell her strong, toxic, juvenile perfume.

"Do you know Roscoe Cousins?" she asked me out of nowhere. It was then that I remembered her from Privé that Friday night, because she asked me the same thing then.

"Kay!" The clerk called my name just in time, so I declined to respond and went to grab my food.

Old girl followed me up to the counter, and then out of Green Bean. Her walk was extra brisk like she was about to jump on my back or something.

Dropping my food on one of the tables outside of Green Bean, I questioned, "What the fuck do you want?"

"I asked you a question!" She folded her arms. She was a pretty black girl; smooth light skin, blue eyes, and curly blond hair that she'd obviously dyed. She looked very ghetto though.

"Yes, I know Roscoe, bitch! Do you know, Roscoe? Oh, I forgot, a lot of bitches probably know Roscoe or his dick at least!"

"Look, calm yourself. You need to learn your place, because I am his woman and you're the side. I saw you blowing him up earlier and I don't appreciate it. When he doesn't answer, that means he is at home with wifey! Girls like you make me sick!"

Laughing, I replied, "Oh really? Well, technically I'm not anything because I haven't dated that man in months. But for the record, I was with him five years before that and I'm sure your number is smaller."

Her lips slightly parted as I nodded my head 'yes' with a smug expression.

"Fi—five—"

"Years. Yes, five years, ma. But please do not let me stop you from chasing behind every woman in his phone book."

"We've been together a little over four, and we have a baby," she whimpered. "Please just let him be. I'm getting tired of tracking all of y'all down. Our child is four years old and—"

This must have been Roscoe Jr.'s mama.

"RJ is your son?" I asked.

"Yes."

"Shamaria?" I guessed, but my teeth clenched since I knew I'd fucked up when she frowned in confusion.

"Shamaria is my sister. My name is Christelle." She pointed to her chest. "How do you know my sister?"

"Never mind. Look, I have to go. Don't worry about Roscoe and me because that will never happen again. As long as he takes care of his son, we won't have any problems."

"Son?" Her voice trembled as tears pooled in her eyes.

"Girl, get your shit together and stop walking around with your eyes closed. I was doing the same thing, and when I opened them my vision was very clear and bright." I snatched my food up and walked to my car. Once inside, I could see through my rearview that Christelle was still stunned and standing there.

As much as I liked to play tough, every time I found out more shit about Roscoe, I got a sharp pain in my chest, because at the end of the day, I was the one who he was ultimately messing around on for years.

That night...

I got out of Waayil's nice shower feeling so refreshed. After spreading lotion all over my body, I slipped on my panties and then wrapped my robe around my body. Stepping out of the bathroom, I heard Waayil talking, so I followed his voice to the extra bedroom. The room was fully Lonan's now, filled with all his baby furniture, and designed with colorful walls that Waayil worked on every night until the wee hours of the morning.

Standing in the doorway, I smiled seeing Waayil sitting down on the floor with little Lonan sitting between his legs. My baby was in his signature white onesie and a diaper, with his curly hair all over the place. Waayil was shirtless, wearing boxers, socks, and basketball shorts. Together, they were playing with one of Lonan's shape toys as Waayil spoke to him.

"I'm gon' be honest, I don't really fuck with yo' pops at all. I don't think you do either, but I think he loves you. And if that nigga doesn't, just know I do." Sighing, Waayil added, "Yeah, I know you don't know me like that, but I already love you, little man." Lonan tilted his head back every so often to look up at Waayil, who kissed his forehead, before Lonan turned his attention back to the toy they were playing with. "And I'm sorry for disappearing on you and ya mama for a little bit. I had a little problem, but that won't happen anymore, I promise. Because I love her, and she only deserves the best, which is what I'm gonna give her, you know? You deserve that shit—excuse me, stuff too, because you's a dope ass baby."

I smiled at Waayil's words as Lonan responded in baby talk. He tilted his head back, and touched Waayil's face. Waayil kissed his small hand, before they both turned their attention back to the toy.

Lonan was supposed to still be with his father, but Miss Loughton said she had somewhere to go, and unbeknownst to me, Roscoe left town, so I picked my baby up. Waayil and I had to cancel our initial plans, and instead, the three of us went to dinner where Waayil taught Lonan how to dip his French fries in ketchup before eating it. And once he learned, he couldn't stop. My Snapchat was full of that cute ass scene.

"Good job, Lo." Waayil grinned when Lonan dropped the square into the right shape opening. He then scooped him up and brought him down to kiss his cheek. "You're smart as hell, you know that?"

Finally, I walked into the room and sat down on the playmat they were on. Waayil pecked me and then sat Lonan back between his legs to start on the next toy.

This was my kind of night.

CHAPTER NINE

Waayil

Some odd days later...

$\mathcal{E}$ko and I were at this park getting a run in since they had a lot of open space. There was a park for the kids and shit too, and even though it was a Tuesday morning, a nice amount of people was out here. I didn't expect that shit, and didn't want it, but I needed to get my cardio in. Being in jail had me addicted to fitness a little bit, but I made sure to only lift weights here and there because a nigga wasn't trying to be walking around here looking like Arnold Schwarzenegger.

After running seven damn miles, the two of us decided to take a little break. I thought working out would clear my damn mind from that DNA test Alba brought to me, but it didn't work.

That paper looked legit as hell. I'd googled fake DNA tests and everything, and the shit on Google Images failed miserably in comparison to the shit Alba had brought to me.

Alba may have been crazy as hell, but I just couldn't imagine her stupid ass going this damn far as to fake a damn test. If she did that shit, I might kill her. And I'm not just talking. A nigga might actually stop her ass from breathing if she took shit that far. However, as much as I didn't believe she would go to such extreme measures, I was definitely gon' get another test done.

"Now, nigga, I know yo' ass is quiet as fuck, but you ain't usually this damn quiet." Eko chuckled before downing some of his water.

"Too much shit on my mind. Nusef getting shot and how we have no fucking idea who did it, then this shit with Alba."

"Yeah, that shit about Nusef is wild. I mean, niggas in Memphis have always been on some bullshit, but homie ain't even in shit like that."

"Niggas get shot for nothing every day, but as many bullets that hit him and they didn't rob him or nothing? Nah, someone was coming for him, for a reason. Some type of revenge or some shit."

Eko nodded as he stared out at the kids playing at the park. I was doing the same when I noticed something.

"What happened with Alba?" Eko inquired.

"Brought me a DNA test that said I was the fucking father of her child. And I know bitches get fake shit done, but if I showed you that paper, you'd be convinced."

"Damn, I know you were hoping the baby wasn't yours."

"I was. I'm still gon' get my own shit done just to be safe, but after seeing that damn test, I feel like I pretty much know what the results are gon' say. And now a nigga feels bad and shit because I don't want my kid to know I was denying the fuck outta them."

"Aye, if it's a boy, just let him know his mama was a scheming ass hoe and he'll understand."

We both laughed in unison as I dapped him up, with my eyes still on the park. I'd been watching this nigga play with this little boy, trying to see if he was who I thought he was.

"Give me a second, E." I got up and jogged across the park to where Roscoe and whom I'm guessing was the four-year-old son Yikayla told me she'd met. "Where is Lonan?" I questioned as soon as I got to the table he was sitting at with his son.

"Why?" he spat, looking up at me.

"I mean, this is your time with him but I don't see him here," I smirked, fucking with him.

Under it all, I was hot as hell that he'd left Lonan at home. I was getting super fucking attached to little man, and anytime I felt he was being mistreated, it bothered the fuck out of me. I'd fallen in love with that little boy like he was my own.

"First off, Lonan is too small for the park. Secondly, don't worry about where my son is, nigga. He's good."

"That's funny because Yikayla and I take him to the park all the time, so I don't know about him being too little. And I'll worry about yo' son if I want to, muthafucka. Some male figure has to." I grinned, enjoying how mad he was becoming.

"Man, look."

When he started to stand up, I said, "Don't make no sudden

moves unless you ready to throw down, my nigga. Keep that shit in mind." I was no longer smiling.

Instead of standing up, he resumed his seating position and replied, "Like I don' already told you, mane, I got Lonan, and I don't need you worrying about him. I'm the one that nutted in Yikayla's pussy, not you!"

"Daddy!" The little boy whimpered when he saw me snatch Roscoe up by his collar.

"Waayil! Man, not in front of this little boy." Eko ran over and gripped my shoulder.

Roscoe stared up at me, still trying to be tough, but I could see the underlying fear in his eyes. This nigga had me fucked up.

"Nigga, I bet not ever hear you mention my bitch's body parts again. I swear to God, I'll knock yo' shit clean off yo' shoulders, bruh. You keep fucking with me, its gon' be a muthafuckin' wrap," I gritted lowly as I grasped his collar tighter.

Nigga was a bitch because if another muthafucka snatched me up by my shirt, I would have swung on his ass. But nah, this wannabe ass nigga didn't do shit but stay silent and take in every muthafuckin' word I spoke.

"Waayil, come on." Eko tugged on my shoulder again.

The little boy's cries and whimpers snapped me out of my trance, and I let that nigga Roscoe go. He straightened his shirt, and then got up to go around the table and comfort his kid. That nigga had better be glad his son was there, and Eko too, because I wanted to whoop his weak ass so bad I could taste it.

Eko and I left the park because if I stayed there any longer, I might haul off and fuck Roscoe up with his kid being there and everything. I texted Yikayla to see if it was okay if she and I picked Lonan up from Roscoe's mother so we could take him somewhere. My mood had improved that quickly when she told me it was a go.

When I pulled up to my apartment, Alba started calling my phone, so I decided to answer while I was in the car. I didn't want to hear Yikayla's mouth because she felt until it was proven that my kid was inside of Alba, we didn't need to have any dealings. And right now, I didn't want to let Yikayla know about Alba's DNA test because I had fucked around and assured her that it wasn't mine. I told her I'd calculated and the time didn't add up, knowing damn well that shit wasn't true. I just hated that look on her face whenever Alba was mentioned. Shoot me for trying to put my girl at ease. Fuck.

"What, Alba?"

"Do you mind bringing me some—"

"Yes I fucking mind." I hung up. Don't even know why I answered. I guess I was hoping she told me the damn test was a mistake. Wishful thinking.

I got out of my car, and when I got up to my door, the mailman had too, so he just handed me what was mine after greeting me. I was sifting through, when I saw an envelope from the same medical center that had supposedly done the DNA test. Putting the rest of the mail under my arm, I ripped that envelope open to see it was a copy of the DNA test. Snatching my phone out my pocket, I dialed Alba's ass back.

"Fuck is wrong with you, huh?"

"What are you talking about, Waayil? I just wanted you to bring me some—"

"Sending this shit to my crib! And I know you just had it done, because you didn't know my address until recently when you came to show me this shit!" I growled lowly, pacing in front of my apartment.

"I thought you wanted a copy!"

"No, you wanted Yikayla to see this shit!"

"Well shouldn't she know?"

"Listen, ma, and listen good. If you do anything in attempt to sabotage my relationship, once you give birth, I will have you torn limb from limb by horses. And don't wonder how I'm gon' get the damn horses, just know I'm that nigga and I can make that shit happen. You got it?"

"Yes, Waayil, but I just—"

I hung up in her face before going into my spot. Why did so many muthafuckas have to test a nigga fresh from the pen?

CHAPTER NINE

Eko

Friday evening...

"Arms out," one of Neo's henchmen barked to me.

Neo was this new supplier that I'd gotten for Gavin and me. He ran pretty much every area of Memphis, and when shit went wrong, we had to answer to him. The nigga had so much power, that even when he went to jail for eight years this last time, he was still running shit from the inside. Pretty much, if you wanted to make good money, then Neo was the nigga you went to for your shit. Any muthafucka who was getting supplied by someone else was making nothing but chump change, shit to spend on a couple hoes just to be broke again.

Since working with Neo, which hadn't been long, I'd saved up 80% of the money I needed to buy the barbershop I managed. And as soon as I did, I planned to hand this shit over. Initially, it was gon' go to Gavin since he was my partner, but not only was he in jail, he attempted to betray me so it was over for him.

After Neo's big buff ass helper finished patting me down and taking any weapon I had, well that he could find, he typed a code into some door and held it open for me. As soon as I stepped into the dimly lit hallway, some other dude grabbed my bicep.

"Bruh, you better get the fuck off me," I snapped, snatching my arm from him.

He tried to grab on me again, so I shoved him back and hemmed his ass up. He looked scared as fuck as I gritted out threats to his ass for trying to manhandle me like I was a bitch out here. Suddenly, I heard loud ass clapping, and Neo appeared from the darkness. I dropped old boy, who before he even hit the ground good, ran off down the hallway to be next to Neo.

"Have a seat." Neo chuckled and gestured for me to come sit at the table a little further down the hallway. The area lit up some more so that I could see, and I saw a big ass rat jet by, hugging the wall.

"Neo—"

"No, see, it's my turn to talk, Eko." He sat down across from me as his bitch ass flunky stood by the door, chest out like I didn't just rough his ass up. "You see, Gavin wants to get out and I can do that for him, but I just need to know what the fuck happened to my shit."

"Neo, as I explained to you over the phone, I don't know. I wasn't even there. Tic called me, frantic as fuck telling me the trap had been raided, and by the time I got there, they'd already taken Gavin and the others. Have you asked him?"

Nodding, Neo replied, "I have talked to him and he believes it was a setup."

"That's obvious. The shit was too random, and that was the only trap they got. I don't know who it was, but I'm looking."

"Are you looking? Or are you too busy cutting heads down at Coney's?"

"I'm doing both, my nigga. I know how to multitask," I spat, irritated as fuck by him insinuating that I was slacking on my duties. And shit yeah, truthfully, the shop was more important to me, but as of right now, I needed this drug shit for a little longer in order to pay the owner the rest of the money to own Coney's.

"Good. I'm just making sure. But the reason I called you down here to meet in person is because Gavin brought to my attention the other day, that he thinks you set him up." Neo intertwined his fingers and sat forward some. "See, he says for the past couple of months, you've been acting strangely."

"I ain't been acting like shit. If anything, he's the fucking snake. Bruh is just mad about something that bitch ass niggas get mad about."

See, I could have easily put Neo up on game about Gavin trying to get him to work with him solely, but I wasn't no fucking snitch, and I had confidence that whatever game Gavin was trying to play, he was sure to come out with that young L. Not to mention, I was doing the same shit Gavin was trying to do.

"Which is?"

"Nothing. Neo, are we done here?"

I wasn't about to put Rori in the middle of this bullshit just because Gavin wanted to be a crybaby ass nigga. Rori was on my shit list right now, but I still had love for her and unfortunately wanted to protect her crazy ass.

"Yeah, we're done. But the longer you take to tell me who did it, the bigger price you'll pay. You and Gavin."

"Least of my worries," was the last thing I said before getting up and walking out. When the initial henchman saw me, he handed me my gun and I snatched that shit from his ass.

Neo had me meet him all the way in fucking Germantown, so it took me over half an hour to get back to my area. I was hungry as hell, but since I was too tired from the long ass day, I just decided I would raid my damn fridge and see what the fuck I had up in there.

When I walked into my spot, the smell of food immediately hit my nose. Scowling hard as hell, I slammed the door and darted towards the kitchen to see Jenni standing there in a thong and no top, with some tall ass heels. As good as she looked, I needed to cut this shit I had with her off. The longer I kept letting this bitch suck my dick and sit on it, the longer it would take for her to give the fuck up.

God, please help me get this hoe out my spot without whipping my dick out.

Shorty's ass was sitting up right, and after the day I'd had, busting one sounded like heaven.

"Jenni, you gotta go."

"Why, baby? I'm making you dinner and—"

"Wait, how the fuck you get in my crib?" I questioned, finally realizing that I never gave this bitch a key to my shit. I would never. Only one I gave a key to stupidly was Rori, during that short-lived ass affair we'd had. Damn, she had a nigga pussy whipped like a muthafucka.

"A couple days ago when I slept over, I woke up before you and had one made. I figured I could handle that for you."

I felt my eyes widen because this bitch had to be crazy as hell. She had to be. I was still upset, but I was also getting a strange feeling in the pit of my stomach. I didn't do shit but drop dick off in her and she actually thought I would want her to have a key? No sane person would come to that conclusion.

"Handle that for me? You actually think I want yo' ass having a key to my spot?" My brows dipped in utter confusion.

"Yeah, I mean—"

"Jenni, we dated once and it was aight for what it was at the time. You were barely hanging on then, but when you fucked the homie it was a wrap, and it's gon' forever be a wrap."

"I'm sorry I hurt you—"

"Nah, ma, you ain't hurt me." I palmed my chest. "Like I said, you was cool, yo' pussy was good, and you can suck dick like a damn champion, but outside of that, I had no feelings for you. You fucking Daniel was just a reason for me to stop claiming yo' ass, which I was barely doing."

With tears in her eyes, she whispered, "So you never cared for me?"

"Yeah, when I was smashing, but it was more of an 'oh I know her' tip, not no 'I love her and I wanna be with her.' And it ain't gon' never be that way. Any chance you did have of actually locking a nigga down, which was slimmer than Holly from *Power*, it vanished the moment you let the homie hit."

"No! I'm not leaving! You are going to eat what the fuck I cooked you and then we are gonna have a good time!" she shouted in her proper ass voice. The shit was funny, and I was too busy watching her titties move to actually take her threats seriously.

Grabbing her arm, I damn near dragged her half naked ass out, snatching her purse up from my couch on the way. I tossed her out my damn crib, and threw her purse at her as well. I slammed my door, and then went to cut the stove off. She already had some of the food ready, so I made a plate and sat down on the couch to eat it.

For some reason, I'd been thinking about Rori's ass all damn day. I hated to admit it but I missed her.

After downing my drink, I picked my phone up and sent her a text.

Me: Wya?

Rori: Minding my business nigga.

Me: That doesn't even go with what I asked smart-ass. But I wanna see you if that's okay.

She took a little longer to respond to that one.

Rori: Fine. But only for a moment.

Me: Nah, bring some clothes for the night.

I was prepared to wait a cool minute so I got in the shower, but as soon as I stepped out and wrapped the towel around me, I heard someone knocking on my screen door hard. I was just waiting for the shit to collapse.

"Aight! Hold the fuck up!" I opened the door to see Rori's pretty ass rolling her eyes.

Her sexy dark cocoa complexion was vibrant as fuck, and her pretty ass face was looking extra beautiful since she had her brown curly hair down. Dressed in jeans, an oversized shirt, and some retro 11's, she barged into my spot, nudging me like she lived here.

"Aye, come here." I closed the door with one hand and then grabbed her arm with the other.

"What?" she barked when I pulled her body into me and made her drop her bag.

"I'm sorry, mean ass." I chuckled. "But truthfully, you should be apologizing to me."

Rolling her damn eyes again, she said, "I'm sorry," before pouting.

Picking her fine ass up, I carried her to the back as she held my face, planting kisses on my lips hungrily. It wasn't long at all before our tongues became entangled, and our breathing pace picked up.

Placing her to her feet, I yanked her shirt over her head to see she wasn't wearing a bra. My mouth seemed to gravitate towards her nipples, as I cuffed one breast while sucking on the other. Rori let out soft moans as I passionately sucked her nipples, switching back and forth between each. Trailing my lips down her stomach, I began unbuttoning her jeans, yanking them down along with her panties. When they got to her ankles, I lightly pushed her back onto the bed, before removing her shoes, and then pulling her jeans and underwear past her feet.

"Spread ya legs for me," I demanded.

Nibbling on her plump bottom lip, she laid back some, propping herself up via her elbows, and then spread those sexy chocolate thighs for me. I moved closer, and gripped her hips before latching my mouth onto her clit. I started off slowly, paying close attention to certain areas, lingering on others.

"Fuck," she mumbled, as I palmed her inner thigh to push it outward some more. "Eko," she whimpered.

Her pussy started to juice up nicely as fuck, and I began lapping it all up in between sucking on her bud softly. She pushed her pussy more into my mouth as she cried out, and I welcomed that shit, spreading her legs some more so I could really feast. She released hard, making her body shiver as I kept eating. I had to groan because the shit tasted good, and the texture against my mouth was some shit I loved. Rori's body stiffened, and a damn river flow came from her and right into my mouth. I damn near cleaned her up before rising to my feet.

She sat up, licking her lips while staring me up in the eyes. I stroked my dick, which was so hard that if she wasn't careful, it may chip her damn tooth. She eased me into her mouth, allowing her tongue to snake around my head before easing me in further. She started slow, allowing her saliva to completely coat my shit as she let it glide in and out.

"Rori, baby," I mumbled. She was giving Jenni a run for her fucking money right now.

Suddenly, she started repeatedly letting my head tap the back of her throat, while letting her spit continue to drown my shit. I could barely take it anymore, so I yanked her off by her soft ass hair, and then laid on my back. I grabbed a condom from my nightstand, and after I rolled it down, Rori mounted me backwards.

"Wait, ma." I placed my hand on her back once I felt my head get inside of her tight drenched pussy. I needed a moment so I wouldn't bust immediately.

Finally, I gripped her hips and guided her down on me. She whimpered upon me filling her up, and was paralyzed for the moment, so I began moving her up and down on me gently.

"Shit," I grumbled.

"Mmm, shit," she cried, starting to take control.

Her pussy was choking my dick in a good way, and the view of her smooth round ass bouncing a little bit every time she moved up and down was unexplainable. By this time, Rori had a handle on shit, so she began to ride me a little faster, as I spanked and groped her ass roughly as fuck. Once she creamed, leaving the condom glistening, I flipped her over, putting her face in the pillow.

"You mine, Rori?" I quizzed, pounding her pussy hard as hell from the back.

"Ye-yesss!"

Our skin continued to slap together as I beat her pussy up while gripping the shit out of her hips. She exploded yet again, and by that time, I couldn't hold out anymore so I filled the condom up. Yanking her up, I hugged her back into my chest as my dick still sat inside of her.

Running my hand down her thigh, I kissed on her neck while groping her breasts with my free hand.

"I love you, Eko," she panted.

"You better," I replied cockily.

CHAPTER NINE

Dree

"Great job today, guys, and remember the test coming this Thursday," my professor spoke as everyone got up from their seats.

I was feeling good again about everything, including school. Before, I used to think I was gonna flunk out, but ever since I joined that study group at the urging of Canyon and my classmate, Monroe, the information had been much easier to obtain.

Speaking of Canyon, he was just everything. He was damn near perfect, always had been, and it angered me to even think about how I'd left him for Sean. The mere thought of me possibly marrying Sean and leaving the extraordinary, yes extraordinary, man that Canyon is to another bitch, made me shudder.

"How did you do?" Monroe asked as we left the class together. I showed her my A- and she squealed.

"That was probably the easiest test I've ever taken."

"I told you Tyson's study group would really help you. And trust me, girl, that test was not easy because I saw a few long faces back in there."

We both laughed in unison as we continued to walk.

"I am starving."

"Me too. Do you wanna get food together and just walk to the next class since we both have the same one?"

Smiling, I replied, "Sure."

When I first started law school, Monroe was extremely annoying because she was always too friendly and trying to help someone out. I think because I wasn't too happy with myself, she irritated the shit out of me. Now, I realized she was just a sweet person, and I enjoyed having someone to talk to about my law school woes. My family didn't understand, and even though Canyon was great, he didn't get the specifics like Monroe did.

We made it to the dining area that consisted of a few well-known fast food places, and some that I'm sure the school had created. After we ordered our food, Monroe went to the bathroom, so I just waited at our chosen table for my number to be called. I saw a text from Canyon come through, which prompted a smile to spread across my face.

Canyon: Come straight here after class.

Me: I have to get clothes.

Canyon: Aight then right after that... no stops...

I was grinning so hard just from those few texts, that my cheeks were starting to hurt.

"I miss that smile." Sean's voice interrupted my moment as he sat across from me. "You look nice today."

"Sean, what do you want?"

"I saw the other guy you call yourself dating now, and I know that's not what you want, Dree."

"Sean, you don't know the first thing about me, other than that I want to become a lawyer someday."

"You can tell me mo—" He stopped speaking when Monroe came to the table. "Can you give us a minute, Monroe?"

She looked to me and I replied, "No, it's fine, Monroe. Sean was just leaving, right?" I raised a brow.

"No, I wasn't. Dree, I want us to be back together again. Everything was fine and then all of a sudden—"

"I'm gonna go pick up our food," Monroe interrupted and walked away.

"Anyway, all of a sudden you started acting weird. And now you have your new thing coming up here and threatening me? Dree, you're better than some thug who thinks just because he has a couple degrees that he can afford to be with a woman like you."

I had no idea Canyon brought his ass up here, and I was wondering when the hell he even had the time. I mean, granted we were apart when he went to work, when I had class, and the occasional nights I spent at home, but I just didn't see Canyon threatening anyone while on the clock.

"I'm sorry, just a few weeks ago you wanted nothing to do with me, Sean."

"I know, but now that you've had the abortion and everything, I figure we can pick up where we left off."

For a moment, the tough shell that surrounded me cracked a little bit because I couldn't believe he'd just said that to me. He spoke as if before I was damaged goods, but now that I was somehow reformed or clean, I was worthy of his time.

"Excuse me?" was the only thing I could utter at the moment, because I was baffled. Baffled that I'd even contemplated being with this man. Baffled that I'd wasted my precious ass time, over his house, eating dinner with him, and doing things that I wanted to and should have been doing with Canyon. Just for him to take advantage of me, get me pregnant, treat me like a slut, and then come crawling back. This was one of the worst relationships I'd ever endured.

"I know that the umm… little problem you had is all gone now, so I was thinking that maybe we could link back up." Sean grinned like what he was saying wasn't the most selfish, disgusting shit I'd ever heard. "And hey look, that woman you saw me with, she was just temporary, baby, I promise." He grabbed my hands, and when I snatched them, he gave me a perplexed look. "Baby—"

"Sean, I have no interest in being with you at this moment. And the only reason I ever wanted you in the first place was because of what I thought you could give me from being well off, and in law school. But Canyon, that man that you don't think is good enough for me is actually too good for me. I can't even believe I wasted time with your reedy voiced, skinny, wimpy, only-got-money-because-his-mommy-and-daddy-does ass. So the next time you open your mouth to speak to me, just don't. I no longer associate with peasants, so please leave my table."

His lips were tightly pursed, and his nostrils were flared like a raging bull as he glared at me from across the table like he wanted to slap me. I was angry too, so if he did hit me, we'd be tussling in this bitch.

"Yeah, well, I already got what I wanted from you anyway and it wasn't even that good." He rose to his feet.

"Probably because I was passed out, you rapist!"

Right when the word rapist left my lips, he got down in my face, finger damn near about to poke me in the eye. I admit I jumped back some because of how off guard he'd caught me.

"You better stop saying that bullshit! I know you told your little boy toy about that, and if one more person repeats that shit, you're gonna regret it!"

"Oh will I?" I laughed.

"Yeah, you will."

"I'm so scared of you and what you will do."

Chuckling, he replied, "I may not be able to fight, or have connections to enough street people to knock you off, but I have connections in way more meaningful places." He stood up straight and put his arms out at his sides, gesturing that he somehow had our school in the palm of his hand.

Monroe returned with our food, and looked back and forth between Sean and I like we'd lost our damn minds, as she took a seat where he once was.

"Everything okay?" she questioned.

"Yeah, everything is perfect. Right, Dree?" Sean looked to me. I gave no response, I just scowled up at him, which made him smile.

He turned around to leave, but before he was completely facing the other way, I saw his smile fade.

That nigga honestly thought he could come in here and get me to be back with him. Not only did that irritate me, but it angered me because he must have thought I was one shallow ass bitch to think I would agree to resume our relations after the way he dissed me.

As bad as it may sound, I just could never bring myself to have a child by Sean, which was another reason for the abortion; the main being how the baby came about. I know it should have been about my baby and me, and not the man, but after that fiasco just a few moments ago, I was so happy I did what I did. No child deserved a father like that.

"I guess you guys aren't getting back together." Monroe's voice brought me back to reality.

"Nope, never. It never was anything really. We were just mostly hanging out. We only had sex one time."

"Yeah, I wasn't trying to eavesdrop, but I heard you call him a rapist." Monroe cocked her head, sandwich in hand.

"I was just being dramatic because I was really drunk when it happened, you know?" I giggled nervously.

Sometimes, I wanted people to know what he'd done because I hated him, but on the other hand, I wondered if it was really 'rape.' I was drunk so I probably did tell him he could sleep with me. And if so, . how could I want to have him penalized for something he thought he could do? Not to mention, crying rape would totally kill my reputation. I was always known as the tough and smart Goode sister, so telling everyone that I drank so much to the point where I let myself be taken advantage of, didn't really coincide with that reputation.

Monroe and I finished our food, and then went to class together. Sean was in there, and even though I was focused, I felt him looking at me from across the room with a deep frown. It was almost like he hated me. I didn't care though. I was here to get my degree and that was it.

That was my last class, so once it was over, I stayed about five more minutes so Tyson could let a few of us know the upcoming study group schedule.

As I was leaving the classroom, Tyson gently grabbed my hand, and when I turned to look up at him, he was smiling.

"I just wanted to tell you how great you're doing in the class. I admire how dedicated you are."

Slowly moving my hand from his grasp, I replied, "Thank you."

"Hey, I was wondering if—"

"I have to go… Tyson." I hurriedly left the class. It was like any man that wasn't Canyon Dennis gave me a nasty feeling, especially when they touched me. As much as I tried to be normal again, the incident with Sean had really messed me up. Every day I regretted dating him more and more.

I stopped at home to get some clothes, and saw my mother had cooked, so I made a plate for Canyon and myself. I actually made him two plates because he could really put it away. I loved how tall and built he was though, which was different from the skinny college guy I used to be best friends with. He told me he ate a lot of brown foods; steak, potatoes, rice, and more, then stayed in the gym so he could shed that scrawny exterior. He was sexy back then, but even more so now.

When I got onto the floor of his apartment and started down, I saw his sister, Jupiter, coming towards me, leaving. A queasy feeling came over me, because I knew she hated me and rightfully so. She and I used to be good friends, around the same time as Canyon and I were. But then when Canyon did the unthinkable, I went on a downward spiral for like a week, sabotaging many relationships, including the one with Jupiter.

"Hi," I spoke softly and nodded since my hands were full.

She looked to me and then stopped in her tracks.

"You may have my brother fooled with your new act, but I know you're the same old shady ass Dree, using people until they are no more use to you. And don't think I won't be watching you. Do one thing I don't like, and I'm telling him what I'm sure he doesn't know."

"Jup—"

"Good day." She cut me off and adjusted her purse as she kept walking.

Anyone else would have gotten a tongue lashing for coming at me like that, but like I said, Jupiter had reason to be angry with me.

Just before she got on the elevator to go down, she scoffed and rolled her eyes. I continued down the hallway until I got to Canyon's door, then knocked with my elbow. When he opened up, he was staring down at his phone with a frown.

"Hello!"

"Oh, hey, ma," he cheesed sexily before kissing me.

I smiled, satisfied with his greeting before setting the plates on his mid-level bar.

"Who is that?" I inquired, since he was still obviously irritated by what was on his screen, even after his phone was shoved into his pocket.

He inhaled and exhaled sharply while looking at me like he didn't want to tell me. We'd been friends for a long time, so I knew what he was thinking sometimes just by his face. So whoever was on that phone, he didn't think I wanted to know.

"Jodi."

"Jodi, my mom's waffle house employee?"

"Yes." He ran his hands down his face before taking my duffle bag off my arm. "I don' blocked the bitch on every social media site. She just found me on Twitter. I ain't used that shit in forever. Forgot it was even on my phone."

"I'm sorry, I'm just shocked. You slept with her?"

"Uh, yeah, I told you that."

"No you didn't! You told me not to worry about who you were fucking!"

"Exactly!"

"I-I just thought you meant in general!" I slapped his hard bicep, making him laugh even though nothing was funny.

"No, I fucked. But only once, and in the back of my truck."

"Ugh, Canyon! You're disgusting!" I turned my lip up as he doubled over in laughter.

"Don't be mad, ma." He slinked his big hands around my waist and leaned down to kiss my lips gently.

Those soft pecks soon turned into hungry kisses, and he immediately yanked my shirt over my head. We started towards the bedroom, still kissing and undressing one another, only parting our lips when needed. By the time we fell onto the bed, we were naked as the day we were born, and kissing so hard I was sure our lips would be swollen by the next day.

"Hey," I stopped him. I wanted to laugh because I could tell he was silently praying that I wasn't changing my mind about fucking. We hadn't had sex since we'd rekindled for the second time.

"What?" he panted, maneuvering himself between my legs. His rock-hard dick was knocking at my hole, making my pussy salivate.

"I just wanted to say that I love you, and I'm for real this time. I always have, but before, I was stupid, immature, and ignorant. That won't happen anymo— mmm," I whimpered, as he pushed himself inside of me. I didn't remember him being this big; then again, I hadn't had it in a while.

"I know, ma," was all he said against my lips as he started to stroke me nice and deeply.

CHAPTER NINE

Jonaya

Saturday morning...

Leighton and I approached Wednesday's house and rang the doorbell. She hadn't been answering her phone lately, and we both were worried. At first, when this whole thing with Waayil blew up, she was down but seemed okay. However, over time, I guess the longer he didn't talk to her, she got more and more depressed.

What she did was horrible, even pretty much unforgivable, but she was still my best friend since childhood and I loved her very much. I didn't blame Waayil at all for wanting nothing to do with her, but I'd be lying if I said I didn't want him to just forgive her already.

"Good morning, ladies. Thank you for coming by," Freya, Wednesday's mother answered the door. "She's upstairs in her room, of course."

"Great. Thank you," I replied as Leighton followed me in.

We made our way upstairs, and saw Emil pass us by. We spoke

to him, but he didn't say anything to us as he briskly moved past us. Leighton and I just gave one another a look as we continued to Wednesday's room. I knocked a couple times, and then finally Leighton and I just walked in. I expected to see Wednesday balled up in a corner, but she was in her large bed, watching TV and eating some big ass pancakes.

Her dark hair was tied up, and her caramel complexion looked a bit flushed. She was still pretty though.

"You don't seem to be doing too badly." Leighton smiled, but Wednesday just rolled her eyes.

She said that Leighton hadn't really been talking to her much since that night she admitted to us her secret. It was hard for me not to be distant as well, but I think Wednesday and I were closer than she and Leighton, so it was harder for me to keep away.

"How are you feeling?" I sat on the side of her bed as she cut up her pancakes into squares.

"I have my days. Today is an okay day, so I'm not feeling too down, you know?" She kept her eyes on the TV as she doused her food in syrup.

"There is a party tonight!" Leighton exclaimed.

"I don't think I'm in the mood for a party, especially not if you're gonna be there. If you haven't noticed, you and me are no longer friends."

"We're no longer friends, when Jonaya is the one who spilled your secret?" Leighton frowned.

"I did not spill shit! We were having a damn conversation that he overheard, which is a big ass difference, if you ask me!" I interjected.

"We're not friends because when I needed you, you were off somewhere, probably chasing after my brother. I don't want a friend like you. Plus, I only made nice with you because Jonaya started bringing you around."

"Okay, y'all, calm down. We don't need to let something like this tear us apart. Wednesday, your little secret made it hard to be around you sometimes, and you need to understand that." Lowering my voice, I added, "You were responsible for someone's death, okay? You practically orchestrated a murder, which made us see you differently."

I noticed Wednesday's body language calm down as she looked at Leighton. I understood both sides, so I couldn't just choose one or the other.

"Not to mention, you never told us why you did it, Wednesday. Telling us you were young and immature is just not enough," Leighton explained.

Taking a deep breath, Wednesday finally began to explain her actions as she ate more of her pancakes. Unfortunately, her reasoning didn't seem like enough to have someone killed, but I guess it made sense that she didn't think Waayil would actually kill Harry. Then again, Waayil was always a little off, especially when it came to someone he loved as much as Wednesday. As my mother used to tell me, watch out for the quiet ones.

I was all for her explanation pretty much until she said she didn't think to tell Waayil about the rape until she saw him in bed with

Yikayla. That part I didn't like at all because it showed her malicious side. It also made me think back to the day Yikayla read my ass for not getting why she was so mad. Wednesday said she neglected to tell Waayil about that part because she was too afraid.

"Can I ask you something?" I looked to her and she nodded. "Are you still… jealous of Waayil and Yikayla?"

"No, I swear I'm not. It was just a simple crush that I grew out of while he was in jail. I swear I love him and Yikayla together, Jonaya."

"Good," I nodded.

After about an hour or so, Leighton and I decided to leave and go have some lunch at Outback Steakhouse. Once we were seated and had ordered our food and drinks, Leighton decided to talk.

"I think it's time for me to move on," she huffed.

"Move on as in what? Like school?" I silently hoped I was right, because I still hadn't told her about Nusef and me.

He'd stopped answering her calls and texts, and when I was with him, I'd tell her I was studying. I was lucky no one really knew about her dating Nusef because the people we knew mutually didn't feel a need to report back to her what they'd seen.

"No, from Nusef. He used to be hot and cold all the time, but now it's like he has cut me off. Niggas do not cut me off, especially after I let them fuck. By then, I usually have to get them off me with a fly swatter."

I wanted to tell her, I did, but she really liked Nusef. This was another reason I didn't want him messing with her. Yes, I had feelings for him the whole time and was ultimately jealous, but I knew Leighton really wanted his ass, and the more time they spent together, the more attached she would become. Now how, as her best friend, could I tell her that the reason he wasn't returning her calls was because he was my man now? I couldn't imagine being on the receiving end of some news like that.

"Hey, not all these guys are the same. Plus, you knew that Nusef was a bit of a player, right?"

"Yeah, but like I said, niggas don't ignore me. I've turned some of the most savage of men into putty in my hand, Jonaya, and you know it."

"Nusef is different." I shrugged as the waiter set down the appetizer.

"I don't think so. I'm gonna find out why, but just not right now. I need to focus on my grades before my parents get on me."

I nodded, shoving a shrimp into my mouth.

"That's what's best," I replied finally.

"So that party, what are you wearing tonight?"

"Oh, I'm not gonna go. I'm not really in the mood to party. I'm just gonna highlight some chapters and watch TV."

"Damn, I guess I won't go either. I need to be studying too anyway."

We continued having conversation over our meal, and then we went our separate ways.

I took a nap when I got home because I'd eaten so much, and when I woke up, I saw I had a text from Nusef.

Boo Bear: *What time you coming to the party?*

Me: *I don't wanna go.*

Boo Bear: *Jonaya. You better come ma. Have someone else drive you so that you can leave with me aight?*

Me: *Yes.*

I sent the eye rolling emoticon because he hated that one. Not wanting to show up alone, I dialed Wednesday and after fifteen minutes, I'd convinced her to go. I made sure to hurry her, so she wouldn't have time to contact Leighton.

"Thanks for driving," I said to Wednesday after I'd gotten into her car.

"No worries. Do I need to pick up Leighton?"

"No, you don't need to. I told her I wasn't going tonight, and she said she wasn't going to come."

"Okay... what am I missing? Why did you tell her that? I mean, I guess because you don't want her to come, but why?"

"Originally, I wasn't going, but I didn't inform her of the change in plans because I'm dating Nusef now and he's gonna be there." I stared out the window as Wednesday drove.

"Oh my gosh! Finally! Everyone has been waiting for you two as much as we've been waiting on Waayil and Yikayla to make things official!"

"Y'all have?" I frowned, not even the slightest bit aware of that.

"Girl, yes. I mean, everyone as far as our families. Of course, Leighton knew nothing about it because it was like a secret wish."

Wednesday chuckled. "But damn, I thought it would never happen. If I had known you'd mature and get with him, I would have never urged Leighton to pursue him."

"I know, me either. I didn't think I would ever get with him despite his efforts, but I eventually caved and now this shit is a mess."

"You're gonna have to tell her. And now that I know Nusef is coming to the party, I will be dropping you off and not staying."

"What? Why?"

"Because he's been on me, trying to find out what secret I'm holding, and I'm not ready for two brothers to be angry with me."

"Nusef won't be as mad."

"Yes he will. You know him, Jonaya, but I know him better. I've seen his dick and everything," Wednesday joked.

"Shit, me too. I just hope you've never felt it."

"Ugh, bitch, you're about to make me throw the fuck up." Wednesday shuddered, making me laugh loudly. "But no, I cannot right now. I need more time. And at this party, he will corner me."

"Fine." I sucked my teeth as she pulled onto the street where the house party was.

I got out and entered the house, scanning the living room to see if I could spot Nusef. My eyes landed on Moses, and then eventually Nusef, who was eating some of the chips and salsa, while bobbing his head to the music.

"Aye, ma—"

"My boyfriend is right over there," I replied, cutting the thirsty nigga off. He looked to Nusef, and chose his battle wisely by letting me go.

"Damn, look at you," Nusef greeted me when I got into the kitchen. He bit his lip sexily with his perfect teeth, before kissing me gently. "I wanna show you something."

"Okay."

"Damn, hi, Jonaya. This nigga taking you away already." Moses shook his head before hugging me.

I followed Nusef out of the kitchen, and he led me into the bathroom.

"Sef!" I squealed when he lifted me onto the sink.

"Just let me slide in for a little bit."

"Baby, no, we can do that when we go to your place later. And you just barely recovered," I whined as he kissed all over my neck and collarbone, getting me hot.

BAM! BAM!

Someone started banging on the door because I guess they had to pee.

"Fuck outta here!" Nusef shouted.

"Sef, no. If you want, we can leave the party now."

The cutest smile graced his face as he helped me down from the sink, and let me straighten my dress. He hugged my body from behind as I opened the door to see a smiling and laughing Leighton.

"Excuse me—" She stopped speaking upon seeing Nusef hugging me and kissing on my neck.

"Leighton—"

"Are you serious?" she barked at me, prompting Nusef to let go and sigh. "This is why he's been distant? You shady ass bitch!"

"Watch yo' mouth, ma," Nusef interjected, and I put my hand to his chest to stop him. She didn't deserve his wrath, but I *did* deserve every name she'd called me.

"Leighton, I was gonna tell you—"

"Fuck you, Jonaya," she spat before leaving the party.

Fuck my life.

me

CHAPTER TEN

Waayil

Couple days later...

I was in my office, replying to a few email inquiries about some tattoos. A lot of them were pretty big ass projects, so I had to schedule that shit properly to make sure I would have enough hours to actually take my damn time.

Once I was done, I looked up some places that I could get a DNA test done. I needed to hurry the fuck up according to my mother, because she said it was a time frame that I had to be within to get the child tested when it was still in the womb. I didn't know when that would be over, but it definitely put some fire under my ass to start looking up how to get that shit done.

I wrote down a couple addresses, just as I heard a knock on my door. I yelled for them to come in, and when I saw my brother, I closed down my laptop.

"So this shit is overdue," he said, leaning up against my door until it closed.

"Have a seat."

He sat across from me, then leaned back, crossing his arms being all serious and shit like he was a mob boss or something. Shit was comical. I contemplated for a moment, trying to figure out how I wanted to tell him. I just decided to get straight to the damn point with it.

"Well, Wednesday was *not* telling the truth about what she claimed Harry did to her," I said.

His glare immediately went away as he sat up some.

"Nah. What?"

"He was threatening to tell me some shit he'd found in her diary; basically, that she had a crush on me. So she lied."

Hearing this shit again and remembering how stupid her reasoning was just made me shake my head. Her explanation only made me more upset than I was before.

"Damn, man. Are you sure? That's not like Wednesday to—"

"My nigga, this shit was uncovered a minute ago. I'm sure. I heard it come from her own mouth; well, hers and Jonaya's, so it's true. I tried to have a sit down with her, but I can't look at her stupid ass for more than a minute without wanting to shoot her."

"You can't do that, Waayil."

"I know. I know I can't. But I would. I sure as hell would, so it's best to keep my distance until I get a little bit more calm, you know?"

The simple thought of Wednesday made my chest ache. I loved

her because she was my little sister, but after finding out about that bullshit she'd done, it made me look at her differently. It was almost like I didn't know her. For the longest, my baby sister was this harmless young girl who'd gotten taken advantage of. Now, all I saw was a sneaky, scheming ass young girl who'd set me up; set Harry up too.

"I can't believe I'm just now finding this out, Waayil. You're supposed to be my damn brother and you wait to tell me?"

"My bad, I'm sorry. I didn't think about you as soon as this shit dropped into my hands. Instead of reacting and taking time to process the fact that I'd killed somebody and went to jail for life almost, over a lie, I should have called you to make sure you were up to date. You're right."

Exhaling heavily, Nusef nodded. "I get it. I just hate that every damn body knew, even Jonaya, before me."

"Shit, she knew before *me*," I replied, making him laugh some. "But I'm gon' get at Wednesday soon, hopefully. Just tell her ass to leave me alone because if she hits my line again I'm gon' snap."

"I can definitely do that." He looked over his shoulder as if my door wasn't closed. "Aye, you know Sax is fuckin' with Rebecca?"

"Word? Where that shit come from? Was he watching her the whole damn time?" I frowned.

Yeah, Nusef was very happy with his situation, but anytime a muthafucka moves in on yo' ex that quickly, it's because they've had their eye on them the whole damn time. That, or the two of them have been fucking around. So I can understand him being a little bothered, more so with Sax than Rebecca though.

"That's the same thing I said, mane. But shit, long as he doesn't have an infatuation with bitches I fuck with and try to come for Jonaya, we good."

"What nigga would have an infatuation with bitches you fuck with? Like you get all the fine bitches or some shit."

"I do." He chuckled.

"Negro, please. You got lucky twice with Rebecca and Jonaya, but before them, all you smashed were paper bag over the head hoes."

Nusef stayed fucking ugly bitches, and parading them hoes around like they were fine or some shit. It was a little embarrassing at some point, but funny as fuck too. Even while I was in jail, he'd shoot me pictures to the little cell phone I had, and they were always mud ducks. I guess he got tired of me clowning him because I'd never seen Rebecca until I got released. It was funny that he kept her a secret, because she was actually pretty as hell.

"Fuck you, bruh. That's a damn lie. Remember Kerri?"

"Nah, nigga. That was some *Shallow Hal* shit, because you were the only nigga thinking she was cute. She had a body on her though."

"Exactly, she had a banging ass body. Shorty was a ten."

"Nigga, having only a nice body does *not* make you a damn ten!" I exclaimed, while chuckling because he was deadass.

"Yes the fuck it does! Shit, in my book it does, fuck you talking about?"

"No." I shook my head, laughing. "A ten means the bitch's face, body, and personality is the shit. If any of them are lacking, she ain't a ten."

"I see you on yo' hater shit." He stood up as I snickered.

"Nah, get yo' ass back with that gay shit, Sef." I laughed when he came around my desk to try and hug me.

"You need to learn how to accept this shit, bruh." He hugged me from the side and as soon as I could, I pushed his ass back like always, making him roar with laughter.

"Fuck out of my office." I walked past his mushy ass so I could leave. "I'm going to get some food, anybody want anything?" I quizzed as Nusef and I entered the lobby.

"Ooh, go to Arby's!" Chiara grinned.

"Don't nobody want no damn Arby's!" Sax hissed and shook his head.

I looked his way, because that nigga was a little suspect to me now that he was dating Rebecca. That shit was weird though because at work, Rebecca stayed to herself, or sometimes talked with Venus and Chiara, but was never on this nigga. I guess they knew how to keep the shit out of the workplace.

"I already ordered barbecue for everyone." Rebecca entered the lobby. "Here is the amount you need to pay me back." She handed a Post-It to Nusef and then went back towards where she'd come from.

"Rebecca puttin' you in yo' place now?" I raised a brow at Nusef, while grinning.

"Shut yo' ass up, Waayil. And just go to the liquor store to get some drinks and shit then, since she don' took care of lunch," Nusef spoke as he scanned the Post-It Rebecca had handed to him.

Everyone told me what they wanted to drink, even Moses, who was damn near about to shit on himself when I asked him what he wanted. I felt bad but the shit was jokes. He needed to find his balls and man the fuck up ASAP.

Chiara tried to accompany me, but when she went to get her purse, I left. Hopefully she found a damn hint in that purse that said I didn't have any interest in her. Letting her suck me off in one of my weak moments was becoming the worst decision of my life.

I ended up at the liquor store down the street, and dapped up a few of the niggas that were hanging outside. I didn't fuck with the liquor store next door to our tattoo shop, because they never had shit and always tried to overcharge. I almost got sent back to jail when that bitch ass nigga told me $2.95 for a little ass can of grape soda, despite the price saying it was $.95.

"What's up, Mooney?" I slapped hands with the homie before going in. I stopped once I saw Emil come out and call his name too.

"You don't fucking know me!" Mooney hissed to Emil, darting his eyes to me nervously before turning them back to Emil. That nigga was trying to play, but I'd already peeped game.

"Waayil…" Emil said, but didn't add any more words.

"How you know my little brother, Mooney?"

"I don't." He shook his head repeatedly, making it obvious that he was lying. "But no disrespect, Yil, I didn't know that was your brother."

"Yeah." I squinted my eyes, not liking what I was seeing. I didn't know if I was more upset that my little brother was fucking with this nigga, or that Mooney's bitch ass was trying to deny him. "You need a ride home?" I asked Emil.

"Nah, man, I'm good." Emil sucked his teeth and shook his head disappointedly as he walked off. Before I went into the store, I saw Emil look over his shoulder at Mooney, before shaking his head yet again.

When I came out of the store with the drinks, I spotted Mooney's car across the street and Emil getting in on the passenger side. It took so fucking much for me not to say anything, but I just headed to my car to get back to work. I needed to stay calm these days. A nigga was stressing too damn much.

As I walked into Monarch, I saw the food was already there and on this big ass fold out table that we used during lunch hour. As Chiara put up the sign and locked the front door, the phone rang. Rebecca answered since Chiara was busy, but then she reached it out to me.

"For me?" I inquired and she shrugged.

"This is Waayil," I answered, but then realized it was a collect call from a damn prison. I wasn't buddy-buddy with no damn body in prison for them to be calling my ass, so I was thoroughly confused. However, I accepted out of curiosity, especially because the name Gavin was very familiar.

"What's good, Waayil?" Gavin asked smugly.

"Where do I know you from?"

"Who knows? I get around. But I just wanted to thank you in advance for taking care of Alba and my baby."

"Nigga, what?"

Click.

CHAPTER TEN

Rori

That same afternoon…

I was at Victoria's Secret, looking for some new thongs to wear, and some sexy ones to wear for Eko. I hadn't been this excited about a relationship in a long time, so I wanted to wear something nice for him. Eko wasn't really the type to need lingerie because as soon as I even made eye contact with him, he was ready. I chuckled, hoping he didn't nut in his boxers from seeing me dressed up… or dressed down.

As I dropped down to sift through the drawers for the size and color I wanted, someone bumped into me. When I looked up I saw it was Alba, Waayil's super clingy ex-girlfriend that was supposedly pregnant by him. Her stomach wasn't large at all, but her dress was so tight that you could see a small bulge. And if you knew Alba, you knew washboard abs was her usual, so something was going on.

"Oh my gosh, girl, I am so sorry! It's Regina, right?" She grinned as I rose to my feet, thongs in hand.

"Rori, Alba. You know my name is Rori."

"Oh yes, it is. I can't remember every little name, only the important ones these days like my baby daddy, and my friends."

"Wow, if you can remember *all* your potential baby daddy's names, well surely you can remember mine. You've known it for years."

"Excuse me? I don't know what your naive sister put into your head, but I know who my child's father is, okay?"

"Right." I laughed and turned my back to her to continue browsing the underwear on the top layer.

"So umm, are you still with that guy you used to date?" She leaned on the square shaped display that held the panties.

"I don't really think that's any of your business. And I'm not too sure why you'd even want to know."

"Oh, it's just that I used to see him with another girl all the time. I actually know her pretty well. She told me they were very much in love and that he was gonna leave you. I meant to tell you, but we don't quite hang in the same circles anymore. And then after he got locked up... I heard, I had forgotten until... well now!"

Hearing that did make me feel some type of way, but I refused to let that bother me. I couldn't live in the past any longer.

"Well, whomever that girl is does not have to worry about me whether Gavin is in jail or out of jail."

"I see." She looked peeved by the fact that I didn't react like she'd wanted me to. "I applaud you, Rori. Sometimes we have to be the bigger woman and understand that in some cases, our men will find better women, like Gavin did."

"And like Waayil did." I smiled, loving watching hers fade. "I wonder if they sit down and discuss how much better their new bitches are? You know, before Gavin got locked up."

"No, honey. Waayil will realize what a horrible decision he's made one day. I just hope it's before I move on."

"From the looks of that belly, you already have." And with that I walked away. I didn't even know why I gave her as much of my time as I did.

"It is his!" she shouted after me, but I just continued to the counter to pay for my things. Eko had given me a knot of cash that I didn't need or want to use. Plus, when I pulled it out, people looked at me like I was some queen-pin on the low.

After leaving Victoria's Secret, I went home to pack some clothes for overnight since it was the weekend for me from school, and then I let my mom know where I was gonna be until tomorrow afternoon.

When I got to Eko's place, he wasn't there yet, and when I texted him, he told he was picking up some tamales. This guy out here named Albert had these good ass tamales that he sold frozen. I couldn't wait to dig into those later.

I entered Eko's place and put my bag down in the bedroom. I then removed my lingerie from the Victoria's Secret bag, along with the receipt, then trashed the bag in the garbage. As I looked around the kitchen for something to make along with the tamales tonight, I heard some footsteps come from the back.

"Need some help?" Jenni smiled, entering the kitchen.

"Uh—"

"You used me," she gritted.

"No I did not." I frowned, taking some potatoes from the sack since I was gonna make scalloped ones.

"Yeah you did." I admit she was freaking my ass out a little bit. "I asked you for help, and you convinced me that making a copy of Eko's house key while he was asleep was a good idea."

Yeah, I was shady as fuck. Not my fault the bitch was dumb enough to believe he'd like that shit.

"Okay, and? I mean, yeah… I thought he would like that. He didn't?" I played dumb with her.

"No!" She slammed her hand on the cabinet I was opening and forced it close. "He was angry as hell!"

"Well look, Jenni, I don't know what to tell you. But if you slam this cabinet again, you're gonna have a bigger problem than Eko being angry, ma." I gave her stern eye contact to let her know I'd be bashing that pretty face into the wall if she did that shit again. Then I went back into the cabinet with no problem. "He didn't want you anyway! I didn't have to do much, as you can see!"

"And the lingerie in his kitchen, he didn't like that either." Her tone was much calmer and softer. "You did all this so you could have him. I know you did."

"So what if I did, bitch? Huh?" I moved closer to her after slamming my seasonings down. "What the fuck are you gonna do about it?"

"You'll see," was all she said before turning on her heels and leaving.

I stormed to the back for my phone, and immediately called Eko.

"You need to have your locks changed," I spat as soon as he answered.

"Why?"

"Didn't you say Jenni broke into your house, nigga? Or made a key or what the fuck ever?"

"Yeah. I'm gonna get that done this weekend."

"No, you do it today, or I am not sleeping here tonight."

"Aight, ma. Aight."

CHAPTER TEN

Canyon

Later that same evening...

"What do you want, babe? Chicken or fish?" Dree asked as she stood in my kitchen.

Having home cooked meals almost every night, was the shit I tell you. Dree had been staying with me most nights out of the week, and in between law school, she was making me breakfast and dinner every time she was here. The other day, she even washed a nigga's clothes. I ain't never experienced some shit like that. Had me feeling like a damn king 'round these parts.

Dree's mood had improved too, but certain times, I would catch her in deep thought and looking gloomy as hell. I knew why, and it only made me hate Sean's ass more. What he did to her took a little bit of her confidence away and I couldn't let that shit slide.

"Doesn't matter. Whatever you make is gon' be good as hell. I already know," I nodded. "I gotta make a quick run though."

"Noooo! I'm about to make the food for you and Cade," she whined.

Smiling, I inquired, "Why did you cut me off years ago? I mean, I know you said you weren't ready to be with me, but you didn't stop fucking with me until months after I expressed my feelings for you in which you turned me down."

My question was random, but had been on my mind for a minute now.

"Uh, well you know how when we first started back up I used to get quiet whenever you mentioned Cade?"

"Yeah." I folded my arms and leaned back in the kitchen chair.

"That was why. When I found out you'd gotten Luna pregnant, I couldn't deal with it. Not to mention, I was angry because I just knew that you weren't serious with her, and that you were gonna wait for me to come around. But when she got pregnant, I hated you."

"I kind of did wait though, Dree."

"Yeah, you did." She walked closer to me and sat down in my lap. "I'm so happy you did too. I'm not sure I'd be okay with you being with Luna."

"Trust me, that was never anything to worry about. I barely wanted her back in the day, let alone now."

We laughed in unison before sharing a kiss.

"Don't leave."

"It's only for a minute, ma. I'll be right back."

She got off my lap and I leaned down to kiss her again once I was standing. I went into the living room and made my son move back some from the TV, and then I grabbed my gym bag before leaving. When I got down to the car my homie let me use, I saw my sister calling but I just hit ignore on her ass.

I didn't feel like hearing her damn mouth about Dree, and how I needed to find me somebody else. That shit wasn't happening. Even when I wanted it to, it just wouldn't. Yeah, Dree was uppity as fuck, but she just needed a nigga to manhandle the fuck out of her ass to shake it from her system. I had done that, and now, in my opinion, she was growing out of that shit.

As if today was my lucky day, by the time I got to Sean's crib in Belle Meade, he was pulling into his driveway. I had timed this shit perfectly. It was dangerous using my access to school records for shit like this, but this nigga wanted to go around slipping shit in people's drinks so he deserved it. After parking a little ways down, I calmly made my way back to his spot.

"Aye, can I talk to you for a minute?" I strolled up on him, hat low and hood pulled over my head, with a clear mask on my face. I made sure I had on long sleeves and everything.

Dropping his corny ass briefcase, Sean threw his hands up in mock surrender and said, "I don't have any cash on me! I have credit cards only!"

Bitch ass nigga.

WHAM!

Without another word, I went across that nigga's face with this wooden bat I'd found. He spun around and fell to the ground, crying and screaming as blood poured from his nose.

"Please! Name your price! My father is a very wealthy man!"

WHAM!

I continued to rain blows down on his body until I felt I'd fucked him up enough while still letting him live. As badly as I wanted to give some fatal blows, I knew I couldn't. Breathing hard, I stared down at his body as he shook and cried like a little hoe. I wanted to threaten his ass, let him know what this was for, but he'd put two and two together if I did that. I didn't want this shit coming back to Dree in anyway, or to me.

Not saying anything, I turned around and walked back to the car I came in, bat covered in specks of his blood. Them broken bones should slow up his Bill Cosby shit for a minute.

CHAPTER TEN

Nusef

About an hour later...

Waayil and I had left the shop for the day, and since our mother told us she'd cooked some of her pecan and lemon meringue pies, we both decided to roll through there and partake in that shit. With the way Jonaya cooked for me, in combination with my mama's pies, it was imperative that I kept my ass in the gym, which I did nowadays.

My brother and I both pulled up to the crib at the same time, and when we got out, I checked to see if his mood had changed. Nigga had been looking like a deranged serial killer ever since he got that phone call at lunchtime earlier. He wouldn't say what the person said to his ass, and frankly, that shit was pissing me off. He'd held enough muthafuckin' secrets from my ass and I was over that bullshit.

"Who called?" I got right to the point as we met one another at our parents' door.

"Nobody."

"Waayil, quit fucking lying, bruh. You think I don't know when yo' ass is lying?" I frowned, even more irritated than before.

"Nusef, drop that shit, please. When I'm ready, I'll tell yo' ass. Quit crying all the got damn time about what the fuck I don't let yo' bitch ass in on."

I shoved the shit out of that nigga as soon as our father answered the door. Of course, Waayil charged me, and we started tussling as my parents yelled for us to stop. Right now, I wanted to fuck this nigga up for coming at me sideways and for keeping shit to himself.

"Stop it right now! Nusef!" My mom called out to me because she knew I was more likely to listen to her. Waayil didn't give a fuck at times.

Not wanting to hear my mama scream, and see my father get decked from trying to break us up, I stopped. Waayil did too, and I laughed when I saw his lip was bleeding and at the fact that we'd started this outside, but were now in the foyer.

"Fuck you laughing at? Clean ya nose, bitch," he hissed to me as blood dripped from my nose onto my lips.

Our parents were standing in the middle of us with their eyes wide as saucers, while on the edge of their seat, hoping we didn't go at that shit again.

"Fuck you," I replied.

"Where them damn pies, Mama? I gotta go," Waayil barked lowly.

"Follow me. Theo, get my kit to clean these fools up." My mama shook her head and started towards the kitchen, in which we followed.

"Bitch." Waayil shoved me, I pushed him back, and we got into a miniature shoving match until my mom turned around to get us straight.

She cut us a slice of one of the pies before wrapping up whole ones for us to take. She wouldn't let us eat the slices though, until my dad returned with the first aid kit, and we cleaned up and washed our hands. While eating, Waayil and I started to make conversation, and our parents just shook their heads at us.

"Mama, I was wonder—" Wednesday came skipping into the kitchen, but stopped walking and talking when she saw Waayil and me.

"Come here," I told her.

She hesitated, but moved towards me. When she got close enough, I embraced her as Waayil continued to smash that pie like it'd disappear if he didn't move fast enough, and like Wednesday wasn't right there.

"Hi, Waayil," Wednesday spoke lowly to him as she stared at the side of his face.

He downed some of his ice water, and went back to eating like he didn't hear shit. The kitchen was quiet as hell as we all waited to see what the fuck would happen next.

"Waayil, your sister said hello," my dad spoke up.

"And obviously, I don't give a fuck." Waayil shoved the last spoonful of pie into his mouth, before standing up and finishing off his glass of water. "Is this mine?" He pointed to the whole pie covered up and my mom nodded.

"Waayil, I'm sorry! Can we just talk—"

"Back the fuck up," he gritted to Wednesday, who stepped back some so he could walk around her.

"Waayil, don't be like that," my mom sighed.

"Just let him be," I told Wednesday.

"He needs to talk to her!" my father barked.

Waayil just ignored our parents, as he made sure he had all his shit, before starting towards the exit of the kitchen.

"Waayil, wait!"

"Back the fuck up, Wednesday! I'm not fucking around with you, ma. I swear to God if you don't step back, you gon' regret that shit!" Waayil warned.

"Wednesday, leave him alone!" I shouted to her as all of us left the kitchen to follow Waayil. I saw that look in that nigga's eyes, so now wasn't the best time for Wednesday to try to talk.

Wednesday didn't listen to anybody's warnings, and grabbed Waayil's arm once we were all in the foyer. He quickly pulled his gun from his waist with his free hand and pointed it at her.

"Waayil!" my mom exclaimed.

"Didn't I say back the fuck up? Now I'm gon' count down from five, and if you're not over there next to Mama and Pops, you gon' have a big muthafuckin' problem."

"Wednesday!" I hollered when she didn't move as Waayil started counting down. She clearly didn't know how off Waayil was. People needed to stop letting his quiet and calm persona fool them.

He chuckled crazily as fuck before saying, "And one."

POP!

"Ahhh!" Wednesday screamed piercingly, collapsing to the floor. My parents hollered in shock as well.

"Nigga, you shot her in the foot?" I yelled, looking at Waayil with bucked eyes. Without another word, he left the crib like it was nothing, closing the door behind him.

"Oh my gosh! I'm gonna die!" Wednesday cried hysterically, blood gushing from her foot and through her fingers.

"Call 911, Theo!" my mom shouted, and my dad did just that.

"Look, baby, when they get here, we gon' tell them some nigga coming down the street did this to you okay?" I said to Wednesday who was sobbing so damn hard that it was crazy. This nigga really shot her.

Wednesday nodded as much as she could in response, before I scooped her up and ran her outside to make a blood trail. I then brought her back inside, and placed her back in the middle of the floor so it'd look like we'd carried her in. I was angry at Wednesday for lying on Harry and getting my brother locked up, but I hated seeing her in this much pain. But that's what people get for fucking with Waayil.

"We need to tell the truth! He's reckless!" my mother spat angrily, pacing the foyer as we waited for the ambulance. Waayil wasn't reckless; he was too smart for that shit. The nigga planned everything out, no matter how quickly he reacted to something.

"Yeah, and then we also need to tell them how she lied. You know she'd go to jail for that shit, right? Probably for first degree murder because she knew what the fuck she was doing." I looked up at my mama.

Her angry expression turned to a somber one before she said, "I know. I know. I didn't mean what I said."

"I hope not." I turned my attention back to Wednesday. I hated to put Wednesday out there like that, but if they wanted to send Waayil back to jail, I'd make sure Wednesday's ass was going too.

"How is it that Yikayla can get Waayil to be so soft?" my mother inquired out of nowhere. It was silent before we both laughed, with Wednesday's cries in the background.

That shit was so true. If you wanted Waayil to calm down, call Yikayla. It was like as soon as she stepped into the room, his demeanor would change if he was angry.

"Maybe she was a lion tamer in her past life," I replied.

My mom nodded as we chuckled lightly, while I still held Wednesday.

Finally, the ambulance showed up and we got Wednesday to the hospital. She was fine though, because even though she'd lost a lot of blood, we acted quickly enough. So after surgery, they let us take her home that night. They also believed our story about some thug muthafucka trying to rob her and shit, thankfully.

I prayed this was the last time I had to make up a damn lie about Waayil's criminal ass acts. First Moses, who he almost killed, and now Wednesday. This shit was too damn much, especially when I had to worry about who the fuck had shot me.

CHAPTER ELEVEN

Yikayla

"Baby, stop, I have to go!" I nudged Waayil off, giggling as he ran his hands all over me.

Just yesterday, he came home mad at the world and wanted to just cuddle all night like a little baby, but today he seemed fine.

"What time you coming back?" he whispered against my collarbone as he reached under my skirt to grab my ass roughly as hell.

"Mm," I moaned shortly and subtly. "Soon, baby. I'm just going out to eat with my friend from work."

He was now brushing his fingers across my clit from behind, as he kissed and sucked on my neck. Lifting one of my legs up some, he plunged his fingers inside of me, sending volts through my body.

"Waayil," I whimpered, nibbling on my lip as he moved his fingers in and out.

"Cum," was all he said in a demanding way as he sped up.

Gripping his strong shoulders, my nails scraped against his supple dark skin since he was shirtless, pressing his rock-hard body against my soft one. My body trembled as I released on his fingers, and when he took them out, he licked my juices off. Placing me on the dresser, he put my legs over his shoulders and moved my panties to the side. I wanted to deny him, but he had me too hot to stop now.

He released himself from his basketball shorts, and pressed hard against my opening. He struggled a bit because of his girth, but eventually he got the head inside of me.

"Baby. slow," I cooed as he started to stroke me, opening me up to accept more of him while gripping my hips. "Ahh," I sniveled at the pain.

"Fuck," he groaned once he was all the way inside of me. "Mmm, this shit is tight." He panted in between sucking my lips.

When he stared me in the eyes with his beautiful honey colored ones, the feeling of our sex intensified. The pain I was feeling soon started to go away, and he could tell, so he began to speed up, fucking me hard and making me cum. I was so wet it was crazy, and he was loving every minute of it, watching himself pound into me. I released three more times before he finally filled me up, sucking on my inner thighs since my legs were over his shoulders. He pulled out and tasted my pussy for a little bit, pressing one of my thighs into my chest.

"I love you, Waayil."

"Come here." He let my legs down and pulled me up closer to him so he could kiss me. "I love you more, Kay."

Finally, we snapped out of our Romeo and Juliet shit, once we'd kissed for a million years, so I went to clean myself up and brush my teeth before he hopped into the shower. I left out, and on the way to

Brynn's, I called Miss Loughton because I already knew she had Lonan instead of Roscoe. When my suspicions were confirmed, I told her I was coming to get him after my lunch, instead of tomorrow. I was missing him too much anyway, and loathed having to split my time.

When I got to Brynn's house, I texted her to let her know I was outside. She told me she'd be a minute since she messed up her makeup putting on mascara, so she offered for me to come inside. Her home was nice, and she told me it was a rental like what Waayil and I had.

"Almost done!" she shouted from her bathroom as I paced the living room, looking around. I saw her daughter's toys, which made me smile.

"Where is Haven?" I asked about her daughter.

"Oh, she is over her cousin's house. Or my sister's house. They're going somewhere… I forgot the name."

I nodded in response, even though she couldn't see me. I saw a picture of her daughter on this table, and picked it up to look. She was super adorable, but looked like a handful. I placed the picture back, and then picked up another of her daughter but when she was a little baby.

"Girl, you didn't tell me Waayil had a twin!" she yelled from the back.

"Oh yeah, he does. But he has a girlfriend, which is my sister."

"I don't want his brother, I just thought that was interesting. Waayil is more of my type anyway. He got that mean sexy look." It was quiet as I gave myself a pep talk not to curse her out. "I didn't know he could sing either."

"Oh umm, yeah, he can." I frowned as I checked the time on my watch. "How did you find that out?"

"I Googled him and saw an old video." Brynn walked into the living room dressed. "You ready?"

"Please don't Google my man, and yep, I'm ready!" I finally replied, just as someone started viciously beating on the door. It was almost like they were kicking it.

Suddenly, I realized I didn't know much about Brynn, or what she had going on in her life. This bitch could have been into all kinds of shit, and I was a bit afraid now.

"What the hell!" Brynn's brows dipped as she darted towards her door. I discreetly pulled my iPhone out, ready to dial 911 when she pulled the door open.

"Where is my fucking daughter, Brynn!" Roscoe shouted.

TO BE CONTINUED

Join our mailing list to get a notification when Leo Sullivan Presents has another release!

Text LEOSULLIVAN to 22828 to join!

To submit a manuscript for our review, email us at <u>leosullivanpresents@gmail.com</u>

OSI665571

CPSIA information can be obtained
at www.ICGtesting.com
Printed in the USA
LVHW040616021118
595724LV00018B/1493/P